FATE'S IMAGE

Each one knew at the same instant that he faced death. One was a man who excused himself by talking about his country. The other was a man who had faced death a thousand times, in the cause of humanity, usually in the cause of his country. One was a man who would kill for whatever he was about, no matter who, no matter what . . . and mostly for money or power. The other was a man who judged his cause and wouldn't have fought for it if he couldn't find it right.

Mack Bolan, the Executioner, squeezed his trigger and sent a lethal shot into the face of the other man.

''Mack Bolan stabs right through the heart of the frustration and hopelessness the average person feels about crime running rampant in the streets.''
—*Dallas Times Herald*

DON PENDLETON's
MACK BOLAN.
BLOCKADE

A GOLD EAGLE BOOK FROM
WORLDWIDE.
TORONTO · NEW YORK · LONDON · PARIS
AMSTERDAM · STOCKHOLM · HAMBURG
ATHENS · MILAN · TOKYO · SYDNEY

First edition March 1991

ISBN 0-373-61422-5

Special thanks and acknowledgment to
Carl Furst for his contribution to this work.

BLOCKADE

Printed in U.S.A.

Whose bosom beats not in his country's cause?

—Alexander Pope
1713

Patriotism is the last refuge of a scoundrel.

—Samuel Johnson
1775

Terrorists talk about freedom, patriotism, anti-imperialism. What most of them really want is to line their own pockets.

—Mack Bolan

CHAPTER ONE

Two hard-eyed men sat in the Washington, D.C., office of Hal Brognola, director of the Sensitive Operations Group, United States Department of Justice—Mack Bolan and Inspector Michael Harrigan of the Irish Constabulary.

"Watch carefully," Brognola instructed.

Bolan leaned back in a leather armchair and focused his attention on the big television monitor built into the opposite wall.

Brognola pressed the Play key on a remote control. The picture that appeared on the screen was black and white and had been taken, obviously, by a camera equipped with a telephoto lens. Nevertheless it was clear enough for Bolan to see what was going on.

The video might have been a travelogue from fifty years ago—the kind of thing shown in movie houses as a "selected short subject" before the main film began. The camera panned across the docks of a small fishing village, which were lined with boats. Some were still coming in. Fishermen slid their crude boats up to the ramshackle wooden docks, and buyers jumped aboard to buy the catch of the day. Once a buyer made a deal, the fish would be quickly unloaded from the boat and packed into a refrigerated truck to begin its journey perhaps to a market or restaurant in Dublin, Belfast or London.

The village and the business were picturesque. In the whole scene, old-fashioned and vaguely romantic, there was one jarring note. The waterfront was swarming with police and soldiers.

"Ballykillen," Brognola announced.

The camera centered on one boat. A man stood at the rail, beaming, watching a group of children running toward him. There were five of them, ranging in age from about six to twelve. They wore school uniforms and carried book bags, and though there was no sound on the tape, it was obvious they were shrieking and laughing.

All five of them jumped aboard the boat and into the arms of the man, who embraced each in turn, laughing and talking with them.

They all went inside the boat's small cabin, and after a minute or so they came out. The man began to wave his arms, laughing and gesturing that they should leave the boat.

Still laughing, the children jumped back to the dock and ran off toward the street. A fish broker stepped aboard and engaged the fisherman in serious conversation.

The tape ended.

"So?" Bolan prodded.

"Innocent, hmm?" Brognola said. "Not so innocent. Right, Inspector?"

"No, not so innocent. What you have just witnessed, Colonel MacKenzie, was the transfer of roughly ten kilograms of purest cocaine—or maybe that much heroin—from the boat to the dock and on into the village. In the book bags you saw those children carrying. We knew it, of course. But what are we to do? If our men had stopped those children, there might well have been a riot on the waterfront of Ballykillen.'' He shrugged. ''Of course, we could have been wrong. What if we had stopped those children, forcibly opened their book bags and found nothing but schoolbooks? What then?''

Colonel William MacKenzie was the name Brognola had given Inspector Harrigan when he introduced Bolan. The Irishman, a detective with the Irish Constabulary, was a man of sixty years with a strong but deeply wrinkled face—a jutting jaw, a sharp nose, thin lips, bushy black eyebrows in contrast with his bristly white hair, pale blue eyes and ruddy cheeks. His hair looked as if the wind had just blown through it, and his body was thin under his heavy tweed jacket.

Harrigan continued to explain. ''You must understand, Colonel MacKenzie, that a few parts of Ireland, particularly coastal towns like Ballykillen, are effectively under the control of the Irish Republican Army—the IRA. The government's writ runs there, but it runs cautiously. The government could establish one hundred percent effective control, but we could do it only at the cost of moving in troops and fighting a small-scale civil war.''

''Since when,'' Bolan asked, ''did the IRA get directly involved in smuggling drugs?''

"Let me assure you, Colonel," Harrigan replied, "that the IRA isn't engaged in smuggling drugs."

"The problem," Brognola put in, "is with a small new group of terrorists who call themselves IRA but really aren't. They're accumulating a major arsenal of sophisticated weapons, which they pay for by trafficking in narcotics. Most of the drugs being sold on the streets over there come through Irish villages like Ballykillen."

"Through Ballykillen and a score of other villages," Harrigan added. "The difficulty is that they make themselves appear to be Irish patriots, which inspires the villagers to protect them. That's why I say we could have precipitated a riot if our officers had investigated those children's book bags. The Irish are sensitive about their freedoms—as well they might be—and are quick to protect and defend anyone who presents himself as a fighter for Ireland."

"They call themselves the Curran Brigade," Brognola said.

"Curran?"

"John Philpot Curran," Harrigan explained, "was a genuine Irish hero, a man deserving of all the respect the Irish people can give him. It's a profanation of his name that a gang of drug smugglers should call themselves the Curran Brigade."

"But they know what they're doing," Brognola observed. "They're using the name of a real fighter for Irish freedom to cover their criminal machinations."

"Where are the narcotics coming from?" Bolan asked.

"Sicily, the south of France, Corsica. If you trace it back far enough, the heroin comes from the Middle East and Asia, of course, and the cocaine comes from South America. The Curran Brigade is allied with the Mafia and with Union Corse, as well as some terrorist gangs in the Middle East."

"And the fishing boats rendezvous with freighters, I suppose," Bolan concluded.

Harrigan nodded. "At night."

"Can't you intercept the incoming boats before they reach the fishing villages?"

"Colonel MacKenzie, there are thousands of boats out there at night. Of those thousands maybe ten or twenty rendezvous with ships and take on illicit drugs. We stop boats at random, but we almost never find narcotics. When they see a cutter coming, they throw the stuff overboard in weighted bags."

"The boat you showed us on the tape?"

"We knew about that one. An informer told us he'd be bringing in narcotics. We could have stopped him, but we wanted to make the tape to show not just you and Mr. Brognola, but a lot of people, something of how these people work. That boat goes out every night. Every day after school those children come to greet their daddy. He brings in narcotics once a month—maybe not that often."

"That's another element of the problem," Brognola said. "There are hundreds of fishermen willing to cooperate with the Curran Brigade. Some of them because they think it's a way to help drive the British out of Northern Ireland, some of them just for what they're paid. But because there are so many of them, the Brigade doesn't have to use the same boats very often. So the constabulary searches a boat known to have carried narcotics before and doesn't find any. But that same boat may be carrying stuff again next week or next month.''

''Drive the British out of Northern Ireland...'' Bolan said. ''A tall order.''

''The weapons they're accumulating are powerful enough to fight an army,'' Harrigan told him. ''Kalashnikovs, American M-16s, pistols, grenades, plastic explosives. And something far more troubling—rocket launchers. We've captured two MILAN launchers. Have you heard of those, Colonel?''

Bolan nodded. ''Guided antitank missile. A little obsolete on the battlefield, but effective and dangerous just the same.''

''Think of one being fired at a limousine,'' Brognola growled, ''from half a mile away. Or even a mile.''

''Assassination.''

''Exactly,'' Harrigan said. ''That, we very much fear, is just what the Curran Brigade has in mind.''

''Whose assassination?'' Bolan asked.

Harrigan sighed. ''Well, it could be anybody's. What we most fear is that it will be the queen.''

The three men fell silent for a long moment.

Bolan stood and walked to the window. He needed a minute to think through the impact of what Hal Brognola and Inspector Harrigan had just told him.

"The Man knows all about it," the big Fed told him. "The Irish prime minister—"

"Entirely unofficially," Harrigan quickly interrupted.

"Entirely unofficially asked if we could help. Specifically what he was worried about was the possibility that some Irish American hotheads might be financing the Curran Brigade. But we've looked into that, and it's no go. I'm not going to tell you that no American of Irish descent is in any way involved, but the vast majority of Irish Americans, even those who sympathize with the IRA, reject the Curran Brigade. They don't like its tactics, and they don't like its use of the name Curran."

"The IRA itself emphatically rejects the Brigade," Harrigan added. "There are some rough boys in the IRA, especially in the Provisional Wing, but they see the Curran Brigade as nothing better than brutal terrorists involved in terrorism for the sake of terrorism, doing nothing for any legitimate Irish cause."

"What does the Brigade really want, then?" Bolan asked.

Hal Brognola leaned across his desk. "Who knows better than you? You know what terrorists really want."

Bolan nodded. "Yeah, I know. They talk about freedom, patriotism, anti-imperialism . . . What most of them really want is money."

"And power," Brognola added.

"They are," Harrigan said quietly, "what I believe you Americans call 'professional losers.' Men who cannot achieve any sort of success, they turn to crime to bolster their fortunes and egos. Like all terrorists, they begin by terrorizing the people they say they mean to serve."

"What the President is concerned about," the big Fed stated, "is the possibility of their succeeding in murdering the queen. Obviously he's worried about her life, but—"

"But he's worried also," Harrigan interrupted, "about what would follow such a vicious murder. If Irish terrorists murdered the queen of England, British public opinion would be satisfied with nothing less than war. Within a week of such a horror, less, the British army would be ashore in Ireland. What's at stake, Colonel MacKenzie," the inspector continued gravely, "is far more than just interdicting the importation of heroin and cocaine into the British Isles. A very great deal more is at risk."

"And routine methods aren't enough to cope with the threat," Brognola said to Bolan. "That's why the President suggested I ask you to go to Ireland. I've explained your sanction and your methods of operation to Inspector Harrigan, and he's discussed you with his government. They're requesting your help."

"Officially, Colonel MacKenzie, my government can't acknowledge you, any more than your own government can. On the other hand, we can give you unofficial cooperation, and we won't interfere with your using your special methods."

Bolan glanced at Brognola. "I see."

"And on the basis of what the President and Mr. Brognola have told us, we have great confidence in you."

CHAPTER TWO

Mack Bolan, the Executioner, stood on the pitching deck of the cutter as it rolled in the churning wake of the small freighter, studying the decks of the other vessel through a sniperscope.

He saw nothing unusual. The rusty little freighter looked perfectly ordinary. It sat high in the water, which meant that it was empty. Fifty miles off Slyne Head, it was moving north. In a few hours it would round Erris Head and might enter Sligo Bay. Or it might be bound for Londonderry, or Belfast, or even across the North Channel for Glasgow.

The cutter was dark, and there was no sign yet from the freighter that anyone aboard knew an Irish cutter was in its wake.

"International waters, you understand," Michael Harrigan said.

"If he's carrying narcotics, I don't care," Bolan growled.

"We have to care," Harrigan replied. "Portuguese registry. Flying the Portuguese flag—"

"Look, coming out on deck to the right."

The Irish detective put a sniperscope to his eye and looked. Four men were wrestling a rubber boat out onto the deck. They lugged it to the rail and abruptly shoved it overboard. "Stop engines," Harrigan directed the captain of the cutter. "Dark and quiet."

The cutter came to a dead stop. The rubber boat, which had landed upside down, rose and fell on the waves fifty yards astern.

"We wait," Harrigan said.

"Why not get the cargo off?" Bolan suggested.

Three minutes later Bolan and the inspector were in another rubber boat, paddling toward the upside-down boat. When they reached it, Bolan grabbed one of the nylon lines that ran around it, pulled it closer and flipped it over.

"Just what we expected," Harrigan said.

What they saw looked at first like a bundle of life preservers, but it wasn't. It was a watertight package of heavy vinyl, securely sealed and securely lashed inside the rubber boat.

"Don't have to guess what's in that," Bolan growled. Drawing a knife from its scabbard on his belt, he slashed the vinyl. White powder spilled through the slit. It was heroin, or cocaine—one or the other. Bolan slashed the package repeatedly. The precious poison spilled out into the little boat, mixing with the seawater in the bottom. "This'll spoil somebody's profits."

Inspector Harrigan tapped a little steel box with his paddle. "Radio locator transmitter. Somebody's homing in on that and will be here shortly."

Bolan flipped the boat upside down again to let the narcotic spill into the sea. Then they paddled away toward the cutter.

"Hear it?" Harrigan asked.

Yeah. Bolan heard what the inspector heard—the throaty rumble of a marine engine, throttled down and coming slowly toward the radio signal from the rubber boat. The approaching boat was running dark.

It had drifted while Bolan and Harrigan paddled to the rubber boat and slit the package. It was maybe a hundred yards away, all but visible, nothing but a faint shadow against the western sky.

The coming boat didn't need light to home in on the rubber boat. But suddenly light appeared to help the crew lift the dinghy aboard and open the package. It was a fishing boat, one of a thousand of its kind that worked these waters. Simple and rugged, it was a working boat, not a yacht.

Suddenly there was an angry yell. They had found their slit package. The angry drug runners switched on a powerful searchlight and swung it across the sea. In seconds Bolan and Harrigan glowed in the powerful beam. A moment later automatic fire chopped the water a few yards away.

Harrigan drew a revolver and began firing on the vessel. Bolan had come better equipped. He had a Heckler & Koch G-11 caseless assault rifle. The weapon fired bullets set into a block of propellant and didn't eject cartridge casings as it was fired. The Executioner had chosen it for the night mission for its rapid rate of fire, but more for its ability to fire reliably even if immersed in water.

He raised the G-11, and as the gunners on the boat corrected their range and their rounds chopped closer, he fired at the fishing boat. He had set the weapon to fire 3-round bursts, and he squeezed off three of them.

Slugs fired from a G-11 are small, but they come fast and they penetrate. He couldn't tell what he'd hit, but the assault from the fishing boat stopped for a moment.

Bolan swung the G-11 around and let loose two bursts into the rear of the hull. He meant to penetrate the boat's fuel tanks and start a fire if he could.

The crew of the fishing boat yelled and cursed. One of them opened fire again. Inspector Harrigan took careful aim on his muzzle-flash and silenced him with a single shot from his revolver.

Now the cutter opened fire. It had a deck-mounted machine gun, and a storm of heavy stuff flew over the water and began to hack the wooden fishing boat to splinters. Then the fishing boat burst into flame. In an instant it was a roiling ball of fire.

"I'm afraid," Harrigan said, "that we won't have an opportunity to interrogate those chaps."

MACK BOLAN WALKED through the shattered bathhouse adjacent to a small swimming pool. The last of the injured children had been loaded into the ambulance, which had just pulled away, its blue lights flashing and its Klaxon blaring. The vehicle was transporting four children to Oliver Cromwell Hospital. One of them wasn't expected to survive.

Debris floated on the water in the little pool—bits of shattered wood, some of it charred, paper, some clothing.

The area was deserted, save for the grim men of the Irish Constabulary and a squad of British soldiers in combat uniforms. The soldiers raised their rifles from time to time and peered through their telescopic sights, looking at windows in nearby buildings, checking cars and vans that were passing on the street.

"Damn fools!" Captain Donald Fraser growled.

"Why attack children?" Bolan asked, at a loss to find an explanation for the carnage.

The captain sighed and shook his head. "In the afternoon the pool is for children. Evenings, two nights a week, my lads are allowed the use of the place. They come here to swim, to cool off after a hot, dusty day's work. The bomb was meant to go off when there were twenty British soldiers in the bathhouse or around the pool. The damn fools didn't set the timer right." He sighed heavily again. "Tomorrow somebody will issue a statement saying they 'regret the error.' But, they'll say, it was a patriotic act. And they'll say it was the fault of the British, who keep troops on the sacred soil of Ireland. What's worse, a lot of Irish people will believe them."

Bolan glanced around. The pool was small, with stained and cracked tiles. The bathhouse had been a dirty old brick building. The explosive charge had been hidden somewhere inside, probably in a locker.

The neighborhood was modest but respectable. Closely packed houses lined the streets, their brick walls black with industrial grime. But the windows were clean and draped with lace curtains. Pots of geraniums sat on many windowsills, and tiny beds of other flowers grew around the door stoops.

An armored personnel carrier blocked the street. More soldiers, with rifles carried high, alert and nervous, patrolled the street.

"So, welcome to Belfast, Colonel MacKenzie," the British captain said bitterly. "Welcome to cloud-cuckoo-land."

To Captain Fraser, Mack Bolan was Colonel William MacKenzie, an American intelligence officer unofficially assigned to look into the most recent wave of terrorist bombings by the IRA. Whether or not the captain believed that, it was what he had been ordered to believe, and he accepted it. He had not, in fact, ever heard the name Mack Bolan, or of the Executioner. He only hoped that this grim-faced, quiet American would take home an accurate report of what he was seeing in Northern Ireland and that the government of the United States would be moved to help restore peace in these troubled counties and this tormented city.

"Climb into the personnel carrier with me, Colonel, and I'll give you a ride out of here."

"I think I'll walk."

"The streets aren't safe."

Bolan shrugged. "I'm not wearing a British army uniform. Nobody knows me, and nobody's interested in me. I'll be okay."

"Good luck, then. I'll see you at headquarters."

BOLAN WASN'T WEARING a British army uniform. That much was true. It was *not* true that nobody knew him or that nobody was interested in him.

Behind the curtains in a house across the street, a man with powerful binoculars had been watching Mack Bolan talking with the British captain. He'd seen him arrive in a British army vehicle and now saw the big man walk away from the captain with a friendly wave and cross the street.

"That one," the watcher said, pointing. "Mark him."

The man had spoken to a woman who turned without a word and hurried after the big man. The watcher in turn left by the rear door of the house, rushed to a telephone booth in the next street and dialed a number.

"Maggie's marking a civilian friend of Captain Fraser. Either he was helping the Brit with the investigation or he's an informer. He's altogether too friendly with the army. North on Harry Street. Let's have his British ass, shall we?"

THE WARRIOR HAD BEEN FIGHTING in the urban jungle far too long not to become quickly aware that he was being followed. The old woman was in too much of a hurry, and her turns matching his were no coincidence.

He could shake her, but Bolan knew it would be better to find out why she was back there, determinedly keeping half a block's distance.

He stopped and pretended to study something in a shop window. She stopped. He moved on. She moved. She obviously didn't want to catch up with him. All she was doing was keeping track of him. Which meant, likely, that she wasn't working alone. Someone else was around, or someone else was going to join her.

He was being set up for something, and whatever it was, he'd be ready.

The warrior stared hard at a dark blue van as it drove slowly toward him. He tensed, waiting for a blast of gunfire, but the vehicle cruised past.

The van appeared innocent enough, but Bolan recognized a drive-by when he saw one. The vehicle would continue on around the block, then the gunmen would make their move.

Bolan turned slightly and watched as the van rolled down the street. As it passed the old woman, she nodded almost imperceptibly.

He stepped out a little faster, heading for a Ford that was parked on the street. The vehicle would provide enough cover.

The warrior didn't duck too soon. He watched for the guys to make their move.

And they did make it. The muzzle of a submachine gun poked through the window of the van. At that instant Bolan bent his knees, and to the gunman in the van the target disappeared behind the parked car.

Even so, the guy pulled his trigger. The tension of the situation had gotten to him, and slugs stitched the parked Ford, shattering its glass.

Brakes squealed, and the van skidded to a stop. The gunner threw open the door and jumped into the street. Apparently it hadn't occurred to him that the man he'd been sent to kill might be armed, too, and might be able to defend himself.

Bolan's big-bore automatic, the .44 Magnum Desert Eagle, was in leather under his jacket, and he jerked it free. He squeezed off a shot just as the gunner started to take aim. The authoritative blast from the huge weapon echoed through the street, and the man with the Uzi was hurled against the open door of the van and crumpled to the pavement.

The van shot forward, and Bolan fired again. The slug punched through the rear door of the little van, and abruptly it ran up over the curb and crashed into a door stoop.

People in Belfast didn't go running toward violence. They hid from it. Bolan leathered the Desert Eagle and walked away. The old woman ran in the opposite direction.

CHAPTER THREE

The woman called Maggie sat with her back to the wall, sucking into her lungs the last smoke from a cigarette that had burned down almost to her fingers, occasionally lifting a mug of dark ale and drinking thirstily. She was approximately sixty-five years old, gray and wrinkled. She wore a tattered old raincoat, and her head was covered by a scarf knotted under her chin.

A younger man sat facing her across the table, himself drinking ale and smoking a cigarette. It was difficult to judge his age, except to say that he was young, because his hair was black and thick, and a heavy black beard covered all his lower face. He wore big, plastic-rimmed eyeglasses, and his smile, as he talked with the woman, was broad and toothy.

The man's name was Timothy Finnerty, and he used the title chief of staff of the Curran Brigade. He was, in fact, its commanding officer.

"A cannon, I say, Timothy. It was the most horrible explosion I ever heard from a gun. And the poor lad just flopped like a fish once or twice. Then the man fired the thing a second time, and—"

"Yes," Finnerty said calmly. "The bullet tore our man's arm off. But that's not what I need to know,

Maggie. I want you to go through it again. What did the man look like?''

"He's big, and handsome, I suppose, in a hawkish sort of way. Black hair. More than six feet tall.''

"Did you get a look at his eyes?''

"No. Not up close.''

"Would you know him if you saw him again?''

"I think so. He's not like most men. I mean . . . there's somethin' about him. How can I say it? Uh, confident, wise. Yes. That's it. When he looked back—and he looked back at me a couple of times— what I saw was . . . well, he's a *fighting man,* Timothy. Powerful. When our lads came, I wanted to warn them. But I didn't have a chance. The lads made a big mistake. They underestimated the man they'd been sent after. They weren't ready.''

"We'll be ready for him the next time, Maggie. If there is a next time.''

Finnerty glanced around the pub. Most of the people in the bar he knew by sight, and they knew him. Six of the men were members of the Curran Brigade, as were two of the women. Of the rest, nearly all were sympathizers. It was only the strangers they couldn't be sure of.

Three of the Brigade men and one of the women were his bodyguards. Finnerty wasn't armed. All of them were.

"I'd like to know where he is, that man,'' Finnerty mused. "I want him eliminated. I want you to consider yourself on duty for a while, Maggie. Full-time.

We'll be looking for him, and you're the one most likely to recognize him."

Maggie shook a cigarette from Finnerty's pack and lit it with his lighter. "It'd be easier if we had any idea where he is."

MACK BOLAN WAS no longer in Belfast. Two hours after he shot his would-be murderers on that Belfast street, the warrior had crossed from county Armagh to county Monaghan. At the boundary between Northern Ireland and the Republic of Ireland he'd been passed through by the British authorities without examination of his baggage, and on the Republic side he'd been met by Inspector Harrigan.

"If it were known that the Brits passed you through and that I concurred in it, neither of our lives would be worth much."

"I've seen a little of how they operate," Bolan said grimly.

"I'm not sure you've encountered the Currans. The men who tried to kill you may have been Brigaders, and they may not."

"I'm learning a little more about the IRA," Bolan told him.

"Then you've learned that it's not a unified organization."

"Some of them are Marxists."

"Some are," Harrigan agreed. "An old-fashioned political idea, discredited and all out of style. Not many IRA lads are Marxist anymore, but some are....

What would you call them? Maoists? Just plain terrorists.''

"Some IRA people just want to unify Ireland," Bolan said. "Some want to establish a socialist government in unified Ireland."

"Most want to achieve their arms peacefully," Harrigan agreed. "Unhappily a few, like the Curran Brigade's leader, Timothy Finnerty, have become vicious fanatics.

"Finnerty's father was a fighter. He shot down an Irish policeman—get that, an *Irish* policeman—and was hanged for it. His mother went out on the streets as a prostitute to earn her living and his. She needn't have done that. The lads would have taken care of her. But she did, and so did Tim's sister. Two Irish whores. Something very unusual in our country, Colonel MacKenzie. Our faith condemns that kind of thing, and few women turn to it. But the Finnerty women did, and young Tim grew up the son of one whore and the brother of another. It embittered the lad. When his time came to marry, he married still another whore. It's an odd thing, you'll agree. An odd thing."

"Things like that happen to people," Bolan said. "It doesn't have to turn a man into a terrorist. It can turn him into something better."

"Agreed, my friend. Timothy Finnerty is a psychopath, beyond any question."

Bolan and Harrigan were in a pub in Ballyjamesduff. The room was thick with tobacco smoke and the smell of men's sweat. A young woman had just kicked off her shoes and climbed on a table, and men were dragging other tables up to make her a dance platform. Someone sat down at the piano and began to bang out a rhythmic song. The patrons clapped their hands and sang.

The young woman stamped hard on the table and began to dance. She wore a thick sweater and a long wool skirt, and nothing about her dance was immodest. The dance wasn't improvised; it was a dance that had been performed for a century and more. She stamped, whirled and clapped her hands. Sweat gleamed on her face; her blond hair swung to and fro as she turned.

Bolan turned from the conversation and frowned at the young woman. He glanced at Harrigan, then turned away from her abruptly and reached for his pint of ale.

"You interested in her?" Harrigan asked.

Bolan shrugged. "She's . . . attractive."

"She's Kathryn O'Connor, an officer of the Irish Constabulary. She's assigned to us."

The warrior stared again at the young woman. She swung, and her skirt whirled high—not high, but above her knees, revealing a few more inches of bare leg. The dance, which exposed nothing more than the three inches above her knee, was somehow interestingly erotic.

The men in the pub cheered the dancer. Their enthusiasm was expressed in easy banter, not in raucous words. She acknowledged them with a wave and a smile.

"She's beautiful," Bolan said simply.

"She carries a gun under that thick sweater, and she's an effective policewoman. We came here this evening because she's found—or thinks she's found—a cache of arms that may belong to the Brigade."

"How did she—"

"She won't tell you," Harrigan interrupted. "She's well-known around here, and she won't speak to us. We'll see her later, somewhere else."

"Then why are we here?" Bolan asked.

"Because I wanted an ale and some supper," the inspector replied.

O'CONNOR HAD STOPPED her car along the road, and when Harrigan pulled in behind it and flashed his lights, she got out and walked back to the constabulary car—as if she were receiving a speeding ticket.

"Kathryn..." Harrigan said.

She opened the back door and entered the car.

"This is Colonel MacKenzie."

"I noticed him earlier."

Bolan turned around to look at her and nodded. He couldn't see her as well as he had in the pub, but he could smell her—an aroma of damp, fresh air that had dispelled the smoky atmosphere of the pub. She had been driving with her car wide open to the night air.

"Tell us where the arms are," Harrigan requested.

"A distance from here," she replied calmly.

"This gentleman has come to help us. He's an independent who works his own way—"

"I heard about what happened in Belfast," she interrupted. "It was Colonel MacKenzie, was it?"

"Suppose it was? Are you willing to work with him?"

"Yes." She thrust her head forward to have a better look at him in the light. "American," she observed. "Well, I'm in control. I found the cache, and I control the operation against it."

"Understood," Bolan replied. "I wouldn't have it any other way."

O'Connor grinned. "If you could, Colonel Mac-Kenzie, you'd have it so that a woman wouldn't have a part in the operation. But you don't have that option."

"I don't ask for that option."

"You want to know where they have a thousand AK-47s?" she asked.

"We'll get a warrant," Inspector Harrigan stated.

"By the time you get a warrant, Michael, the clerks in the court that issued the warrant will have sent the alarm halfway across Ireland. It's my understanding that Colonel MacKenzie works without a warrant."

"He has a special sanction."

"I'll work within that sanction. So then, go away, Michael, so you don't hear the details of what we're going to do. If you don't know what we're up to, you won't be able to answer anyone's questions."

WITHIN MINUTES Bolan's weapons were transferred into the back of O'Connor's car, which was an MG. The vehicle was painted British racing green and was obviously maintained with loving care. As a driver she was on the borderline between professional and over-confident amateur. She knew all the tricks of driving, which were very useful on Irish roads, and she sped west through the night at sixty and seventy miles an hour.

O'Connor shoved a knitted cap down over her head to prevent her hair from being whipped by the wind, and she reached into a pocket by her door and handed Bolan—of all things—a blue-and-white baseball cap bearing the logo of the New York Yankees.

"Don't ask me how I found this cache of arms. It wasn't by accident, but it wasn't in accordance with the rules of police procedure."

"I'm not scornful of the rules of police procedure," the warrior told her.

"Neither am I—except when they make it impossible to protect the innocent."

O'Connor stared at the road ahead and drove with both arms high on the wheel, except when she downshifted and upshifted, keeping the MG just at the limit of its ability to cling to the road.

"These weapons," she said abruptly, "will be guarded by three or four heavily armed men. If we have any luck, they'll be asleep. I've seen the hiding place. I did a reconnaissance this afternoon and looked at it in the daylight. There were no guards in sight, and no one noticed me. At least no one gave any sign of noticing me. The weapons are stored in a stone barn and in some outbuildings. There are explosives as well as rifles and ammunition."

"How do you know?" Bolan asked bluntly. "Don't you think I ought to have some idea why you think there are arms in this place?"

"In its history Ireland has suffered three terrible plagues, Colonel—the potato blight that starved tens of thousands 150 years ago, the English and informers. Whatever the Irish try to do, someone invariably carries the word to the opposing side. I'm confident that my information is correct."

The road they had taken from Ballyjamesduff was no superhighway. Now the Irish policewoman turned onto narrower roads that wound through the countryside, and from those she turned onto country lanes wide only enough for one car.

The moon was three-quarters full, intermittently shining bright and disappearing behind cottony clouds. The land smelled of rain-wet green foliage and of the manure dropped by cattle and sheep.

O'Connor drove beyond the end of the pavement, into a lane that was rutted and bumpy. She slowed, but even then the car's crunching on gravel was loud enough to be heard across the fields.

"We stop here," she said, pulling the car over and stopping in front of a gate in a fence. "We've got some distance to walk."

Getting out of the car on the driver's side, O'Connor startled Bolan by hauling her skirt and a half-slip up over her head and, wearing only white panties below her heavy sweater, bending over to lift from the rear of the car a camouflage jumpsuit. She pulled those up over her legs, then stripped off the sweater, revealing for a moment generous breasts spilling from an inadequate bra—plus the shoulder holster in which she carried a Walther PPK, the concealable 7.65 mm automatic favored by European police forces. She unstrapped the holster and laid it on the hood of the car, shoved her arms through the sleeves, shrugged them up and zipped the front. Lastly the police-woman donned the holster.

Bolan was surprised at the weapons she pulled out from under a canvas cover in the back seat. Besides the PPK O'Connor would be toting a mini-Uzi.

She buckled a heavy belt around her waist, which would hold ammunition pouches containing extra magazines for the Uzi and the PPK. Four tear gas grenades hung from clips on the belt.

The Executioner hadn't anticipated this night raid. He wore a black nylon jacket, black pants and boots. He did what she did—unstrapped his leather holster and switched it outside his jacket. He was carrying a .44 Magnum Desert Eagle and a Beretta 93-R, equipped with a silencer and flash-suppressor. He had extra ammo, but nothing else. He hoped it was enough.

O'CONNOR OPENED the gate and entered the field. She'd told Bolan that the farm buildings were beyond a low rise just ahead, and they trotted forward, moving a little away from the fence. In two minutes they reached the top of the rise and dropped to their bellies on the damp ground. Nearest the road was a stone cottage, a small, square building with a sagging tile roof. Yellow light gleamed in the windows.

"Not farmers," O'Connor whispered. "Farmers don't stay up this late."

A big stone barn dominated the farmyard behind the cottage. It was four times as big as the house and was in better repair. Beyond the house and between the barn and the road was another small stone building. It was, most likely, a spring house where cool water kept temperatures moderate and preserved the milk from the dairy herd. Behind the barn, out of sight from the house, were two wooden animal pens.

The policewoman touched Bolan's arm and pointed to what he had already seen—five cars drawn up in the yard between the cottage and the spring house.

Too many cars for a simple farmstead.

Too many cars for a cache of weapons guarded by two or three gunmen.

"They've brought in reinforcements," she said.

"Maybe. Or maybe they're moving weapons out for some operation."

"Or a new shipment is coming in."

"That could be, too," the warrior agreed.

The Executioner rose, and in a crouch he trotted over the crest of the little rise and down toward the farm buildings. O'Connor followed.

Bolan knew that a farm this size should have had a few dogs, but he couldn't hear any barking. They moved quickly down the soft, moonlit slope toward the outbuildings.

Yeah. Now he could hear the dogs—big dogs. But inside one of the buildings—deep inside, like in a cellar.

"Luck," Bolan whispered to his companion.

"What luck?"

"They locked up the dogs. Too many strangers around. Two more strangers don't make them bark any more."

"Which means," she concluded, "that there are extra troops around taking in a shipment or sending one out."

"You got it."

"We might be moving in on more than we can handle."

Bolan nodded. "Want to back off?"

O'Connor shot him a piercing glance. "Let's move!"

She had guts. You could say that. He returned her gaze for a moment, then moved down the slope.

Ahead was a woven-wire fence, with vines tangled in the rusting wire. It was no cover against gunfire but afforded them a hiding place where they could crouch and look.

They were only twenty-five yards from the near end of the big stone barn, and they could clearly see the five vehicles drawn up in the farmyard. They could also see the points of orange fire on the ends of half a dozen cigarettes. Men were lounging around the cars and vans.

"I wish we had a sniperscope," O'Connor whispered.

"We don't need one to see the deal. What I'm looking at is hardmen with heavy stuff. I see two assault rifles, and where there are two, you can figure there are more."

"That says it for us, doesn't it, Colonel?"

"Not yet. Too many guys with too much iron make too much confidence. I could go around behind and get close, signal you, and you toss a tear gas grenade. What could we do in the confusion?"

O'Connor peered through the misty night at the farmyard. "There are others in the house," she pointed out. "I don't like your plan, and I'm not sure I could get a grenade in from here. Here. You carry one. And let's move in together. When it gets tough, this—" she patted the mini-Uzi "—works better at close range."

"It's not smart to work too close together. You work around to the left. Get back on the road and slip past the house. I'll give you five minutes to be in place. Don't toss a grenade until I fire a shot. Then toss one in among the cars. Let them have a burst or two from the Uzi, then move out. They'll be concentrating on you, and I'll take out as many as I can."

O'Connor nodded. As she slipped away along the fence, Bolan threw himself over and dropped to the ground on the opposite side.

He hadn't told the policewoman exactly what he intended to do. The warrior figured he could take out some of the gunmen with his Beretta before any of them knew what was happening and before she heard a shot and threw the grenade.

He drew the 93-R with his right hand and crept down the slope toward the farm, working his way to the right to make it possible to put the stone barn between him and the armed men around the parked vehicles.

It seemed to the warrior that the moonlight had to be casting its light on him as he made his way down the slope. Yet he knew from long experience that men tending a perimeter were not often alert, not often sharp-eyed. They were bored and focused their thoughts on other things—women, alcohol, glory. Few of them could be counted on to scan the area constantly. Sentries were rarely as responsible as their commanders hoped.

Coming within fifty feet of the barn, Bolan dropped to the ground and lay studying what was ahead of him. One man stood on the wooden back porch of the cottage. In the light from a window Bolan could see the assault rifle slung over the man's shoulder. Another gunner stood to the side of the house, also carrying an assault rifle and staring at the road. For a moment the warrior wondered if this man had spotted O'Connor. Then he decided he hadn't. The guy was too calm. He smoked and walked around, alert but bored.

Hardmen. No question about it. Something was going down, and they were waiting for it.

The Executioner didn't move against any man until he could be sure of who and what he was. The policewoman's intel, plus what he saw, dispelled all doubt as to what these guys were and what they were doing.

Bolan crawled forward. The man by the side of the house jerked his assault rifle around and prowled toward the road, weapon up and ready to fire. Had he seen O'Connor?

The warrior still doubted it, but there was no doubt that the guy was nervous, ready to fire on anything. He turned and stalked toward where Bolan lay, as if he'd seen him.

The Beretta could be fitted with a folding wire stock for long shots. Bolan rarely used that, but he did sometimes fold down the front handgrip that made it possible to use both hands effectively when aiming. He pulled down the leverlike grip and took careful aim.

A single, silenced 9 mm round punched through the gunman's chest. He dropped the assault rifle and fell, first to his knees, then quietly to the ground. No one had heard the shot.

Bolan was up and sprinting toward the downed gunner. The sentry on the porch stood directly in the bright light spilling from the house, his eyes not yet adjusted to the moon-bathed night. The Executioner watched the man closely as he moved toward the prostrate gunman, but his movements weren't detected by the man on the porch.

The warrior reached the dead man and, more importantly, the assault rifle, a Kalashnikov. He checked the weapon, then the body. The gunner had an extra magazine, which Bolan shoved into his waistband.

So, okay, now he had a heavy weapon, like the ones he faced. Carrying the Kalashnikov, he circled the house to the front and came around to where the cars and vans were parked.

The terrorists weren't careful. They were like hired guns, just standing around waiting for orders. He could hear them talking. They talked like their kind everywhere, all the time—loud with braggadocio, their voices coarsened by smoking and drinking. They weren't devoted to anybody's cause. They were gunmen. And armed. He recognized more Kalashnikovs.

How many? Six. Maybe seven or eight. Not good odds. The warrior set to work to even them.

He crouched at the corner of the house. First he looked back at the road to where O'Connor might be waiting. He'd given her five minutes to get in place before he opened fire and she threw her grenade, and that five minutes had all but elapsed. He wondered what she would do if she thought he'd been too long silent.

A gunner leaned against one of the vans, visible in the moonlight and visible also in a narrow beam of yellow light from the house. Bolan focused on him. He carried a Kalashnikov in a sling over his shoulder, and he was sipping from a pint bottle of something.

Bolan laid his own Kalashnikov on the ground and drew the Beretta. But suddenly the whole road before the house was lighted, as was the front of the house where Bolan lay against the stone foundation. A truck had come around a curve in the road, and its bright headlights lit everything.

The man by the van tossed his all-but-empty pint aside and unslung his rifle. He barked an order to another man, and the two of them moved toward the road, the second man bringing an Uzi.

It wasn't Bolan they'd spotted in the beam of the headlights. They'd seen O'Connor. She was lying on the short bank between the road and the farmyard, with her face up for a quick look, which would have been safe enough in the cool, dim moonlight, but wasn't at all in the fierce beam of headlights.

The man who'd dropped the pint raised his Kalashnikov and aimed toward her. But he crumpled to the ground suddenly, neutralized by a 9 mm slug from Bolan's silenced Beretta.

The second man stopped dead still and stared around, looking for the source of the shot that had killed his confederate. Another shot blew away the flesh of his throat, and he dropped to the ground.

Bolan turned his Kalashnikov toward the truck and let loose a long, deadly burst, then a second burst that emptied the first magazine. The policewoman took the cue. She, too, fired a burst at the vehicle. The headlights went out, and the truck drifted to the side of the road and into a shallow ditch.

O'Connor remembered the plan. She pitched her tear gas grenade among the suddenly alert men around the vans in the farmyard. It burst and spewed forth the choking gas.

Bolan had reloaded the Kalashnikov, and he sprayed the area with concentrated fire. The magazine ran empty, and he raced forward to grab the Uzi dropped by one of the gunners.

Confusion. Bedlam. The gunmen around the cars and trucks fired wildly as the tear gas spread over the ground on the quiet night air and rose into their noses and throats.

O'Connor ran forward and joined Bolan. She stood beside him and fired repeated short bursts from her mini-Uzi. The Executioner still had the tear gas grenade she'd given him, and he tossed it through the window and into the house.

He'd fired the Uzi until it was empty, and now he threw it down and grabbed up the Kalashnikov dropped by the man who had been drinking. The terrorists were retreating. A car bumped away across the field, dropped over the bank and skidded across the gravel lane. A van followed. Two men raced after them, yelling.

For a moment they stood at the front corner of the house—Bolan and O'Connor, weapons ready, alert, looking for targets. Suddenly it was apparent there weren't any. The survivors had run. Only Mack Bolan and Kathryn O'Connor were left in the field.

He looked at her curiously. In the yellow light from the house he could see her face plainly. It was streaked with sweat and flushed beet-red. And he'd never seen on a woman's face before such an expression of triumph.

He'd known men who liked combat—and maybe a worse way to put it, liked killing. The war lovers, some had called them. And it looked as if Kathryn shared the addiction.

"Let's make sure we've got the right place," she said.

The policewoman led the way into the barn, and it was apparent immediately that they had zeroed in on the right target. The barn was an arsenal. She'd said there were a thousand Kalashnikovs here. There seemed to be closer to two thousand, and, best guess, half a million 7.62 mm rounds. Plus fragmentation grenades and perhaps a thousand 9 mm pistols— Brownings, Walthers, Berettas, Colts, Smith & Wessons...and hundreds of thousands of 9 mm rounds.

"You know how to handle it?" she asked.

Bolan nodded.

"So do I."

In twenty minutes they'd set their charges in the barn and in the truck, which turned out to contain more assault rifles and a grenade launcher with ammo. The terrorists had supplied themselves with a variety of devices to detonate their explosives, including radio-controlled detonators that Bolan and O'Connor used. Half an hour later, as the headlights of approaching police cars at last reached the farm, they set off their charges.

They blew the truck first, which flew apart in a ball of fire. Then the barn, which dissolved in a bright burst, spraying stones, timbers, armament and ammo over a hundred acres of peaceful Irish countryside.

CHAPTER FOUR

The hot touch of the explosion roared across them. It snatched the breath from their bodies for a moment because it took all the oxygen from the air. Then, though Bolan and O'Connor were behind the crest of a hill, they were pelted with debris. They should have put more distance between them before they detonated the charges in the barn. Grenades were exploding, some of them high above the main explosion. Secondary explosions flashed inside the fire that submerged the wreckage of the barn.

Bolan rolled his body over O'Connor's to protect her from the falling debris, and he folded his arms over his head. The wreckage of an assault rifle fell not far from them. The warrior took some painful hits before the torrent stopped.

Finally he was able to roll off his companion. "Damn it," he grumbled as he got to his knees. "I think we set off too much of the stuff."

The policewoman lay prone, blinking and staring in disbelief at the farm. Not only was the barn gone, the house had collapsed, and the cars and vans had been blown into a jumble, some in the wreckage of the house, some out on the road. "Couldn't leave any of it," she said. "It has a way of showing up where it kills people."

Police cars were approaching. They had slowed down and were coming on more cautiously.

"Time to move," Bolan stated decisively.

They turned and trotted across the field toward where they had left her car. The gate wasn't far, and they reached it in a few minutes.

"Hold it," Bolan whispered.

Once again it was someone's addiction to cigarettes that had given warning. Little orange points of fire pinpointed the man's position.

O'Connor nodded. "I think I see two of them. Or is the second one something else, like a tree trunk?"

"Could they be police?" the warrior asked.

"Impossible. Officers wouldn't be hiding from me. They'd know the car, and they'd be waiting at the vehicle, not back in the trees across the road." She ejected the magazine from the mini-Uzi, checked it and shoved it back in.

"You've got one more tear gas grenade," Bolan pointed out. "I'd like to use it. I'd rather be sure those guys aren't police or military before we open fire."

"Suit yourself." O'Connor shrugged and handed him the grenade.

Bolan crawled forward, and when he was within twenty-five yards of the stand of trees across the road and a few yards behind the car, he threw the grenade. It bounced into the grove and burst, spewing a thick cloud of choking gas.

Two men raced into the road, screaming curses. Both were armed with assault rifles, and they opened fire, sending unaimed bursts of fire toward the field where they guessed the grenade had come from.

Before Bolan could draw the Desert Eagle for a shot, O'Connor's Uzi chattered viciously. She knew how to handle her weapon, and her burst cut down one of the gunmen. The other fell to his knees and began to scream.

"Hold your fire!" Bolan shouted. "I want him alive."

The policewoman joined him, nervously raising and lowering the muzzle of the mini-Uzi. "I'm not sure I want a survivor who's seen me."

"Then hold back. I'll let him see *me*." The Executioner walked toward the man, who knelt in the gravel of the lane rubbing his eyes with both fists. "Curran?" Bolan asked coldly.

The man lowered his fists and peered up. Kathryn O'Connor needn't have worried about being seen. The man wasn't going to see anything for a while.

"I asked if you're with the Curran gang."

"We aren't a gang," the man muttered hoarsely. "We're soldiers in the war for the freedom of Ireland."

"Ireland is already free," Bolan replied.

"Free? In the hands of cowards who're afraid to fight for the unity of the sacred soil? I don't call myself free, governed by what's in power now." The man lowered his head again and covered his burning eyes with his hands.

"I have a word for your gang."

"If I could see you, you'd be dead," the man mumbled.

"But you can't see me, so listen."

Bolan pulled the slide on the Desert Eagle and ejected a .44 Magnum round. He caught it, reached down and shoved it into the man's shirt pocket.

"Give that to the animal that calls himself the head of the Curran Brigade. He's seen others, and he'll see more. Tell him the fun's over. The game has just been changed, and I'll be looking for him."

"KATHRYN O'CONNOR! At such an hour! And dressed... Well, come in, lass! Come in. With your friend."

"Let me introduce Colonel William MacKenzie," she said to the innkeeper. She looked up into Bolan's face. "Himself is O'Dougherty," she said, nodding toward the cherubic, pink-cheeked, white-haired little man.

"Well, it's a fine hour you've chosen to appear on my doorstep, lass," O'Dougherty said. "By law I'm not even supposed to give you a drink. But, you bein' of the constabulary, I suppose we could say you were checkin' my stock to see that my whiskey's not watered. Hmm? Come in! Come in, Colonel. And welcome."

The inn was dark, but as they stepped across the threshold and into its common room—the bar and dining room—O'Dougherty switched on lights and bustled behind the bar.

"A drop, mind you," he warned as he half filled two coffee mugs with Irish whiskey. "Just enough to see it's not watered." He paused, eyed the quantity in the cups and splashed a little more into each. Then he poured one for himself. "There's not a thing in the house to eat at this hour," he said as he crossed the room and put the mugs on the table. "Well, maybe a joint of beef I could carve on a bit." O'Dougherty took a swallow of whiskey and hurried off toward the kitchen.

"The Irish." O'Connor smiled with warm affection.

Bolan nodded. He tasted the room-temperature, straight whiskey. "Is this how you drink it?"

"No, like this," she replied, tipping back the mug and drinking a third of the contents.

Bolan laughed and took a healthy swallow. The whiskey was fiery and smoky, like Scotch but heavier, with a more pronounced flavor.

"Understand something," she said solemnly. "We can't go any farther in the MG. That's why I pulled it around behind. O'Dougherty will pull it into the barn. By now the word's out. The Curraners will shoot at that car, and not just them. Sympathizers. I wouldn't want to drive it into Dublin in the morning."

It *was* morning. In these latitudes the sun rose early at this time of year, and it hovered in an overcast sky.

"We can stay here awhile," she went on. "We need some sleep. A little later I'll telephone for another car."

Bolan nodded. He couldn't argue with her even if he wanted to.

The innkeeper returned, carrying a tray loaded with mammoth slices of roast beef, bread, mustard and pickles. He shrugged as he put it on the table. "I told you," he said. "At an hour like this there's not much."

There was plenty, and Bolan was hungry.

"I'll not ask what you're up to," the innkeeper said. "Makin' Ireland safe for honest men like me, I imagine."

O'Connor nodded. "It'll be reported on the telly in the morning."

"Aha. So. The politicals. I hope you're bein' careful. We fought for freedom once. Now . . ."

O'Connor spoke to Bolan. "O'Dougherty's father was killed by the English military police. He's got good reason to be a patriot."

"And I am a patriot," O'Dougherty replied. "But to paraphrase what it says in the Good Book, not every man who cries 'Patriot, patriot' is, in fact, a patriot."

"Colonel MacKenzie," she said, "has come to help us fight the false patriots."

O'Dougherty rose from the table, picked up his cup of whiskey and drank the last of it. He walked behind the bar and took two big keys from a board. He returned and put them on the table. "I bid you goodnight," he said. "I'm glad you came. I'll hide the car now and I'll see you in the mornin'."

TIMOTHY FINNERTY TOSSED the .44 Magnum round onto the table in front of him.

"He said that, did he? He said that? He called us 'animals,' and threatened. Well. So. Very well. So be it."

"'So be it'? 'So be it,' Finnerty?" the woman sneered. "What the hell does that mean?"

"This man has declared war."

He sat over eggs and smoked fish in the tiny kitchen of a house in Belfast, eating hungrily, drinking coffee with every bite of food, and glaring back and forth between a man and a woman.

The man's name was James McIlhenny, and Bolan had dropped the .44 between his knees the night before. His eyes were still red and watery. He was a thin man with a long jaw and high cheekbones, thinning black hair and sullen pale blue eyes.

The woman was Molly Finnerty, Timothy's wife. She was a forty-year-old woman who looked her age—still pretty but loosening, showing too much flesh around her jaws and on her arms and legs. She had sandy red hair, a light, freckled complexion and intense blue eyes. She had been a street prostitute fifteen years ago, just as Harrigan had told Bolan, but she had turned since into a tough and dedicated terrorist.

"Who *is* the man?" she demanded. "Who the hell is he, Tim?"

"If I knew that, I'd have some idea where he is, and I'd go get him."

"You'd *send* to get him," she said.

Finnerty looked up at his wife with anger he had to contain. He had learned to detest the woman, but he had learned to... Not to respect her. Not to fear her. What he felt for her was something between fear and respect.

She'd given him reason to hate her, too. Some men laughed at him behind his back.

"The slugs that killed our man here in Belfast yesterday were .44 Magnum," he said. "They—"

"And crippled another," she interrupted.

"And crippled another," Finnerty agreed—and tried not to let her see that he really didn't care, since that man was one of the ones who laughed at him, he was almost certain. "Anyway...that's an unusual caliber. An American caliber, hardly ever seen anywhere else. A few American weapons are chambered for it. So, are we to believe the man who hit us on the streets of Belfast yesterday afternoon is the same man who hit us last night in county Roscommon?"

"Maybe Captain Fraser can tell us," Molly Finnerty suggested.

CAPTAIN DONALD FRASER was stark naked and hung by his ankles on a rope tied around a pipe on the cellar ceiling. He had screamed, but screams couldn't escape the confines of the old cellar deep under what had been a brewery a hundred years ago but had recently been abandoned. Now it was a storage warehouse for empty beer kegs.

Molly Finnerty wondered if the fumes from the hissing gasoline lantern were going to asphyxiate them all before long. It filled the room with intense white light, and because all of the light came from that one source, the room was filled also with stark shadows.

Tim Finnerty had beaten the man. That was Tim's idea of torture—bully-boy beating. He'd broken the captain's right arm and had destroyed his kneecaps, but the man stuck to his story. He hadn't changed an iota of it since they'd brought him here.

Molly sucked on her cigarette, generating a bright point of fire. She reached out and touched Captain Fraser on the scrotum. He groaned and twisted, as if he could somehow draw himself away from her, but said nothing.

"The son of a bitch," Tim growled.

"It's possible he's telling the truth," she said to him.

Finnerty picked up his truncheon. The English captain's eyes widened, and he shook his head.

"Wait a minute," Molly said. "Why not let the doctor try his way?"

Finnerty glanced across the cellar room, where a compact little man with bristly gray hair sat drinking whiskey. "All right. Try it your way, Doctor."

The doctor rose reluctantly, with an air of weariness, and picked up a worn black leather bag. He put the bag down on the table by his bottle, opened it, rummaged around and came out with a syringe and a vial of clear liquid. With hands that trembled slightly but that were obviously experienced, he shot down the plunger to drive the air out of the body of the syringe, then pushed the long thin needle through the rubber cap on his vial. As he pulled the plunger up, the body of the syringe filled with fluid from the bottle.

"So..." he muttered. The little man crossed the room and, for a moment, stood looking at the English captain, who stared at him, acknowledging defeat and complete resignation. "Hold him still."

Molly encircled the captain with her arms and steadied him. The doctor chose a spot on the man's upper left arm, jabbed the needle in, pressed down the plunger and injected the fluid into the captain's vein. Then he glanced at his wristwatch. "Two or three minutes," he announced, and returned to his table and his bottle.

Molly watched the naked man, and she saw the tension seep out of him. Incredibly he relaxed. His muscles softened, and his flesh settled downward.

"How long's two minutes?" Finnerty muttered.

"Patience," the doctor soothed.

When he'd finished another glass of whiskey, the doctor rose again, this time more purposefully, more briskly, and came to the side of the hanging man. "Now, Captain," he prompted. "Tell us about this man you were seen with at the swimming pool. What's his name?"

"His name is Colonel William MacKenzie," the captain said dully.

"How did you come to know him?"

"He was at headquarters when the word of the bombing came in. It was Colonel Tavener who suggested he go with me to the swimming pool."

"Who is this Colonel MacKenzie?"

"An American."

"Why was he at your headquarters?"

"I don't know."

"Do you mean to say the man accompanied you in your command car when you went to investigate a bombing and you don't know why?"

Fraser blinked but didn't answer. Finnerty stepped forward with his truncheon.

"No, no," the doctor said firmly. "That was too complicated a question. He couldn't understand it."

"I'll knock his bloody teeth out!"

"Right now he wouldn't care."

Finnerty stepped back, kept the truncheon menacingly in his right hand and watched.

The doctor resumed the interrogation. "When was the first time you saw Colonel MacKenzie?"

"At headquarters."

"Did someone introduce him to you?"

"Yes."

"Who?"

"Colonel Tavener."

"Who did he say Colonel MacKenzie was?"

"An American who was going to help us."

"Help you do what?"

"Fight terrorism."

"How was he going to help you?"

Fraser was silent for a long moment, then said, "I don't know."

"When did you last see Colonel MacKenzie?"

"At the swimming pool."

"Haven't you seen him since?"

"No."

"Did he kill a man on the streets of Belfast not long after you last saw him?"

"Yes."

"How do you know?"

"Colonel Tavener told me."

"Were you then looking for him? Was he wanted by the military? By the police?"

"No."

"Why not, if he killed a man?"

"He killed a terrorist."

"And that made it right?"

"Yes."

"Do you mean he is *authorized* to kill anyone he thinks is a terrorist?"

"Yes..."

"Who is he, Captain?"

"Colonel MacKenzie."

Finnerty advanced again. He struck the captain across the bridge of the nose, but the Englishman seemed hardly to notice. Molly stepped between her husband and the captain.

"Who gives Colonel MacKenzie his orders?" the doctor asked.

"I don't know."

"When he came to Belfast, where did he come from?"

"From the south."

"He came up from the Republic?"

"Yes."

The doctor turned to the Finnertys and smiled. Then he returned his attention to the captain and asked, "Does the British military have any weapons that fire .44 Magnum ammunition?"

"No."

"Did Colonel MacKenzie, then, bring his pistol with him when he crossed from the Republic into Ulster?"

"I don't know."

"But a pistol in that caliber couldn't have been issued to him by the British forces?"

"No."

The doctor turned to the Finnertys again and shrugged.

Molly spoke. "What else can you tell us about Colonel MacKenzie?"

"He is a big man. Some sort of . . . special man. Special . . . That's all I know."

"I believe that," Molly said to Finnerty. "I believe that *is* all he knows."

Finnerty slapped his truncheon against the palm of his left hand.

"You can kill him with that if you want to," the doctor said. "You won't find out anything more."

Finnerty pondered for a moment, then tossed the truncheon across the room. "You kill him, Doctor."

The little man returned to his medical bag, took out the syringe and loaded it with a liquid from another vial. He paused for a moment beside Captain Donald Fraser, then jabbed the needle into him a second time.

INSPECTOR MICHAEL HARRIGAN arrived at the inn about noon. "The whole country's in an uproar," he said after perfunctory greetings to Bolan and O'Connor. "They're talking about nothing else. The whole world, in fact, is talking about it. Some think the terrorists blew themselves up while making bombs. But that theory doesn't explain the bodies lying about dead of bullet wounds. I wish it did explain it. I'd like that explanation to be accepted."

They sat in Bolan's room upstairs. It was important that O'Connor not be seen in Roscommon for a few days. Though O'Dougherty was completely trustworthy, IRA sympathizers were to be found in every town, in the common room of every inn, and some of them—by no means all—would regard the destruction of a huge cache of weapons as an outrage against Irish nationalism.

"In all the circumstances," Harrigan went on, "it might be wise if Colonel MacKenzie were to switch his attention to the source of the funds that purchased those weapons. I mean, of course, the narcotics trade."

"We hit them where it hurts," Bolan said. "Why back away?"

"A problem right now is, we don't know where there's another cache of weapons like that. If I knew, believe me, I'd say let's go get it."

"But you do know something about the narcotics?"

Harrigan nodded. "Yes. Hitting them in their drug supply would be just as hard a blow."

"I've got some leads on that," O'Connor announced.

"Ah." Harrigan turned to her. "I have orders for you. From Dublin."

O'Connor frowned skeptically at Harrigan. Over breakfast she had told Bolan she expected trouble from constabulary headquarters.

"They want you to investigate allegations of child abuse in a school in Cork. You're to report to headquarters there tomorrow."

"No."

"What do you mean, no? You can't say no."

"I told you last night," she said, "there would be those who'd take offense at my moving against the stash of weapons. We mustn't do anything *too* effective against the IRA. The political consequences might—"

"It's not the IRA," Harrigan said firmly.

She shrugged. "Curran Brigade. Sinn Fein. This branch of the IRA. That branch. Some inside the law. Some outside. It's a struggle for civilization against terrorism, and I'm not backing away. I didn't join the constabulary to investigate allegations of too-severe paddlings of unruly children."

"Your orders—"

"I won't obey them. I'll resign if that's what they want."

"They may want it," Harrigan said grimly.

"Then they'll have it. In the meantime I'm going with Colonel MacKenzie to continue the fight against the terrorists."

"Himself may have something to say about that," Harrigan warned. He turned to Bolan. "Do you?"

The warrior turned up the palms of his hands. "She's an effective fighter, Mike. I don't want to be involved in a disagreement within the Irish Constabulary, but I will say it would be a waste of her courage and skill to turn her into an investigator. It's not my decision to make, of course—"

"Nor mine," Harrigan said curtly. "We shall see. So, it's to Dublin..."

THEIR CAR WAS a Humber, a big old sedan, black, heavy and sedate, unmarked. The driver was another detective of the Irish Constabulary, a bland, humorless man who drove the car and kept out of the conversation. Inspector Harrigan sat in the front seat by the driver. Kathryn O'Connor and Mack Bolan sat together in the back.

Harrigan filled them in about what they had done the previous night. "The man we found on the road 150 yards from the farmstead—dead from a burst of 9 mm rounds—was definitely a member of the Curran Brigade. Do you want to tell me, incidentally, what he was doing there, so far from the rest of the action?"

"He was trying to steal my car," O'Connor replied.

"He was there to kill us," Bolan added.

"Very well. Of the identifiable bodies—that is, those so far identified—at the house and barn, two have been identified as Brigaders. Two have been identified as members of the Provisional Wing of the IRA.''

''So it all fits together,'' O'Connor concluded.

''Yes, I suppose it does. Of the vehicles, two have been identified as stolen. One has been tentatively identified as a van used in a bank robbery in Galway two months ago. Repainted and so on, but—''

''Bank robbery?'' Bolan interrupted.

''Any way to get money,'' O'Connor told him.

IRELAND WASN'T KNOWN for its superhighways. Two-lane roads, the kind on which O'Connor had sped through the night, were choked with traffic in the daytime. Their progress toward Dublin was slow.

A light rain began to fall, and drivers switched on headlights that gleamed on the wet pavement. A truck passed them, cutting in close ahead. The constabulary driver shook his head and said nothing, but Harrigan muttered an angry curse. Then, having cut in ahead of them, the truck driver abruptly slowed down. The constabulary driver edged the Humber out to pass, then ducked back as he saw oncoming traffic in the other lane.

Bolan looked out the back window. Another truck was all but on their rear bumper, and he recognized the situation.

''We've got trouble,'' he growled, and drew the Desert Eagle from under his jacket.

O'Connor jerked the mini-Uzi out of her bag.

What happened next was what the Executioner had expected, and it happened too quickly for him to warn the constabulary driver. The truck driver ahead jammed on his brakes. The constabulary driver hit his hard, but he didn't have nearly enough time, and the Humber skidded into the rear of the truck.

The hood of the Humber caught under the rear of the truck body and was crumpled into a tangled mass of sheet metal. Held by their seat belts, Harrigan and the driver were spared impact with the windshield. But, since they were wearing belts and not shoulder harnesses, their heads crashed down on the padded dashboard.

Ready for the crash, Bolan and O'Connor had turned and pressed their shoulders against the back of the front seat. As soon as the car was stopped, they threw open the doors and rolled out.

Just in time. A gunman standing on the running board of the truck behind—resting a foot on a front fender to steady his aim—sprayed the rear window of the Humber with a burst from a Kalashnikov.

It was the last action of his life. O'Connor was on her knees on the pavement before he could swing his muzzle toward her, and she swept him off the truck with a short burst from her mini-Uzi.

The truck driver spotted the policewoman, and he took aim on her from his window with an automatic. Bolan's .44 Magnum slug punched through both windshield and driver.

There were others. O'Connor didn't wait to see what was in the rear of the truck that had caused the accident by its sudden stop. She stitched the canvas cover with two quick bursts and saw a man topple out of the back and onto the crumpled hood of the Humber, Kalashnikov in hand.

Bolan edged along the side of the Humber, noticing that traffic was skidding to a stop in both lanes of the road, and hearing the crash of fenders. The driver of the lead truck, unaware of what had happened behind, jumped to the ground and raised the muzzle of still another Kalashnikov—just in time to meet a .44 Magnum slug that blew his chest open as though it had been hit by a cannonball.

The Executioner ran to the door where Inspector Harrigan sat stunned, his nose bleeding from the impact with the dashboard. O'Connor stepped up to the lead truck and fired another burst through the canvas.

Harrigan shook his head. "I . . . what . . . ?"

O'Connor circled the vehicle to stand beside Bolan, rain streaming down her face. She looked past Harrigan and saw that the driver was stunned but not seriously injured.

"Mike," Bolan said, "can you hear me?"

Harrigan nodded.

"Kathryn and I have done the easy part. We're leaving the tough part to you. I mean, the explaining. Kathryn will know where to find you later, right?"

Harrigan fumbled for a handkerchief and pressed it to his bleeding nose. "Right . . ." he mumbled. "And right to get away from here. You go. She'll know where."

Bolan put his hand on Harrigan's shoulder. "Mike, we probably won't go where you think we will. Whatever you do, don't tell anyone what rendezvous you've worked out with her. Because you've got a traitor. You've got an informer somewhere.''

Inspector Michael Harrigan nodded and sighed. ''My beloved country,'' he muttered. ''One of our curses. We've always got traitors. No matter what we do.''

CHAPTER FIVE

"Does it bother you that we may have just lost our sanction?" O'Connor asked Bolan as they walked across a soggy field. "I mean, I've always worked within the limits of the law."

"In the past two days," Bolan told her, "I've been the target of at least two murder attempts. I'm not worried about sanction."

"You have to understand our country," O'Connor said. "The great majority of our people want to do what the great majority of people want to do anywhere—live in peace, rear their children, enjoy what pleasure they can, die at peace with God. They do resent the Brit presence in the Six Counties. To some extent they sympathize with armed action to drive them out. But they hate terrorism as much as you or I do. That's the Irish people."

"That's the Italian people, who are tainted with the name of the Mafia. Truth be known, that is the great majority of the Palestinians, the Syrians, the Libyans, the Iranians... We don't fight nationalities. We fight gangs who appropriate the names of nationalities."

"I can't go home tonight," she said, ominously, only partly changing the subject. "Like you told

Harrigan, there's a traitor. We've got to find some-place, Bill.''

She called him Bill because she thought his name was William MacKenzie. He hated not being able to tell her who he was. ''Kathryn, call me Mack. My friends do.''

She smiled. ''I'm glad I'm one of your friends.''

''I KNOW WHERE TO LOOK,'' O'Connor said the next morning after spending the night in a small hotel on the south side of Dublin. ''But I don't know, Mack. I'm beginning to wonder...''

''Harrigan?'' he asked as they walked down three stone steps to the street, leaving the hotel. ''Do you have any doubt?''

''No. If I can't trust Mike Harrigan, I don't want to live.''

''Then—''

''Then why don't we call him?'' O'Connor asked. ''We need to keep in touch with him.''

She called the headquarters of the Irish Constabulary from a telephone booth. She reached Harrigan's office but was told the inspector was out of the office and no one knew for certain when he would return.

''So we're on our own,'' she said to Bolan. ''Which may be just as well. I've got some ideas.''

Bolan's thought was that he would much rather work alone. That was his way. But he didn't know the city, and he needed her help—or Harrigan's, and Harrigan was out of touch.

"I need to go to my flat," O'Connor said, "to pick up some other clothes. There's a bit of risk in that."

"We can handle it."

"We need to separate just a little. If anyone's looking for me at my flat, I'll be recognized easily enough. But they don't know you yet. They don't know what you look like. That's an advantage."

They boarded a bus for the center of the city. Separately. She rode in front, he in the rear, standing and clutching a strap so that he could see her.

Dublin was a fair-sized city with a population of about half a million. It was an odd combination of bustling modern city and dusty small town. It reminded Bolan of a New England city during the decades of economic doldrums before recovery began.

When O'Connor got off the bus, he got off. He kept a hundred feet or so between them as she walked to the street where she lived alone in a small apartment.

They had planned what they would do. O'Connor would be on the lookout for someone watching for her. If she spotted anyone, she'd signal Bolan. If she saw no one, she'd go in. When she was in the apartment, she would go to the window to let him see her. He would stay outside, watching the street. He'd wait beside a telephone booth. If he saw anyone enter the building, he'd dial her number.

The policewoman lived on a curving narrow street where identical red brick buildings lined both sides. Shops filled the street-level floors of all but a few buildings, and people lived on the floors above. O'Connor's apartment was in a building about midway in its block and, as she had told him, on the third floor.

She wasn't subtle about staring around her as she walked along the street. A woman sweeping the stoop in front of a shop paused and said good-morning as she passed. The policewoman stopped for a brief moment to return the greeting, then walked on, glancing around her.

The street-level floor of the building where she lived was occupied by a shoe repair shop. She waved at the man working just inside the window as she opened the door to the left of the shop.

Bolan had been following on the opposite side of the street, and he stopped at the telephone booth. He watched the window she had told him to watch, and after a minute or so she appeared in it and looked down.

So far so good. White sunlight bore down hard on the narrow street, evaporating the last of the water that remained along the curbs from the previous day's rain. Two children ran along the sidewalk, one chasing the other, laughing and shrieking. O'Connor had said that she'd need no more than ten minutes to gather some things, and it looked as if she wouldn't have an unwelcome visitor in that ten minutes.

The thought had barely appeared in the Executioner's brain when a car pulled up and a man got out. He was tall and thin and wore a black jacket, a pair of gray slacks and a black hat. He stood by the car for a moment, then was joined by another man who left a doorway and hurried across the street. He was shorter than the first man, but just as thin and similarly dressed. They glanced up at the window of O'Connor's apartment.

Bolan didn't wait for them to make their move. He stepped inside the telephone booth and dialed her number. "The two by the car. You can see them from the window."

"Let me look." In a moment she returned to her telephone. "The little weasel could be a man I've seen before. Look out for others. They could have backup."

The two men walked to the door and entered her building. Bolan crossed the street. He couldn't follow immediately behind them, so he took time to open their car and place a .44 cartridge on the dashboard. Then he entered the building and headed up the staircase.

He heard them knocking on her door. What would she do? He didn't hear her respond. Knowing the woman, he was afraid she might fire a shot through the door. And at this point it was possible they could be vacuum cleaner salesmen for all he knew—though he didn't for a moment think so.

They pounded harder on the door, and Bolan climbed faster, drawing the silenced Beretta. The warrior reached her floor just as the smaller of the two men shoved the tip of a crude burglary tool into her door lock. It was a carbon-steel blade at the end of a jimmy, and when it was turned with leverage, it would destroy the lock.

They were so intent on what they were doing that they didn't notice the Executioner. He stood a little distance from them, with the light from a window at the end of the hall at his back. "Gentlemen," he growled.

The two men whirled, both digging for guns. But then they saw the Beretta leveled at them, and they let go of their weapons and stepped cautiously away from the door.

"You work for the leader of the Curran Brigade?" Bolan asked coldly. "Tell him I'm looking forward to meeting him."

The door opened, and O'Connor faced the two men with her machine pistol aimed at waist level.

"Tell him how lucky you are that you didn't force that door," Bolan went on. "I think I stopped you about five seconds from the end of your lives."

The two hit men stood stock-still, terrified.

"Why should we let both of them go to carry the message?" O'Connor asked. "One can do it. The other—"

Bolan shook his head. "I don't want to cause a panic." He wasn't entirely sure she didn't mean it, that she wasn't really suggesting they kill one of the two. "Besides, it would leave a mess somebody would have to clean up."

She nodded and gestured with the muzzle of the mini-Uzi. "Get out of here."

A TELEPHONE CALL from another phone booth reached Inspector Harrigan. He agreed to meet them.

They got into his car, a blue Ford, and talked while he drove. O'Connor sat in front with him, Bolan in back.

"They tried to kill me this morning," the policewoman began. "They sent two men to my flat."

"I suppose they're dead," Harrigan said dryly.

"No. There was no convenient way to get rid of the bodies," she replied caustically.

"I have further word for you from headquarters," Harrigan said. "You've been given five days to clear up whatever you're working on and report for duty in Cork. If you elect to resign, the constabulary will expect the return of the weapons issued to you, and I'm directed to remind you that thereafter if you possess any kind of firearm you'll be doing so illegally."

"God forbid I should offend the IRA, is that it?"

"It's the fact that you're a woman, Kathryn," Harrigan replied. "Some men can't accept the idea of a woman operating so independently."

She glanced at Bolan and shrugged.

"I have something else to tell you," Harrigan went on. He turned to Bolan. "Do you remember the English captain you were with in Belfast? Captain Fraser?"

"Yes."

"He's dead. Kidnaped, tortured and murdered. Probably in an attempt to learn your identity."

"Any leads on who did it?" Bolan asked.

"We can only assume it was Brigaders. Whoever was watching you at the swimming pool and called for the gunmen to try to kill you also saw Captain Fraser talking with you."

"This is getting personal," Bolan said.

For a moment the inspector gave his attention to his driving, turning the Ford onto a main street and threading through heavy traffic. "There's a strong possibility," he finally said, "that a shipment of narcotics is coming ashore tonight. If you're willing, Colonel MacKenzie, we can try to intercept it. For reasons of confidentiality it has to be a small operation. Perhaps just the two of us."

"Three of us," O'Connor contradicted.

Harrigan sighed. "My orders are not to include you. But since the whole thing is going to be highly confidential, I don't suppose anyone has to know you were included. I don't know what would happen if—"

"If I got killed," she said.

"Or injured. I mean, you'll have to take the risk on your own."

"I've done it before."

"Dress like a man, then. I'll pick you up at eight o'clock in front of the Old Harp Pub. You know where it is, Kathryn. I'll draw some heavy weapons."

"Bring some 9 mm ammunition," she said. "The Uzi cycles it pretty damn fast."

"And I suggest you two get some rest for the balance of the day. No more adventures. You'll see plenty of adventure tonight if I don't miss my guess."

"THERE'S NO very great market for cocaine and heroin in Ireland," O'Connor said to the Executioner when they were on the street and Harrigan had driven away. "This is a tight little society, you know. Everybody knows what his neighbor does—makes it his business to know what his neighbor does. So there's not much room for playing with drugs. What's coming in from the ocean is going across the Irish Sea to Britain and on to the Continent. But Dublin's a city, and I think I know where you can make a buy."

She turned and walked through the open door of a pub. Bolan followed.

"Beer or whiskey?" she asked.

"Beer."

She ordered two pints of Guinness, and they carried them to a table in the corner.

"It's not worth your time, Mack," she said, "just to move against a petty drug pusher. But suppose the line ran back to the pair of pretties who came to kill me this morning."

"You think it does?"

"Not necessarily, but I think it's possible. You know what we've got now? What you're here to fight? Call it the Irish Connection. Before the Curran Brigade started financing its arms imports by smuggling narcotics, you could hardly find a gram of coke in Ireland. We still have only a few pushers, but I have to think every one of them is connected to the Brigade."

"And you think you know where you can find a pusher?"

She nodded. "If you want to risk a look."

BOLAN AND O'CONNOR rode a bus—separated once again—to an area of small factories and warehouses. Here, too, Bolan was impressed by how much the city represented a deteriorated New England city. Old factories of soot-stained red brick stood on both sides of some of the streets. The clatter of heavy machines reached the street through open windows. Clouds of steam and smoke puffed into the air. The pavement was dusty.

Brick walls were marked with crudely painted slogans:

VICTORY TO THE IRA!
UNITY OR DEATH—FOR THE BRITS!
IRELAND FOR THE IRISH!

Heavy trucks rumbled along the streets. There were few women on these streets, and there were no homes, only industries, warehouses and pubs.

"Look." O'Connor pointed at a spray-painted graffito—F & F.

"What does that mean?" Bolan asked.

"Finnerty and Freedom," she said. "Timothy Finnerty is the so-called chief of staff of the Curran Brigade."

"Yes. Harrigan told me about him."

"A vicious man. You're his target as much as he's yours."

"Maybe that'll smoke him out," Bolan suggested.

She looked into his eyes for a moment, then nodded. "Maybe," she said quietly.

They walked along the streets. He was conscious immediately that they were conspicuous here. Other people weren't dressed like them. He was wearing a loose nylon jacket—to cover what he had sheathed in leather—over a white polo shirt and khaki slacks. On this street, among men dressed in black wool jackets, even in summer, with baggy wool pants and flat caps, he looked like an American golfer. And O'Connor, in a white cotton blouse and a maroon skirt—carrying both her weapons in her straw handbag—looked nothing like the graying women in flat shoes and black raincoats with scarves tied over their heads.

"The pub across the street," she said to him. "Or so I hear."

It was an exceptionally dingy place called the King James. The door opened on the corner.

"You'll have to do the talking," O'Connor told Bolan.

"Saying what?"

"Saying whatever an American says when he wants to buy cocaine."

They walked into the place, and all conversation immediately stopped. Bolan stepped to the bar. "Two pints of lager," he requested.

The barkeeper was a burly blond man with a shiny pink face. He drew the two pints and shoved them across the bar.

Bolan saluted the man with his mug of beer and took a sip. "Fine day," he said.

The barkeeper shrugged. "We've seen worse, seen better."

"Yeah. Guess so. Uh, do you mind if I ask a question?"

"Not if you don't mind if I don't answer," the man replied. "A man can't answer just every question."

"That's true. The wife and I—" he nodded at O'Connor, who was sipping beer "—actually the wife. We, uh, we've got a certain affection for the white powder. You know. Americans call it different things. Nose candy, for one. We were told not to try to bring any with us, 'cause it might be detected by customs and they would get all excited about it. We were told we could find it here, if we asked at the right place. Then somebody else told us to ask at the King James. Somebody said you don't deal in it, but you might be able to give a traveler a word of advice."

"My advice is to stay away from that stuff."

Bolan nodded. "Not bad advice. But the wife is feeling a little nervous about going without it for so long. So...no harm in asking, huh? No offense intended."

"No offense," the barkeeper replied.

On the street a few minutes later, O'Connor laughed. "Two minutes," she said. "Half a block."

It worked out that way. Before they had walked half a block a man stepped out of a doorway. "Lookin' for somethin'?" he asked.

Bolan nodded. "Right. Can you help?"

"Well, just what is it you're lookin' for?"

"Coke," Bolan said bluntly.

"Can of Coke?"

"Line of coke."

The man was seventy years old at least, Bolan judged. He was gray, his eyes were droopy and watery, and a shabby black suit hung over a ravaged body. His old satin necktie was spotted. His shoes were splitting.

"That's illegal, you know," the old man said.

"Everything fun is illegal," Bolan retorted.

The old man stared at O'Connor for a moment, as if somewhere in his memory he retained an image of her, as if the sight of her sent off some kind of alarm. Then he tipped his head and focused on Bolan.

"Americans, hmm?"

"Americans," Bolan agreed.

"Forty Irish pounds," the old man said.

"Expensive."

"It's scarce in this country," the old man replied.

Bolan pulled out his wallet and took out two twenty-pound notes. The old man reached into his jacket pocket and pulled out a yellow envelope.

"You're sure this is the real stuff?"

The old man nodded. "They tell me it is. I don't use it myself."

"If it isn't, I'll come back and find you," Bolan warned.

"Yes. You should do that. It's guaranteed. I'll give you your money back if it isn't good."

The old man turned and shuffled away.

"Cross the street and keep an eye on him," the policewoman told Bolan. "They'll be watching for somebody following him. They're careful, so we have to be, too."

They crossed the street, stood for a while as if they were examining their buy and kept an eye on the old man. Only when he was almost a block away did they walk after him, keeping to the opposite side of the street.

He had walked a block or so when a young man stepped out of a doorway and confronted him. As Bolan and O'Connor watched, the young man thrust out his hand, and the old man reached into his pocket and appeared to hand over the two twenty-pound notes. The old man walked on, and the young man walked briskly back the way the old man had come, toward the pub.

"Mack..."

Bolan, who had been watching the old man and the young man closely, now turned in response to her warning and saw two big men striding toward them.

They were muscle, no question about it. O'Connor jammed her hand into her bag, and Bolan knew she had closed her grip around the mini-Uzi or the PPK.

"What're you staring at, Yank?" one of the men asked.

Bolan looked up into the bruiser's face. The man weighed about two-fifty, but it was all muscle.

"Nothing," the warrior replied.

"You did your business. What're you standin' around for?"

The bonecrusher was going to use those muscles. Bolan had no doubt about it. The other one, only a little smaller, was glowering at O'Connor—obviously unaware that the muzzle of a deadly weapon was pointed at his belly.

The big man grabbed Bolan by the shoulders.

Okay. If that was how it was going to be... The warrior shot his right knee into the man's crotch. The hardman screamed, but it was as much in fury as in agony, and he didn't loosen his grip on Bolan's shoulders. The Executioner drove a fist into the man's ribs and felt bone snap. Still the man didn't loosen his grip. Instead he tried to shake Bolan. A second punch, driven into the already-broken ribs, was the end. The bonecrusher staggered back, growling and coughing. The Executioner dropped him with a left that shattered his nose.

The second tough guy had drawn a knife, and Kathryn O'Connor's eyes glittered.

"No!" Bolan yelled at her.

He ducked under the man's first thrust, grabbed the arm, turned it behind and wrenched it out of its shoulder socket. His unfortunate assailant stumbled against a wall and began to weep from the pain.

Bolan grabbed the man and turned him around, then dropped a .44 Magnum shell into his shirt pocket.

O'Connor stalked across the street. She'd drawn her machine pistol out of her straw handbag and headed for the pub.

Bolan trotted after her. "You're going to get yourself killed," he growled at her. "Or both of us."

Unless he grabbed her and pulled her back, he couldn't stop her. She burst into the King James pub, the machine pistol menacing the half-dozen men who stood at the bar.

"Out!" she ordered.

The policewoman strode across the common room and down the stairs, toward the cellar. Bolan followed. There was little else he could do.

She found what she was looking for. The young man who had taken the money from the old man was in a stone-walled room in the cellar of the pub. Another man was there. Piled on the table between them was a stock of narcotics in clear plastic bags. The second man—middle-aged, bald—had been measuring cocaine into little yellow envelopes of the kind the old man had sold to Bolan.

On the stone floor beside the young man was a big old leather suitcase. The treasury was in it—loose money, Irish bank notes.

O'Connor pointed at the plastic bags, then at the valise. "That," she said. "In there."

The bald man stared for a moment at the muzzle of the mini-Uzi, then into the burning eyes of the young woman. Without a word he stood and began to shove the narcotics into the suitcase.

"Do you know who that belongs to?" the young man asked.

"I'd like to know," O'Connor replied. "Suppose you tell me."

"To the fighters for the Freedom of Ireland. The money is for the sacred cause."

"What sacred cause?" she asked. "The sacred cause of making people addicts?"

"A few . . . maybe. It's little enough to sacrifice for freedom."

"Finnerty?" Bolan asked.

"A saint, that man. A devoted fighter for the cause."

"Here's something for him." Bolan tossed another .44 cartridge onto the table.

"You're a dead man, whoever you are," the young man snarled. "And you, you bitch. You're a dead woman. You'll never have peace. Never. Neither one of you. From this day forward."

On the street a few doors down from the pub, O'Connor went into a shop and bought two cans of lighter fluid. She and Bolan poured the flammable liquid over the cocaine and the money. When he tossed in a match, the suitcase filled with hot flame.

They left it after a minute or so. As they walked away, people stood far away and watched the contents of the suitcase burn. No one dared go near it.

CHAPTER SIX

When Inspector Michael Harrigan picked up Bolan and O'Connor in front of the Old Harp Pub that evening, the sun was low in the sky.

"We've got a little flying to do," Harrigan told them. "I hope you got your rest this afternoon. It may be a long night."

He drove north out of the city toward the airport. During the drive, O'Connor reloaded the magazines for her mini-Uzi with the boxes of 9 mm rounds Harrigan had brought along.

At the airport the inspector drove to the side of the field opposite the passenger terminal, where some military aircraft were parked. He pulled the blue Ford to a stop beside a Lynx helicopter.

Bolan recognized the Lynx—he'd flown one before. Much like an American Huey, it had been designed and was built by the British and French in a cooperative effort and was something of a standard combat helicopter for Western European forces. It was capable of launching missiles, dropping bombs, working as a gunship or carrying a troop of heavily armed soldiers. It had a long, sharp nose, a fully enclosed body topped by a four-blade rotor, and the warrior knew it was powered by twin Rolls-Royce turbine engines. This one was painted black and sat on skids.

A pilot wearing blue coveralls strode out of the hangar. Harrigan opened the trunk of the Ford. Lying on the bottom of the trunk were three MAT-49 submachine guns. Bolan was familiar with these weapons. A rather simple blowback automatic, the subgun carried thirty-two 9 mm rounds in a long, straight magazine that extended below and was also the forward grip. A heavy wire butt telescoped into the body of the gun when it wasn't being used.

Harrigan had brought along three extra magazines for each weapon. "There's combat dress in the helicopter, if you want it," he told them.

Bolan was glad for that. He climbed in and changed into a set of combat fatigues. They weren't black, which he would have preferred for a night mission, but they were dark, with room in the deep pockets for extra magazines, not just for the MAT-49, but for the Desert Eagle and the Beretta, as well. He adjusted his leather to carry the big .44 on his hip and the Beretta under his left shoulder.

O'Connor donned a set of the ill-fitting fatigues and set to work rolling up legs and sleeves. She'd carry her mini-Uzi, not a MAT-49, and she was able to shove her Walther PPK into a pocket of her fatigues.

The Lynx took off as the sun set. Powered by turbine engines and a four-blade rotor, it wasn't as noisy and shaky as many choppers. Bolan, O'Connor and Harrigan sat on the tube-and-canvas seats in the compartment behind the cockpit, where they could see out through square windows.

Rising to no more than fifteen hundred feet above the landscape, the chopper swung abruptly into a northwestward course. The Lynx was capable of 175 miles an hour fast cruise, and from so low an altitude the passengers had a vivid impression of speed.

As the sunlight turned redder, then darker, the chopper sped to the north of the setting sun across counties Kildare, Westmeath, Roscommon, Sligo and Mayo, lifting to a higher altitude as the land rose and they were flying over hills. By the time they crossed the coastline over the village of Ballycastle, the light was gone, and yellow lights shone in the village.

Over the open Atlantic the helicopter passed over scores of lighted fishing boats heading out. And beyond, forty and fifty miles at sea, the aircraft approached North Atlantic ship traffic.

"We won't identify the ship, of course," Harrigan said. "But one of those carries a shipment meant for Ireland."

"A rubber boat thrown overboard?" Bolan asked.

"More than that, if my information is correct. Much more. The shipment we saw was small compared to this. This is a major movement of the vicious poison."

They stared down from the windows of the chopper at a dozen ships now visible, their lights gleaming against the diminishing light of the sun. Those ships were only a fraction of the number that would pass along that coast that night.

"I wanted you to see the dimensions of the problem," Harrigan told him as the helicopter swung around and headed back toward the shore.

"But tonight we know where to look," O'Connor said.

"Tonight we know where to look," Harrigan agreed.

"An informer," she said dryly.

"Tonight, thank God, *we* have one."

Crossing the shoreline, the chopper flew over a point of land. Harrigan mentioned its name, but that made no difference to Bolan—he didn't know where it was exactly, in any case.

"That's where it will happen," the inspector said.

Bolan surveyed the area quickly. The point was a promontory not very high above the surf. A single country road led out to the end, and a stone cottage was the only sign of human habitation. It was dark and might be abandoned. Behind lay an expanse of fields rising toward the hills. He could see a few sheep grazing, and a few settling down for the night.

Drug smugglers bringing in junk weren't very wise, if this was where they were coming in. It was remote and they could cover it with a few gunners. But there was only one way out—the road running through the fields. A small force could block that road.

A small force.

How about two men and a woman?

THE LYNX SET DOWN in a field behind the crest of a hill, out of sight from anyone near the point. Bolan and O'Connor were out of the aircraft in seconds, armed and ready to move. Inspector Michael Harrigan stepped down with a little more dignity, wearing a tweed hat and a black raincoat over his tweed suit. He carried a MAT-49, just the same, and the pockets of his raincoat were heavy with ammo.

Bolan carried two MATs. O'Connor wanted to carry her mini-Uzi and said she didn't need the French submachine gun, but the Executioner wasn't willing to leave the weapon in the chopper. He carried one slung over his shoulder, one in hand.

"We walk," Harrigan said. "And not on the road. I told you I hope you got your rest this afternoon."

The last trace of sunlight had disappeared. The moon shone over the hills behind them and on the fields ahead.

They walked, staying parallel to the road but a hundred yards north of it. Presently they heard the surf pounding to their right. They were on the promontory, and less than a hundred yards from the cliff that dropped down to the beach. They edged closer and looked down.

The cliff wasn't high, no more than twenty feet. It was broken rock and soil, not impossible to climb. The surf crashed among rocks and on sand, rushing up and retreating.

Soon they could see the little stone cottage, and no lights were visible. Maybe it was abandoned. Maybe not.

Crouching in the field and at the edge of the cliff, they spotted several flashlight beams. And then they heard a vehicle coming along the road.

"So far it's as I was told to expect," Harrigan whispered.

"I want to do a recon," Bolan said.

"Meaning?"

He nodded toward the cliff to their right. "I'll go down. I can get a better idea of the deal."

"I'll go with you," O'Connor offered.

"No," he replied, bluntly and firmly.

She stared at him for a moment, then shrugged.

"How soon do you expect the shipment to come in?" he asked Harrigan.

The inspector glanced at his watch. "Not for an hour."

"Good. That gives me time to check the landing area."

THE WARRIOR CARRIED just one MAT-49 as he jumped down from the brink of the cliff to the first solid landing below. In four more jumps he was at the bottom on the sandy beach.

Getting down was no great difficulty. It would be a little harder to get back up.

He worked his way west, sometimes wading in the surf, sometimes walking on dry sand. As he neared the end of the promontory, he edged over closer to the bottom of the cliff to be out of sight from above. He risked a look up, but saw no one tracking his movements.

The northwest end of the promontory was a heap of jagged rocks over which the sea broke with angry force, as if the waves resented these rocks that wouldn't yield.

For Mack Bolan those rocks presented a problem. Should he try to go around them, or did he have to climb over them?

He waded out into the surf. The rocks were slippery with slimy marine vegetation, and embedded in the slime were barnacles with shells as sharp as knives. The seas rolling in from the west struck the outer rocks and surged up, crashing down onto inner rocks. Torrents of saltwater rushed through the gaps among the rocks, swirling and boiling. Waves hurled water high in the air, floods of it descending hard.

A man could swim around, but it would be a hard swim in rough, cold water—impossible, perhaps, for a man laden with weapons and ammunition. And climbing wasn't going to be easy, either. But there was no other choice—except to work his way back to the top of the cliff and try to circle the cottage in full view of anyone who might be looking from its doors or windows.

The warrior slung the MAT-49 over his shoulder and watched the rhythm of the waves for a couple of minutes. When the water receded, he charged into the gap between two rocks and began to clamber up, knowing he had less than half a minute before the water surged in again.

The rocks were slick, and he had to look for cracks to grab on to. Jamming his feet into crevices, his hands into cracks where the barnacles cut him painfully, he scrambled to the top of one rock and threw himself onto it just as a mammoth wave struck the outer rocks, throwing up a storm of water that fell like a hundred streams from a hundred fire hoses.

Almost as hard and fast as it had come, the wave retreated, making way for the next one. In the time that gave him, the warrior made a jump to a bigger, higher rock, bracing himself for the next onslaught of water.

The wave struck the tangle of rocks with furious power, again was heaved into the air, and again fell. The relentless cadence of the waves continued, and Bolan finally reached a point where he could see beyond.

The rocks served as a breakwater for the beach to the west—the little strip of sand lay sheltered from most of the force of the surf.

And there, on that sheltered sand, a pair of small boats were drawn up. They lay upside down, and a man sat atop each one.

The moonlight was enough for Bolan not just to see them, but to get a good look at their weapons. One had an assault rifle slung over his shoulder. The other held his in his lap. Both men smoked cigarettes, and were staring out to sea. Looking for the shipment, no doubt.

Two men, but obviously there were more at the stone cottage, and there would be still more aboard the boat coming in with the drugs. But surprise would equal the odds. Not to mention Harrigan and Kathryn. When the shooting started, they would know what to do.

The Executioner began to work his way down the far side of the rocks. It was no easier. The cliff was sheer above. The immense surges of water all but covered the rocks and rushed against the lower reaches of the cliff.

Twice he was almost swept off the rocks. He dug in with both hands, though the barnacles cut him, and tried to wedge his feet into cracks. If he had been thrown into the rushing water, it would have thrown him against first one rock and then another until he was swept out to sea, probably unconscious.

After another quarter hour's struggle, he reached the sand in the shelter of the rocks and there dropped onto his hands and knees to catch his breath. He was wet and cold, but he was where they wouldn't expect him to be. He sat in the shadow of one of the rocks at the base of the cliff and checked the MAT-49, Desert Eagle and Beretta. He made sure there was no sand in any of them, no chips of rock, no fragments of barnacle shell. He pulled the clips and worked the actions to make sure each weapon operated smoothly. Before long, his life would depend on them.

There was no way to get warm. He stripped off the fatigues and wrung them out, but then he had to put them back on, no warmer and no drier.

The sand was a little warm—the sun had shone on it all day. He stretched out on his belly and watched the sea and the two hardmen sitting on the boats.

In a moment or two he saw the signal. A light at sea blinked twice and disappeared.

He wouldn't have missed it, but its effect on the men on the boats confirmed that what he'd seen was the signal they'd been waiting for. They jumped down from the boats, and one of them yelled to other men on top of the cliff. Then the two down on the beach turned over the upside-down boats. They dragged first one, then the other, closer to the surf.

Bolan counted five men as they descended to the beach, carrying assault rifles. He began to hear the rumble of throttled-back marine engines, their muffled roar gurgling in the surf when the exhaust pipes dipped under the waves, coughing louder when the pipes were out in the air.

Bolan pressed himself as deep as he could into the shadow of the cliff and the closest rocks, and listened to their conversation.

"Maybe the chief will be satisfied at last. There's a million pounds' worth in this night's haul, so I hear."

"But a lot of good stuff," another man said. "Weapons that will make us more powerful than the British army."

"Don't count on that," the first retorted.

"We'll make 'em pay," another added. "All of 'em."

A man who hadn't yet spoken said, "I wish we could finance the cause some other way. Dope . . . We don't know who gets hurt by it."

"Makes no difference," a companion replied harshly. "When the sacred soil of Ireland is ours, all of it, and we govern it *our* way, we'll get rid of the dope and the dopesters. In the meanwhile . . . it's how we make our money. It's how we buy our weapons.''

''Missiles!'' another gloated. ''Wait till we have our missiles! Then the world will sit up and take notice.''

''Shut up and get to it,'' someone growled. ''Get those boats into the water!''

The incoming boat was now visible, long, sleek and low in the water. It ran without lights and lay offshore half a mile, wallowing in the heavy swell, waiting.

The men strained to push their boats into the surf. The craft were small, but they were heavy and wooden. It took muscle to launch them, even in the shelter of the rocks.

A man sat in each boat as the others pushed. As soon as the vessel was afloat, the man began to pull on oars. Others ran into the surf and threw themselves over the gunwales and into the boats. Three men rode in the first boat, two in the second.

That left just two gunners on the beach, but a yell from above told Bolan what he already knew—that there were more up there.

He stared at the boat offshore. The vessel was no fishing boat. The seagoing racer could speed across the water, and no Coast Guard cutter would have a prayer of catching them.

Chances were the boat was heavily armed, too, and the crew would be ruthless gunmen. Bolan wondered who they were and under what flag they sailed.

THE VESSEL SAILED under the Italian flag, and the boat was of Italian registry. But not a single man on board was Italian or felt that he owed the slightest allegiance to Italy.

Two days earlier the *Santa Clara* had been anchored at a yacht club on the Isle of Wight, and wealthy yachtsmen had come aboard to admire it and chat with Carlos Kafka, its owner, the heir to a Chilean mining fortune. He'd served champagne and hors d'oeuvres to the yachtsmen and their ladies and had accepted invitations to visit their boats. His crew had kept out of sight, except for the captain and a serving boy. In two days the *Santa Clara* would return to the yacht club, bearing no hint of where it had been and what it had done.

It had effected a rendezvous at sea with a Moroccan freighter. Two million British pounds' worth of white powder lay in its main cabin in sealed plastic packages that wouldn't leak the odor of the narcotics. The packages were weighted with lead so that they would sink if thrown overboard.

The *Santa Clara* was heavily armed with twin .50-caliber machine guns and an assortment of other weapons. It would rendezvous with another freighter before the night was over and strip itself of heavy weapons. The crew members were all armed with pistols, but those could be quickly thrown overboard if a cutter or a helicopter somehow managed to stop the vessel for a search.

Carlos Kafka stood on the deck, watching the Irishmen approach in their wooden boats. With a gesture he ordered a crewman to throw more fenders over the side. He didn't want those crude terrorists in their crude boats scraping the sides of his craft.

"Ho, mate," an Irishman, who was standing in the front of the first boat, called. "Beautiful night, isn't it?"

"Identify," Kafka responded coldly.

"We work for the chief of staff."

"What's his name?"

"What's his name, then, is it? All right. It's Timothy Finnerty. The finest man Ireland has produced in many a long year."

"Your password for tonight?" Kafka asked.

"St. George and England." The Irishman growled out the words.

"All right," Kafka replied in a voice icy with scorn. "Keep your boats back. Don't bump against my hull."

Kafka waved his arm, and crewmen came out of the cabin with the packages of cocaine and heroin and began tossing them into the boats.

"Hey! Careful! If one of those goes into the water..."

The crewman ignored the Irishman.

"Can we count these packages?" Finnerty's man asked.

"As you wish. And perhaps you'd like to weigh them," Kafka suggested.

"Well, I—"

Carlos Kafka snapped his fingers, and the man at the wheel shoved in the throttles. The *Santa Clara* moved decisively. The little wooden boats seemed to slide along its hull, and in a moment they were tossing in the wash of its screws. In fact, the man at the wheel turned the stern of the yacht to direct the churning waters from his screws right at the little boats; and the men at the oars were hard put to keep their boats headed into the turbulently writhing prop wash.

Kafka lit a cigarette and took a couple of puffs before he flipped it overboard. He went below to the master cabin, where somebody delicious was waiting for him.

BOLAN WATCHED the boats go out. He heard the engines throttle up and knew the big boat had made its transfer and was moving away.

Now, if ever, he had to stop the shipment of poison that was coming ashore. But he had a problem that had to have priority. One of the gunners left on the beach had walked toward the rocks and was now only twenty feet or so from where the warrior crouched in the shadows.

"Where you at, Bill?"

"Relievin' myself, friend. Relax."

The guy did his business in the sand, looked around, then raised his Kalashnikov and slowly walked toward the deep shadow where Bolan crouched. Maybe he'd seen nothing, but he acted as if he had.

And then, in the minimal light of that rock-shadowed beach, the eyes of the two men met. The tiny glints of light, reflected off the moon or off the sea, were obvious to two men who were looking for just such light.

There was no other option. Each knew at the same instant that he faced death. One was a man who perhaps excused himself by talking about his country. The other was a man who had faced death ten thousand times in the cause of humanity—usually in the cause of his country. One was a man who didn't care about the consequences of his behavior, as long as he could rationalize it as being in the cause of his cause. One was a man who killed only reluctantly. One was a man who would kill for whatever he was about, no matter who, no matter what . . . and mostly for money or power. The other was a man who judged his cause and wouldn't have fought for it if he couldn't find it right.

Mack Bolan squeezed the trigger of the Beretta and sent a silenced but lethal shot into the face of his enemy. Seconds later the boats came in. Rising high on the big rollers, then disappearing in the troughs, they returned to the beach.

The man who had called to his friend Bill had lost all interest in him now. He waded out into the surf, as if that could help bring the cargo of cocaine and heroin ashore. Obviously he was wild for it. He could hardly wait to put his hands on it, for whatever reason.

Who he was and what he did was beyond question. The warrior leveled the Beretta and dropped him in the surf.

Two down, with five more in the boats. More yet above.

Bolan strode to the edge of the surf. A burst from his MAT-49 chopped into the first boat, the one with three men aboard. Splintered wood flew into the air, and one of the terrorist gunmen clutched his throat and fell over the side.

The warrior fired a burst into the second boat. A gunner in the first boat fired toward the shore. He hadn't found his target, and his slugs splattered in the shallow water and in the sand. Bolan cut him down with a short burst of 9 mm death.

The MAT ran dry, so Bolan jerked a magazine from his pocket, ejected the empty and rammed home the full one. The gunmen in the boats hadn't seen him yet, only his muzzle-flash, and they fired wildly at where he'd been. Their own muzzle-flashes gave the warrior his target, and he let loose two short bursts directly at their blue-yellow blasts.

He saw one gunner topple over the side of his boat and into the water, assault rifle still firing from his convulsive grip on the trigger. That was the last gunfire from the two boats. They rose and fell on the churning surf...silent.

Chaos reigned at the top of the cliff. Men shouted orders and questions at one another and began running down the stairs to the beach, their feet thundering on wooden steps.

Bolan waded out into the water beside the boats. The plastic-wrapped packages he saw lying in the bottoms of the boats had to be the narcotics. He aimed the MAT-49 at the heap of packages in the first boat and fired a burst. Slugs ripped through the packages and through the bottom of the boat. Saltwater surged into the boat, mixing with the white powder from the blasted-open packages. Bolan repeated the procedure in the second boat.

Now the men from above swarmed onto the beach. They couldn't see the Executioner. He was waist-deep in the water between the boats.

"What the hell's going on here? If that stuff's lost, somebody—"

A .44 slug from the Desert Eagle cut off the man's threat and punched him onto his back. The remaining gunners learned something from the fate of their confederate. They backed away into the shadow of the cliff. They'd seen the huge, flaring blast of the Desert Eagle, and they laid down a disciplined fire between the sinking boats.

Bolan was careful to keep a boat between him and them. He lowered himself deeper into the water, but the gunmen knew where he was, and their short, economical bursts chopped into the wood above him.

He dropped the MAT-49 into the boat above him and drew the Beretta. Slipping around the rear of the boat, he reached a point where he could see the flashes from the assault rifles that continued to chop away at the wooden boat, which was disintegrating little by little. He took aim at the nearest flash and fired a single shot. The man screamed.

One was down and the other two were mystified. They hadn't heard the subsonic round, and the Beretta's flash-suppressor had completely obscured the blast.

They ceased firing. Bolan searched for their shadows but couldn't see them. His opponents were afraid to fire, and he couldn't because he didn't have a target.

The terrorists turned and ran. He saw them when they reached the wooden stairs and heard their boots clatter on the steps. And then the warrior heard the stuttering chatter of a mini-Uzi.

Kathryn O'Connor had taken up the fight.

There were no survivors.

CHAPTER SEVEN

During the hour when Mack Bolan, Inspector Michael Harrigan and Kathryn O'Connor were flying from Dublin to County Mayo in the Lynx helicopter, a different drama was played out on an autobahn in Germany.

It happened on the autobahn designated E-5 between Cologne and Frankfurt. Specifically it happened two miles northwest of the exit for West German Highway 256, some fifteen miles south of the town of Altenkirchen.

A convoy of three British military trucks was moving toward Frankfurt. The first vehicle was an ordinary passenger car, though painted with military colors, the second was a light armored personnel carrier and the third was a small covered truck. The captain in command of the convoy rode in the car, driven by a sergeant. Another sergeant drove the personnel carrier, with two lieutenants and one sergeant as passengers. Two sergeants rode in the cab of the truck, one driving. In the rear of the vehicle twenty-three enlisted men of various ranks sat on benches.

The convoy was moving a small unit of Special Air Service personnel, the tough paratroopers Britain often called on for difficult duty. The SAS carried full-automatic assault rifles and other special weapons, and they were the best-trained soldiers in British service.

There was no speed limit on the autobahn, and cars constantly passed the British convoy, which was moving at the best speed the armored personnel carrier could make—about sixty miles an hour.

On a slope above the autobahn and about five hundred yards from the edge of the pavement, two men lay on the ground behind a weapon known as a MILAN launcher.

The name MILAN was an acronym for *Missile d'Infanterie Léger Antichar*—light infantry antitank missile. The launcher sat on a low tripod, and the operator lay beside it, squinting into an infrared night sight. He'd been practicing, taking aim at cars and trucks, following them in the sight, familiarizing himself with the technique of tracking speeding traffic on the autobahn.

The other man was watching the highway through binoculars, looking for the British convoy. There was still enough light to see without the infrared sight, but it would give added assurance to the accuracy of the missile launch.

The missile unit was already clipped into position on the launcher, so they were ready to fire whenever the convoy appeared. The missile unit consisted of a steerable solid-propellant rocket nested in a tube. The rocket had a range of about two thousand yards, a little more than a mile.

"Here they come," the man with the binoculars announced.

The operator looked up from his sight for a brief moment and saw the three-vehicle convoy coming over the crest of a rise. It was far out of range, but as it approached he'd track it through the sight and have his aim well fixed when it was within range.

The convoy was moving fast. With another type of weapon, the gunner would have had a difficult shot, but the MILAN was a guided missile that would find its target.

The first vehicle, the car, appeared in the sight. The remaining sunlight interfered a little with the infrared sight. It would have worked better in the dark. Even so, he had a clear view of the oncoming convoy—a view that would get better as the range closed.

Neither the car nor the armored personnel carrier was his target. The truck was. He would kill more Britons hitting the truck with almost seven pounds of explosive.

All right. The truck was clearly in his sight, and in range. But he wouldn't fire yet. He'd let the range diminish a little to make the shot more certain.

He held a tense thumb above the launching button. Two thousand yards, fifteen hundred...twelve hundred...

He pressed the button.

For a brief, sickening moment nothing happened. Then with a roar the missile shot from the tube, and the tube flew to the rear. With the rocket flying one way and the tube the other, there was no recoil.

The missile was launched by a gas explosion in the tube. It was then accelerated by a boost burn of its rocket engine, after which the rocket settled down to a sustained burn that kept the missile flying. It was equipped with wings that unfolded as it left the tube and wouldn't fly an arcing trajectory but would fly flat until it hit a target or the rocket burned out.

What the operator had to do was keep the sight fixed on the target. It didn't matter that the truck was moving rapidly. The missile would follow it.

Through the sight the operator could see two bright flares burning on the rear of the missile. What was more important, sensors in the computerized sighting system could see those flares, too. Seeing where the flares were, the aiming system could tell how much the missile was off target. It sent commands to the steering rudder set in the rear of the rocket engine.

The steering commands were transmitted down a pair of thin, strong wires that unspooled and trailed the missile. Though the missile was flying at more than six hundred feet per second, the wire unspooled and kept intact the electrical connection between missile and aiming system.

As the angle changed, the operator had to swing the sight faster from right to left. The computer analyzed the aiming information, sent repeated signals, and the missile turned and followed the truck.

To the two men on the slope it seemed as if the flight of the missile took forever. In fact, it took a little less than five seconds. The missile hit the truck just behind the cab, and low. The explosion was furious and deadly.

TIMOTHY FINNERTY STOOD at a window, looking down on an ugly Dublin street, where gusts of wind spun trash along the pavement and clouds of dust made pedestrians turn their faces away.

"War," he snarled. "This is war."

Molly Finnerty took a drag on her cigarette and watched as he did the same and blew the smoke out through his nose.

He went on. "Ten men, two million pounds' worth of stuff and we don't even know how, really. No one survived the attack, the boats shot to pieces, the delivery lost in the water. *War,* by God!"

Molly hadn't dressed yet. She sat on the edge of the bed, naked, not fully awake. Her husband had taken phone calls half the night and again from dawn on. She'd tried to sleep while he jawed and cursed on the telephone, but it hadn't been possible. He'd growled and grumbled even between calls. He'd gulped down so much whiskey the previous night that this morning his head ached, which did nothing to improve his temper.

"But who the hell do you shoot at?" he demanded. "I know who did this. That goddamn American with the .44 pistol, plus his confederates. Traitors, likely. But who?"

"You're ahead of the game from last night, Tim," Molly said wearily. It was the tenth time she'd said it, maybe the fifteenth. "Twelve Brits."

"Woman," he yelled, "use your brain! The Brits have a hundred thousand soldiers. How many have I got? Tell me how many men I've lost this week—and what percentage that is of how many I can count on. Plus money! How much did we lose in Roscommon? Add that to the two million we lost last night. Twelve Brits in a truck! I'm *not* ahead of the game!"

"What you did last night in Germany was more important than anything you've ever done, you ignorant bastard," she muttered. "Do you know what that signifies?"

For a long time Tim Finnerty had resented the superior intelligence of the prostitute he'd married. That was why he'd married her, in fact—because she'd been smart enough to entice him into marriage. That had made him suspicious of her. He could never be sure when she was on his side, when she was exclusively on her own.

"Talk, for the love of Christ," Finnerty said sullenly.

"Okay. Yesterday you used the MILAN for the first time. You know what that means? You killed twelve out of twenty-three SAS Brits riding in a truck on a German highway. That means that no goddamn Brit is safe anywhere, even if he's riding in a tank."

Finnerty frowned and nodded. "Right. Yeah, right... If Prince Chuck wants to go out today, he goes in... Like you said, a tank isn't safe enough."

"Which means," she went on, "that none of the Royals can do anything but hide behind the stone walls of their palaces, so long as we have the MILANs. Her

Majesty goes out in her Rolls-Royce...she can't be sure she won't be blown up by a guided missile that takes out the royal maroon limousine. Opening garden shows, trooping the color, the horse races—either they hide behind stone walls or they make themselves targets. Timothy, you're on top of the world!''

AT NOON a helicopter landed on the grounds of the Royal Air Force Museum at Hendon, a suburb of London. The museum had been an air base, its runways were still intact and it was a good place for a secret meeting. It was so public a place that cars or aircraft moving in and out attracted no notice.

A London taxi drove up to the helicopter. Bolan jumped down and got in.

"Hello, Striker," Hal Brognola said.

The taxi was, in fact, an armored car, and the driver was an agent of the Special Branch, the counterterrorist department of Scotland Yard, lately concentrating once again on what it had been originally formed to combat—Irish terrorism.

"In a few days you've done a hell of a job," the big Fed commented.

Bolan shook his head. "That attack in Germany last night, using a MILAN launcher, changes everything."

"You've hurt the terrorists more than you may realize. That night when you sank the rubber boat at sea—plus the fishing boat—you didn't sink much cocaine, but you put a new fear into the smugglers. A lot of fishermen quit volunteering after that night. And last night. Two million pounds' worth! The Curran Brigade needed that money. Their credit's no good. They have to pay cash for arms, and now they're two million pounds poorer. And three days earlier you blew up millions' worth of arms. They're hurting."

"They're going to hurt more."

"That's what I'm here to talk to you about," Brognola said grimly. "Maybe they are and maybe they aren't. I, uh, I've got a problem."

"Spit it out."

"You've done too damn well, it seems. The Irish government has revoked your sanction. They don't want you in Ireland anymore."

The warrior narrowed his gaze and shot his friend an inquiring look.

"Their rationalization is that you work too far outside the law. What they're really afraid of is that it will become publicly known that an American, working in cooperation with the British government as well as the Irish, is going around the country killing Irishmen. The political consequences could be—"

"What will be the political consequences if the Curran Brigade uses a MILAN missile to assassinate the queen?"

"That's a remote problem. You're an immediate problem. Anyway, somebody has gotten to somebody, and the President got an unofficial request to call you off."

"So what does he want me to do?"

"The President," Brognola told him, "reminded the Irish government that he never sent you to Ireland in the first place, that you were working at *their* request. And he reminded them that you weren't an agent of the government of the United States. Then he said he would suggest you come home. Suggest . . ."

"Which means?"

"He'd rather you stay on the job. But it's up to you."

"Some people over there have been trying to kill me."

Brognola nodded toward the helicopter, marked with the insignia of the Irish defense force. "The chopper will go back without you," he said. "Officially Colonel MacKenzie has been withdrawn. If you want to go back, you'll have help from the Special Branch, which will give the Irish another reason to hate you."

"I don't see how we can walk away and leave those missile launchers in the hands of terrorists."

"Okay. It's gonna get tougher and tougher. Be careful. Be damn careful."

JUST TWO TOP MEN in the Special Branch were among the few people who knew that Mack Bolan was the Executioner. They were thankful to have his help in coping with what they called "a devilishly dangerous new manifestation of Irish terrorism." They provided him with what he asked for—a new passport, weapons and ammo, clothes.

He recrossed the Irish Sea that night on the ferry from Liverpool to Dublin, carrying an Irish passport that identified him as Tom Grady. The passport was stamped with visas, indicating he'd been in Spain, Portugal, Italy and Greece and had been away from Ireland for nearly eight years. He wore simple clothes that suggested he was a workingman: a flat cap, a jacket and pants, boots, all worn.

Bolan carried his meager possessions in a stained old canvas bag. He carried a little Greek money and a few Irish pounds. He had no weapons.

Leaving the ferry at about ten, he passed easily and quickly through passport and customs. In a jacket pocket he carried a claim check, and within a few minutes he was in a railroad station where he presented the check to a pink-faced old man who hefted three heavy packages from a shelf and dropped them onto the counter.

Weapons, ammo, money, other kinds of clothes— the Special Branch had somehow smuggled them into Ireland earlier and checked them into the station, so he could enter the country without the risk of being caught with weapons.

The warrior checked into the first cheap hotel he saw and paid for a night's lodging in advance. He had an iron cot and no bathroom, but it would do. He'd certainly put up with worse.

He unpacked the bundles from the railroad checkroom to see what he had. The Desert Eagle was there, as well as the Beretta, plus plenty of ammo and extra clips for each. And his harness. Somebody had supplied a Heckler & Koch G-11. If Brognola hadn't sent it, he'd suggested it to the Special Branch. It was the kind of rifle Bolan had used when he and Harrigan encountered the heavily armed fishing boat off the west coast of Ireland. There was nothing better, and the bundle in which it was packed included plenty of ammo.

He had also been provided with a good knife, a flashlight, a coil of nylon rope, two thousand Irish pounds, a gray tweed suit, white shirt and tie, and a set of blue workingman's coveralls.

The tools of the trade.

The warrior donned his combat harness and settled the Desert Eagle and Beretta into their leathers under his workman's jacket. He pocketed the knife and looped the coil of rope over his shoulder under his jacket. Then he left the hotel.

His first priority was to contact Kathryn O'Connor. The warrior stopped at the first telephone booth he came across and dialed her number. After several rings he hung up.

Okay. She could be a lot of places.

When he left that morning, the word to her and to Harrigan had been that he'd be back in a few hours. Then the chopper had returned without him. He wondered what word had been given to her. That he'd been pulled off this job? That he wouldn't be back?

He'd have to contact Harrigan, though he wasn't sure it was a good idea for Harrigan even to know he was back in Ireland. He had his loyalty, after all.

On the other hand, the inspector need not know from where he was calling. Or why.

Bolan dialed the inspector's number at the constabulary office. The man was still on duty, and after a minute he came on line.

"MacKenzie."

"Where are you?"

"It doesn't matter. I tried to call Kathryn a minute ago. No answer. Do you know where she is?"

"Mack . . . you don't know?"

"I don't know. Where is she?"

"Gone. Most likely dead."

"What happened?"

"What can I say? She was snatched from her flat this afternoon. She shot one man, killed him, but the others got her. Witnesses saw her being shoved into a car, still alive. But—"

"Any leads?"

"I . . . I can't work with you any longer. You know why."

"You can put the word out for me," Bolan growled.

"What word?"

"Word to Finnerty. The only possible chance he has to survive is to release Kathryn unharmed. Put the word out, Mike. The word is that if he releases her unharmed, he'll live. If she's dead, he's dead. He can take that to the bank."

"Where are you? I can't work with you officially, but—"

"Don't sacrifice yourself. I don't need help. My job has just got a whole lot simpler. So put the word out. It's over for Timothy Finnerty. He's history. And so is anybody who goes near him."

CHAPTER EIGHT

The Executioner had asked Inspector Harrigan one more question before he hung up. "Tell me, Mike. Do you have anybody watching her apartment?"

"No. They won't bring her back there."

"Nobody's looking for me, then?"

"Not yet. Officially you're not in Ireland, and unless you do something crazy, the constabulary isn't looking for you."

"Thanks. I may be in touch."

"Do keep in touch. I'll help you if I can, as long as—"

"As long as I don't do something crazy," Bolan said as he hung up.

Yeah. And he had an idea just what was crazy.

If the Irish Constabulary wasn't watching her apartment, he would lay odds that somebody was. They'd figure he'd come looking for her, and where would he start? Where she was kidnapped. He'd go looking for a lead.

He stepped out of the telephone booth and checked the street. Midnight. The street was quiet. Streetlights burned yellow at the ends of the block. The shops and apartments were mostly dark. A little light shone here and there in upstairs windows.

One black car was parked in the middle of the block, a little beyond the building where Kathryn O'Connor lived. The warrior couldn't tell if anyone was in it.

He walked away. If anyone was watching the policewoman's flat, or from her flat, he'd been seen. Better they think he was just someone who'd come up the street to use the telephone.

There were only one or two ways to get into the building without confronting the watchers. One was to find a back door, and the other was to come in from the roof. Since it was unlikely there was an alarm system in one of the modest brick buildings, he could use either way.

Bolan guessed there had to be an alley or passageway behind the rows of buildings. There was no trash or garbage on the sidewalk waiting to be collected. He'd seen none yesterday.

Rounding the block, he found the alley, which was narrow and paved with gravel. Water lay in dark puddles made by the ruts. Each building had a rear door, flanked by cans and bins, and each building displayed a number, either painted on the door or in rusty old wrought-iron numerals attached to the brick. He knew the number of Kathryn's building, and walked directly to the back door.

The door was locked, but the lock was old and simple, and the wood was soft. Bolan had no trouble shoving the point of his knife between the door and frame and jimmying the bolt back. He turned the knob and opened the door, stepping back to wait for a reaction from inside. Nothing.

The warrior stepped inside and closed the door. He found himself in a long hallway that ran, apparently, from the rear of the building to the front. For some reason, though, it wasn't a straight hall, and he couldn't see the front door.

He edged quietly along the hall, listening. Presently he arrived at a right turn and came in sight of the front door. And of a sentry.

He'd guessed right. The man was silhouetted against the faint yellow light from the street—indistinct but distinct enough for Bolan to see the rifle in his right hand.

From the man's frame and posture, Bolan judged he was young. He was dressed in a suit, dark brown or black, with an open-collar shirt. Except when he turned and glanced up the stairs, he kept his face to the door, watching the street through lace curtains.

Sure. He didn't know who he was watching for, but he was there to kill whatever man came to Kathryn O'Connor's flat at this time of night. The gunner knew what he was doing, and the way he glanced up the stairs from time to time told the warrior there was another man upstairs. At least one.

The Executioner crept up behind the sentry and looped one muscular arm around the man's throat, cutting off his wind. Then he eased the unconscious gunner to the floor.

The warrior dragged the guy back into the hall a little, where he was more likely to be overlooked by someone who entered the building—or someone who came down the stairs.

Bolan examined the panel of doorbells. O'Connor, 2B. Right. The third floor. Numbered by the European system, flats on this floor were counted as being on the ground floor, and the floor at the top of the first flight of stairs was the first floor.

He drew the Beretta, expecting trouble. Likely there was another sentry on the street. Maybe two. Then someone in her apartment, probably.

Maybe not. Maybe they wouldn't suppose he could get that far. On the other hand, the chief of the gang would make himself comfortable. And maybe he would want to have access to her phone so that one of his animals could call him, as Bolan had called Kathryn yesterday morning. Most likely there'd be a gunman in her apartment.

With the Beretta up and searching for a target, Bolan slowly made his way up the stairs, his eyes focused hard on the floors above. He was conscious that sleeping in the rooms around him were innocent people, people who just lived there, going about their daily business. They'd been frightened. Harrigan had said Kathryn was kidnapped from her flat and had killed one of her kidnappers. The residents of these apartments had seen violence and blood, and hordes of police on the premises. But now they slept, thinking they were safe.

The warrior hoped they continued to sleep. He didn't want any of them waking and checking their hallways.

The second floor was clear and quiet. He mounted the stairs toward the third. It, too, was quiet, but he could smell cigarette smoke. As he climbed higher, the smell become more distinct, more acrid. It wasn't old cigarette smoke. It was fresh.

Bolan continued up the stairs and made his way to Kathryn O'Connor's flat. Though it was difficult to be sure, it seemed as though the cigarette smoke was coming from under the door of 2B.

He stood beside the door and listened. Silence. But the smell of cigarette smoke was definitely coming from under the door, and someone was awake in that apartment.

He had options, but he decided on the most direct one. He rapped gently on the door.

"John?"

"John" must have been expected. Bolan grunted an indistinguishable reply. The knob turned and the door eased back.

The warrior hit it hard with a boot, and it slammed back into the face of the man who was expecting to see John. When the guy recovered his balance, he saw that he was facing a stranger—and a Beretta 93-R.

The Irishman extended his hands to both sides. Bolan reached out with his left hand and relieved him of a Colt revolver.

"You're the one they call MacKenzie," the man muttered.

"Right. But you wouldn't be Finnerty, would you? No. That would be too easy."

"My name's O'Bannion, and I expect to dance on your grave."

"I wouldn't count on it," Bolan replied.

"Well, on *hers,* then."

"Finnerty's dead if he harms her," Bolan growled.

O'Bannion was a barrel-chested, muscular man about forty years old. The light in the policewoman's living room was enough for Bolan to see the smirk on the terrorist's face.

"You're a babe, MacKenzie," O'Bannion sneered. "The woman's a traitor. We'll sacrifice a dozen men to kill one traitor. She may be dead already. I don't know." He laughed. "Actually she's probably not. The boys would want to have a bit of fun with her before they dispose of her. And when that's over—"

Bolan seized the man by the lapels of his dark jacket and lifted him off his feet. O'Bannion kicked and shoved, desperate to get away from the man he'd goaded too far. The terrorist managed to free a Gerber combat knife from an ankle sheath and started to raise the weapon in a slashing arc. Abruptly Bolan gave the man a powerful shove. Completely off balance, O'Bannion stumbled, then went crashing through the window.

O'Bannion, shrieking in terror, plummeted toward the street. Suddenly the shriek broke into a screech of terminal agony, followed by a gurgling groan.

Bolan looked down. The man had landed across the spear tops of the wrought-iron fence that separated four feet of flowers from the sidewalk. For a moment he groaned and flopped. Then he was silent.

Two men with rifles ran toward him.

KATHRYN O'CONNOR WAS ALIVE. She lay naked on cold pavement in a cellar so dark that she couldn't find a single glimmer of light on which to focus, on which to fasten her sanity. Her hands were cuffed behind her back, and her ankles were pinched by leg irons. As nearly as she could tell, a chain ran from her handcuffs to the leg irons, doubling her back so that she could hardly move.

The pain from the manacles and shackles was bad enough, but it was little compared to the pain in her face and on her ribs. She knew her nose was broken, and she guessed two or three ribs were. Her swollen lips were split and tasted of blood.

She had recognized the man who had worked her over. His name was Brian Connelly, and he'd been furious about the death of the man she'd shot during the kidnapping. He had her chained before he began to use his big, hammy fists on her. He was a pro. He'd meant to hurt her and mark her, but not to kill her.

When he'd finished beating her, a woman had taken pictures of her with a Polaroid camera.

With all the pain it made little difference that she lay in a pool of her own urine. Yet she had held it back for as long as she could. Now she lay in it and couldn't roll out of it. It was even in her hair.

She couldn't at first imagine why they hadn't killed her. Then she realized that she was bait. The Polaroid pictures were for... Colonel William MacKenzie? No... lying here with a lot of time to think, Kathryn had decided she knew who "Colonel MacKenzie" was. She'd heard of the man.

They would sacrifice anything to kill him, and they would use her to lure him.

And they would die.

If "MacKenzie" was who she thought he was, Brian Connelly was a dead man, and so was the man who probably gave orders to Connelly. That would be Timothy Finnerty.

MACK BOLAN HAD PROWLED the night. He'd made himself more familiar with Dublin than he had been before. Without O'Connor to help him find his way around, and with Harrigan reduced to unofficial recognition of him, the warrior had to do his own recon of the city.

It wasn't an easy city to probe in the middle of the night. Taxis didn't run much after midnight. Buses didn't run at all.

Such Irishmen as were on the streets were staggering drunk—boisterous and fun-loving, and ready to welcome another man into their comradeship. He had joined two groups of them, had pretended to be as drunk as they were, and had laughed through the streets, listening to their talk, asking questions and getting answers.

Plainly the Irish were a race of men with great enthusiasms, much dignity, complete honesty. The fanatics among them were a tiny minority. The terrorists were a minority of that minority.

In the light of dawn he stood across the street from what he had identified during the night as a possible headquarters of the Curran Brigade—or an arm of the IRA. All he'd been told was that dangerous men gathered here, killers.

Whoever they were, they kept early hours. At dawn they were in the building, and active. A crudely lettered sign above the door and windows proclaimed Victory to the Irish Republican Army!

The three-story brick building was a little isolated, as if the hardmen who hung out there had frightened other people away. The similar buildings on either side were boarded up, abandoned. Even across the street the buildings immediately opposite the IRA headquarters looked abandoned—as if the people who might have lived there had been frightened by the presence on their street of this particular detachment of the Irish Republican Army.

And at this hour of the morning—five o'clock— hardmen lounged around the front, guarding the door, menacing anyone who wasn't wanted.

They paid no attention to Bolan as he walked past. Even at five in the morning scores of workmen walked through the streets on their way to work. Many of them were on their way to labor exchanges where they hoped to find a job for the day. They looked much the same as Bolan—wearing flat caps, short jackets, baggy pants—and many of them carried canvas bags containing the tools of their trades.

The Executioner's canvas bag contained one of the tools of his trade—the Heckler & Koch G-11 caseless assault rifle.

He stood across the street and watched men coming and going. Even if workmen were on the streets, five in the morning seemed an odd hour for so much activity in a political headquarters—or, if what he had been told during the night was right, a terrorist headquarters.

A car pulled up, and two men got out. Someone rushed out of the headquarters and shook their hands with conspicuous enthusiasm. The hardmen gathered around, as if the newcomers were important.

It was obvious that one of them wasn't Timothy Finnerty. Harrigan had described Finnerty as having a dark beard. The driver of the car had dark hair but no beard. The other man, the one who had the deference of the men gathered around him, was blond, his eyebrows all but invisible against his pink skin.

Bolan stared harder, and recognition clicked. The man was Klaus Schimmel, a German terrorist, number three man in the terrorist organization that called itself Revolutionäre Zellen, RZ. They were the group that had bombed a Cologne shopping mall and killed nearly twenty people, half of them children—for "revolutionary" purposes.

Klaus Schimmel. What was he doing in Dublin? He'd escaped the Executioner in Frankfurt. That was unfinished business. Maybe he'd have the opportunity to finish it now.

But what was Schimmel doing in Dublin? It would be a good idea to find out.

TIMOTHY FINNERTY WAS ANGRY. Molly sneered. He was angry most of the time, and she was bored with seeing his temper. He was angry this time because they'd overslept, and they were going to be late for their meeting with Klaus Schimmel.

Finnerty literally threw himself behind the wheel of his car. Molly was hardly in and hadn't closed her door when he jammed the car into gear and sped off.

"They care nothing for us. You know that," Finnerty said. "The Germans would just as soon walk away and leave us—"

"Except that you're paying five times over for what they're supplying."

"I am if it's not drying up. We've lost—"

"I know what you've lost. Don't tell me again. On the other hand, they're funding *their* operations out of the junk we bring in from the ocean. We need them. They need us. It's a simple business proposition."

"The American—" Finnerty began.

Molly turned and pressed a finger hard against his shoulder. "Keep the men away from the girl," she said with hard, cynical emphasis. "Keep her alive, Tim. She may be your only chance."

"*What!* You buy his threat? Hers? What the hell are you talking about?"

Molly tipped her head and looked at him. "What he did to O'Bannion last night is something like what he plans to do to you. And I think you've had plenty of proof that he *can* do it. Get word to him, Tim. Get the word to him—lay off if you ever want to see Kathryn O'Connor alive."

"See her alive..." Finnerty said quietly, something working in his mind.

"He's never going to see her alive. You know that, I know that and I imagine she knows that. If the American cares for her, he may resist the idea."

KLAUS SCHIMMEL in Dublin. Okay, it figured. If the Curran Brigade cared nothing for the Irish cause but was just another terrorist gang, then an alliance with Klaus Schimmel's RZ was perfectly logical.

What Schimmel wanted out of this "revolutionary" struggle had been made clear a dozen times. What he wanted was simple—wealth and power, other people under his heel. Why think Timothy Finnerty was any different?

A second car pulled up behind the car that had delivered Schimmel. What was going on that generated so much enthusiasm?

Suddenly it was plain enough. Four men began to unload boxes from the trunks of the cars. Bolan realized the boxes contained Semtex, a plastic explosive that was always shipped in those distinctive, Czech-manufactured green cartons. And there had to be a hundred pounds of it.

Who were they going to blow up? Who could guess? It was likely that the terrorists didn't know yet themselves.

Well, the Executioner had an idea about who they were going to blow up. It wasn't their idea, but he liked it.

He opened the canvas bag and withdrew the G-11. A couple of workingmen saw what he pulled from the bag, but they pretended they didn't see. They made no effort to warn the IRA men across the street. All they did was walk on a little faster and hurry out of the street.

Semtex was a stable plastic explosive that could be detonated only by a violent shock—the explosion of a blasting cap. What would be the impact of a 4.7 mm slug slamming into it at three hundred meters per second? Would that be shock enough?

Bolan knew the answer.

He leveled the muzzle of the G-11 on the rear fender of the second car, just behind the wheel. The rifle was equipped with an optical sight so that he could direct his burst very precisely.

One of the hardmen spotted him and yelled, but the warning was too late. A 3-round grouping ripped through the thin sheet metal of the car and into packed boxes of Semtex.

The blast ripped the car to pieces, hurling steel, metal and glass up and down the street and high into the air. It punched hardmen through the collapsing windows of the IRA headquarters. Klaus Schimmel was thrown backward against the brick wall of the building so hard that his neck was broken. The facade of the building sagged as supports broke and fell.

Bolan, fifty yards away, was thrown back against the front of a building. A big hunk of torn sheet steel skidded across the street and barely missed his legs.

He raised the G-11 and took aim on the first car. It was damaged and had rolled forward, but the Semtex in its trunk hadn't exploded. Another 3-round burst took care of that. There wasn't nearly as much plastique in the first car, but the explosion was ferocious.

The warrior watched from across the street, ready to fire on any IRA gunman who lifted a weapon. But none had survived. The street was silent except for the low roar of burning gasoline and a sullen rumbling in the buildings, which began to collapse like a paper bag in a driving rain.

TIMOTHY FINNERTY SWERVED toward the curb, braked and brought his car to a quick stop. Two blocks ahead a furious explosion had just filled the air with dust and debris.

He turned to Molly, the anger in his eyes turning to cold fear. "It couldn't be—"

Then they saw and soon heard the second explosion. Smoke and fire rose above the rooftops ahead.

Molly Finnerty slumped in her seat and shook her head. "What else could it be?" she asked dully.

This was the worst yet. They were on their way to meet Klaus Schimmel, and if Schimmel was already there and was hurt . . . It was beyond contemplating.

"We have to know," she said. "You can get a little closer before we have to turn."

Finnerty nodded. He pulled the car away from the curb and drove toward the rising column of smoke.

What they saw was worse than they could have imagined. The headquarters building—storehouse for arms, ammunition, explosives and records—had collapsed, burying everything under tons of rubble. No emergency personnel or equipment had arrived, but people running to the scene to help were kneeling over a score of shattered bodies.

The Finnertys could see that two cars had blown up. They had to guess that Klaus Schimmel had been in one of them.

"Schimmel!" Timothy Finnerty shrieked.

Molly stared openmouthed at the destruction. "Schimmel . . . my God! The RZ! They—"

"At the very least they'll break off the alliance. It was always a condition that we could control—"

"Could *they?*" Molly asked in a shrill voice. "How well have they done when they came up against MacKenzie . . . you think it's MacKenzie again?"

Finnerty nodded. "I think it's MacKenzie— whoever he is."

"A murdering—" She stopped. "No, Tim, not a murdering fool, which is what I was about to say. No. We should be that lucky. No, he's smart and tough. But beyond that he has experience. You never get ahead of him."

"Never get behind him," Finnerty contradicted.

"Either way. We're talking about a man who's professional. That's the point. He's a soldier, Tim."

"So?"

"The son of a bitch is vulnerable," she went on.

"Meaning?"

"Meaning the girl we've got chained up in the cellar. It's the only chance we've got to stop him."

O'CONNOR WAS BLINDED by the light. It was only daylight, coming into the cellar after bouncing off walls upstairs, but it was the most light she'd seen in many hours. And her eyes received the dim light painfully.

She could only blink against the light, couldn't rub her eyes with her manacled hands. She looked up at the indistinct figures coming down the steps. Her eyelids were stuck together, and she had to force them apart.

It wasn't the man who had used his fists on her. It was another man, maybe Finnerty. She couldn't tell; she couldn't focus her eyes on him. The woman was there, too. O'Connor recognized her without looking at her.

The man poked her with the toe of his shoe, sending stabbing pain through her broken ribs. She cringed. Her body ached from what the other man had done to her, as well as from lying hour after hour on a stone floor, chained and barely able to move.

The man—she could see a little better now and was almost sure it was Finnerty—opened his pants. As she cowered and tried to turn her face away, he urinated on her, directing the hot stream on her head and neck.

"That's a little something in memory of Sean O'Bannion," he growled. He turned and stalked up the steps out of the cellar, leaving her alone with the woman.

"It could have been worse than that," Molly Finnerty said. "He learned of the death of O'Bannion only a minute ago. He wanted to kill you, but you're more valuable alive. So get on your feet. I'm taking you up out of here. You get a bath. I can't stand the stink of you. Then, well, we'll see."

HARRIGAN JERKED the blue Ford to the curb. Bolan opened the door and got in.

"Did anybody run an ID on the blond man?" Bolan asked.

"They're making identifications on all of them."

"When they make one on the blond man, they'll find out he was Klaus Schimmel. Does the name mean anything to you?"

Harrigan shook his head.

"He was a top man in an organization the Germans call Revolutionäre Zellen—Revolutionary Cells. RZ for short. The explosive that went off was Semtex, lately the favorite plastic explosive of the terrorist world. Schimmel was delivering it to the IRA headquarters."

"You're sure of this?"

Bolan shrugged. "I saw what I saw. You can verify what I said through the West German Security Service, the BND, or run it through Interpol."

Harrigan nodded solemnly. "The rumored connection to the Third World crazies, plus connection to the most vicious terrorist gangs in Europe." The inspector steered through the increasing traffic of mid-morning. "Okay," he said several minutes later, "I've got something to show you. Try to keep control of yourself."

Bolan expected to see photographs of Kathryn's body, dead. The Polaroids of her chained and injured were a relief. At least she was alive.

"They also sent a message."

"I don't even have to ask what it is."

"No. It's call you off, send you home, or she dies. We were going to send a message that you'd been called off, sent home, but you were busy last night. The man they found impaled on the wrought-iron fence was named Sean O'Bannion. He was one of Finnerty's most trusted lieutenants." Harrigan sighed loudly as he whipped the wheel around to drive the Ford past a truck that blocked his lane. "So what next? Do I have any influence over it? Does my government? Does yours?"

"What would Kathryn do?" Bolan asked.

Harrigan shook his head. "We can't be governed by that."

"I can. And you can send the word back to whoever sent you these pictures. If you can. Finnerty has just one chance, and it's not a very good one. I want Kathryn."

"Understood," Harrigan replied. "I don't have contact, but I'll do what I can to get the word through."

CHAPTER NINE

Mack Bolan lay across the simple bed in his hotel room. Whatever they said, Kathryn O'Connor was lost. He didn't know where she was or how to save her except by fighting the way he was fighting.

If they had called and said to him, "She's at 383 Patrick Street," he could have attacked 383 Patrick Street and, at whatever risk, rescued her or died trying.

But they were too smart for that. Too ruthless. Too despicable. And he was left with nothing to do but raise the bet.

He slept for a few hours. At about noon he got up, dressed a little differently in a cheap, worn black suit that was among the clothes provided for him by the Special Branch, and went out on the streets. He carried the Desert Eagle and the Beretta in leather under the suit jacket. In a pub not far from the center of the city he drank a beer and ate a sandwich.

The IRA wasn't hard to find. Its neighborhood offices were everywhere. But he couldn't just walk into every storefront IRA headquarters he found and start to shoot. Not all IRA men were terrorists, not by any means. Even though they intended to use force if necessary to drive the British out of Northern Ireland, many of them renounced terrorism and rejected gangs like the Curran Brigade.

So on the streets of Dublin, Mack Bolan was a hunter.

And the hunted, too. He had no doubt of that.

THE TERRORISTS wouldn't return to her apartment, and there was no reason to go there, really. Yet Bolan was drawn to that street.

At the end of the block he stood and looked at the rows of brick buildings. It was the kind of street where honest people worked to make an honest living, where neighbor lived at peace with neighbor—and where the kidnapping of a young woman, and her shooting one of her kidnappers, then the deaths of two more hoodlums last night must have upset a long-standing way of life.

He turned away from the street and walked north. Every street was the same, block after block. Except on a street called Paul's Lane where a small crowd gathered around a scene of destruction. The plate-glass window of a small women's clothing store was shattered. The sidewalk glittered with the broken glass. As Bolan drew closer, he could see chaos inside the little shop. Racks of garments were upset, the clothes dashed to the floor. Worse than that, the merchandise was spattered with white paint.

This was no accident. Someone had trashed the little store.

The warrior stopped at the edge of the murmuring, sympathetic crowd, listening to the voices.

"The devils! They should be put on the gallows, every one."

"Poor Mrs. Dugan. She didn't deserve the likes of this."

"So, what are you goin' to do, Constable? You know who did it. What's the law goin' to do?"

A uniformed man of the Irish Constabulary stood just inside the store, writing in a notebook. He was conspicuously embarrassed and pretended to ignore his heckler.

"What happened?" Bolan asked.

"The damn IRA," an old man muttered—ready to talk but anxious not to be heard by everyone in the crowd. "Mrs. Dugan didn't pay."

"Didn't pay?"

The elderly man looked up into Bolan's face, stared suspiciously and judged him, then decided, apparently, it was safe to talk to him. "They demand what they call their 'contribution.' A contribution to the cause, they call it, and if a shopkeeper doesn't pay... well, you see what happens."

Bolan understood. The protection racket. "Who's the collector?"

The old man glanced around, anxious to see if anyone was listening. Then he said, "For this neighborhood, it's a fellow named Brian Connelly. Husky sort of fellow, sure. Red hair. Carries a little satchel and drops the money in.

"The enforcer?"

"He does it himself, mostly. With help."

"He did this?"

"Very likely. But you'll never find out. Mrs. Dugan won't say. Not now. She won't tell the constable. She's afraid. The constable knows who it was, but since nobody will testify, there's nothin' he can do. There's nothin' anybody can do."

Bolan nodded thoughtfully, as if he agreed. But he didn't. There was something somebody could do. And within the hour somebody did.

It took less than that to find Brian Connelly. When he spotted the burly redhead, he followed him for a while, watching the operation.

It was as the old man had said. Connelly walked into shops, pubs, gas stations, occasionally even knocking at the door of a home. He received something at each stop, usually in a white envelope, and he dropped the envelopes into his small leather satchel.

Bolan decided to get ahead of him, to watch him work a stop. He strode down the street on the opposite side, crossed over and was inside a stationery and card shop, browsing, when the collector came in.

"You have your bit for the cause, I suppose?" he said to the slight, bald man behind the counter.

"I have," the man replied solemnly, reaching under the counter and pulling out an envelope.

Connelly opened the envelope and counted the money. "It may be necessary to ask for a slight increase, starting next week. There have been some expensive losses."

"You'll put us all out of business," the shopkeeper said quietly. "Then what? Where will you get your money then?"

Connelly smiled. "Out of business... Sure, it's what you said the last time we had to have a bit of an increase. But don't worry. We're keepin' you in business, not puttin' you out of it."

"I'm barely making a living."

"We'll see to it that you do make a living," Connelly said. "We've got some ideas of ways to help you."

"By doing what?"

"By setting you up with a new line of merchandise, maybe."

"I know what you mean. I don't want to sell that stuff."

"Well, we'll see. We'll see, my friend. I'll be talking to you."

The collector strolled casually out of the shop. He was, as the old man on the street had said, a burly fellow, a little too heavy but carrying his fat over powerful muscles. His nose was flat and pushed a little to one side. When clenched into fists, his big, scarred hands would make a pair of punishing clubs.

Bolan followed him. The point was to see where he took the satchel he was slowly filling with money.

His next stop was a pub, where he collected money and drank a beer. Then, it appeared his rounds were finished, and he walked away quickly. Bolan followed.

At last Connelly reached a brick house on Casey Street. It was a three-story structure, set on a narrow lot but separated from other houses by a few feet. A low brick wall ran along the sidewalk. To reach the door of the house, Connelly opened a squeaking wrought-iron gate.

The house was in better repair than most on Casey Street. There were others like it, with walls or fences, sitting on little lots with room for a bit of grass and a few flowers, but the brick of this one had been sandblasted not long ago and was fresh and pink, and the window frames bore a fresh coat of white paint. The oak front door was freshly varnished.

Connelly rang a bell, and a woman opened the door. He handed her the bag, they chatted for a moment, then Connelly left. Bolan supposed he could be wrong, but he thought he saw that Connelly treated the woman with exaggerated deference.

He would come back. This place deserved checking out. For now he followed Connelly.

Connelly's work for the day was done, apparently. He returned to the pub where he'd made his last collection, and the Executioner followed him inside. The Irishman called for another beer, and for this one he slapped money onto the bar. Bolan, too, ordered a beer and stood not far down the bar from the burly collector.

"Well, Brian, a successful day, was it?"

Connelly grinned, as he lowered his mug and wiped beer foam off his mouth with the back of his hand. "They're all successful days when you're workin' for the holy cause."

"What about the awful explosion this mornin'?"

"Well, there are those who aren't careful," the collector stated with an artificially casual air. "Explosives can be a useful thing, but if you handle them badly, they can turn around and bite you."

"That what happened?" the man asked.

"When did we begin to ask so many questions? Hmm? You wouldn't be askin' for some reason, would you now?"

The man smiled and shook his head. "You're talkin' to a loyal man, Brian—as you well know. Only curious. Something that damages the cause—"

"In truth," Connelly interrupted, "I don't really know what happened. Luck has run the wrong way the past week."

"Dare I say I think mistakes have been made?" the man asked.

"No, you don't dare," Connelly replied bluntly.

Half an hour and one more beer later Brian Connelly left the pub, and Mack Bolan again followed. The man had taken no notice of Bolan. He was either stupid or, more likely, he was supremely confident. He had used his fists—and maybe worse—in this city so long that he was known as a man not to be challenged, not even to be questioned. Either way, he hadn't noticed that a grim, dark-haired man had been following him.

He was bold enough to return to Paul's Lane. He walked past Mrs. Dugan's ruined little clothing store. Walked past? Ambled past. Swaggered past. The people on the street looked away and pretended they didn't know he was there.

Then he made a mistake: he walked into one of the alleys to relieve his bladder, which was swollen with three pints of beer.

He wasn't a cautious man and didn't seem to care much if somebody saw him. He just walked along the alley a little way and stopped.

Another mistake.

When Bolan walked up, the collector-enforcer was so intent on relieving himself that he took too long to recognize the hazard implied by this hard, dark, American-looking man. Before he could quite button his trousers, a solid fist crashed against his nose and stunned him.

Connelly staggered backward, and Bolan let him have it again, square on the jaw. And not knowing if Connelly was carrying a gun and might go for it, Bolan drove a third punch into his gut.

He didn't let the man drop to the ground. He shoved him against the wall and held him up as he checked under his jacket for weapons. "You know what this means?" he asked Connelly.

The hardman was bleeding from nose and mouth, but he grunted, "It means you're a dead man."

"No, you've got it wrong, pal," Bolan growled. "It means your racket has just ended. I'm letting you live so you can take the word to your boss. But the next time you trash somebody's store—in fact, the next time you try to collect—you're a dead man. And so's the guy you work for."

Bolan shoved a .44 cartridge into Connelly's pocket. The Irishman wiped a hand across his mouth, then reached into his pocket and pulled out the .44 slug. "So," he muttered. "I've heard about you. You figure you can fight the whole army?"

"Just carry the word," Bolan said. "Collections are history. Don't try it tomorrow. Or any other time."

Connelly ran his hand over his damaged face, coming away with a broad smear of bright red blood. "We avenge our blood," he warned.

"Maybe I should finish you. Finding you dead would be just as good a message. Maybe better."

Connelly's eyes—as hard with hate as any Bolan had ever seen—strained to focus. "Maybe you should. 'Cause I have a feeling you and I are going to see each other again."

"I don't kill helpless, unarmed men."

"Good for you," Connelly, grunted. "Next time I won't be unarmed."

BOLAN RETURNED to the house on Casey Street for a soft probe. He walked along the street and around the block. The house was guarded from alley traffic by a high brick wall with broken glass set into concrete on top. The wrought-iron gate was topped with sharp spikes.

Approaching the gate, he saw that it was wide enough to let a car pass through. In fact, a car sat in a wood-and-brick shelter in the backyard.

Back in front he noticed what he hadn't seen before—hardmen, watching the house. Two of them in plain sight.

Somebody important was inside that house. He'd return after dark.

ON A BED in a second-floor bedroom of the Casey Street house, Kathryn O'Connor lay on her stomach. She was dressed in a skirt and a sweatshirt. Her hands were cuffed behind her, and her ankles were chained together with leg irons. She'd been allowed to bathe and use the toilet, and before they put her hands behind her back they'd let her eat a cheese sandwich and drink a cup of coffee.

Molly Finnerty had been with her most of the time since she had been brought up from the cellar. Now a harsh male voice ordered Molly to go downstairs, and the man entered the room.

O'Connor twisted her aching body and looked up at him. "It *is* you."

"Whore," he muttered.

"Not *me,* Timothy," she said.

"Yes, you. You and the American. Traitor and whore."

"Is that why you pissed on me?"

"You richly deserve everything that's happened to you," he said coldly.

"Are you going to kill me?"

He shook his head.

"I don't believe you."

He shrugged.

"I may die on you if you don't get me a doctor."

"No one ever died of a little beating."

"If a rib punctures a lung—"

His chin shot up. "Don't you *dare* die!"

"I can feel the pressure," she said. "The way I'm chained—"

"Molly!" he yelled through the bedroom door.

Molly came trotting up the stairs.

"Take the cuffs off her," he said. "Let her have her hands in front."

Molly shot a quick, skeptical stare at her husband. "You better go down and get on the telephone," she said. "Brian's on the line. He's been hurt. And guess who?"

Finnerty dashed down the stairs and grabbed the phone. "What's going on?" he asked.

It was all but impossible to understand Brian Connelly, but Finnerty did make out some of what he said. "The American...he slugged the hell out of me. Teeth knocked out. I—"

"The American? You're sure?"

"He stuck one of those big bullets in my pocket."

"What the hell did he want from you?"

"He says no more collections. He says we're out of that business."

"He's giving orders?"

"He is to me, Tim. I'm not collecting or enforcing until we get rid of that man. I wouldn't be anyway for a while. I'm going into the hospital. I never saw a man so dead serious. He's damn dangerous. Use the girl, Tim! Use the girl to smoke him out."

"I will if she lives. You smashed one of her ribs in against a lung—or so she says."

"Maybe I did. You said give it to her good."

"I also said keep her alive."

"Listen, Tim, I got something more to tell you. The American must have been following me. I don't know how long, but—"

"You were here!"

"I sure was. I went into the pub and had a couple of beers. He could have picked up on me there. But I got the idea he was following me for a long time. If so—"

"If so, he saw you drop the bag here!"

"Right."

"Where are you, Brian? Doc Kelly's?"

"Right."

"Tell Doc I'm bringing the girl there. I've got to get her out of here fast before the American comes and tries to rescue her. Then I— You have to go to the hospital, you say?"

"That's what Doc tells me."

"But I could use you tonight. The American will probably come here looking for the girl. She won't be here. But some guns will be. Waiting for him."

"Can't join you, Tim. Not tonight."

"We're gonna get him, Brian," Finnerty growled. "Tonight. I swear. He's gone too damn far!"

WITHIN FIVE MINUTES the car Bolan had seen inside the wall behind the house pulled out through the gate and into the alley. O'Connor and Molly sat in the rear seat. The policewoman was blindfolded and still securely chained hand and foot, but with her hands in front. Finnerty drove, and a gunman with an Uzi on his lap sat beside him.

Half an hour later they drove through another gate and into another little backyard. Molly led O'Connor inside another brick house through the back door. Only when they were inside the doctor's examining room did they take off the woman's blindfold, then her handcuffs and leg irons. For the next hour Dr. Robert Kelly worked over her, taping her ribs, setting her broken nose, applying salve to soften the scabs on her lips. When he put her to bed, Molly chained her left wrist and right ankle to the cot. Under a sedative, O'Connor slept.

"I don't entirely understand all this," Molly said to her husband.

"Then don't try," Finnerty snapped. "You stay here with her. I'm going to the confrontation with the American."

Molly knew that he wouldn't. Brian Connelly had known it. Timothy Finnerty invariably found reasons to be absent from any place where guns were apt to be fired. He would find a reason tonight, too.

In fact, he didn't return to the house on Casey Street. He deployed his troops by telephone, and having done that, he drove alone to a house in the village of Clondalkin, a few miles outside the city. He was happily received by a family who considered it an honor to have so great a man as Timothy Finnerty under its roof. They hid his car in their barn, and the elder son of the family hurried along to the pub to fetch the barmaid who would sleep with Timothy Finnerty—to comfort an honored man wearied by his heavy labors in the holy cause.

MACK BOLAN RETURNED to Casey Street an hour after midnight. He couldn't wear a combat suit on the city streets, but he wore rugged black pants, a black sweatshirt and a loose black nylon jacket that covered his weapons. The Desert Eagle and the silenced Beretta rode in leather under the jacket. He carried a canvas bag, as he'd done in the morning. The G-11 was in there, together with extra ammo, a knife, a coil of rope and a flashlight.

He wasn't surprised to see that the hardmen were looking for him—or looking for somebody. He would have been surprised if they weren't. The Curran Brigade had been hit hard the past few days and had taken big losses. They'd have been stupid not to guess that sooner or later they'd get hit here.

They had an advantage in that they knew somebody was coming, and they were ready.

He had an advantage. They didn't know who was coming, or when.

Especially they didn't know when, and that was a big advantage for the Executioner. Nobody could stay alert forever. Few men could stay alert for an hour, and it wouldn't be long before the sentries got careless. Years of experience told the warrior where to look for sentries. Unless somebody was unusually creative, they'd be in doorways, at windows, on the roofs—and some would just walk along the street, probably around the block.

He'd spotted some. Not all. There would be others.

A car cruised slowly along the street. Guns. For sure.

He knew how the block of houses was laid out. All of them had low brick walls or wrought-iron fences separating their narrow front lawns from the sidewalk. Those walls and fences afforded no cover. If there was a sentry behind the wall in front of the house where the enforcer had delivered the bag, the guy was lying on his belly.

In the rear the lots were separated from the alley by higher brick walls or wooden fences—so the people in the houses wouldn't have to look at the unpaved alley or the piled trash. Some of the houses were separated from each other by walls that ran from the front to the back of the lots. Some weren't.

The target house was in the middle of the block. If the street and alley were guarded, there was only one approach—through the lots.

So far unnoticed, apparently, he moved south to the first east-west street. In the dark he watched for a while, looking for hardmen watching this approach to the target house. He saw no one, but a car did keep circling the block, a small black car that carried what he'd figured—guns, gunners.

As soon as the vehicle was out of sight, Bolan crossed the street. A six-foot wall blocked his way into the first lot. He jumped, grabbed hold and was over in seconds. He dropped into the lot and crouched at the base of the wall, waiting for a reaction.

None.

The warrior eased his way along the wall toward the rear of the lot. The high brick wall continued and, except for a gate, separated the house from the alley.

There was no wall between the target house and the next house to the north. He moved cautiously into the next lot, where the house was long and there was almost no space between it and the wooden fence along the alley.

Bolan heard tires crunching on the gravel and tensed, wondering whether the gunners had decided to check the alley. He lay on the ground at the foot of the fence and waited. The car passed on.

Which meant nothing. They could have dropped off a gunner.

Again, no fence divided this lot from the next one north. Working his way along the wooden back fences—passing the gates carefully—he entered the third lot by stepping over a low, square-trimmed hedge.

Grass grew behind the houses on the first two lots, but this one was paved with gravel, and two cars were parked there. The gravel crunched beneath his feet, and he stopped. The crunching continued. Someone was behind him.

Bolan dropped to his knees and drew the Beretta. Light shone dimly in the windows at the back of this house. The Executioner was careful not to stare too long at those windows, not to allow his eyes to accustom themselves to that light. He needed to see what was in the dark behind the house, not what was in the light inside. Even so, he saw a figure move across one of the windows.

Bolan turned his head slightly at the sound of crunching gravel. Whoever was on the gravel wasn't moving much. He was standing, shifting back and forth probably.

A darker shadow moved within the blackness of the shadow of one of the cars. Bolan shifted a little and brought the man between him and one of the windows. Then he could see him—the silhouette of a slouching, weary man, a sentry compelled to stand outside all night and barely able to stay awake. The warrior could see, too, the distinctive silhouette of a Kalashnikov.

Yeah. A peaceful householder enjoying the night in his backyard—and just by chance carrying a deadly assault rifle.

The back door of the house opened, and a man stepped out. "You awake?"

"Hell, yes."

The man at the door snapped a lighter and lit a cigarette. In the brief flare Bolan could see the revolver hanging under that man's armpit.

"Shut up down there!"

Bolan looked up. The voice had come from the roof of the target house, and he could see a man sitting astride the peak of the roof, armed with an assault rifle.

The man in the doorway stepped out onto the gravel and walked over to the sentry by the car. "I'd as soon go to bed," he said quietly, so the man on the roof wouldn't hear. "What would I do with ten thousand pounds, anyway?"

"Jimmy, my boy, nobody's going to earn ten thousand tonight. There'll be no American showin' up at this hour."

"You're right on that, Bill. It's Finnerty's brainstorm," Jimmy replied.

"Right. You don't see *him* standing around or sitting on a roof like a goddamn stork. He's snug in bed with Molly somewhere while *we* wait out here to spring his trap."

"The trouble with his trap," Jimmy said, "is that there's no bait in it. They took the policewoman somewhere."

Bill snapped his lighter and lit a cigarette, and both men stood smoking, glancing up at the sky, peering casually into the shadows. They looked right past Bolan and didn't see him.

Bill flexed his shoulders and arched his back, trying to relieve the ache of standing too long in one place. "Did you get a look at the tits on that girl?" he asked.

"Damn right. Shame to bust up a pretty thing like that. She was in no condition for any fun after Connelly worked on her."

"Well, maybe Tim will want to keep her alive awhile. We may get some fun out of her yet."

"You dream," Jimmy scoffed. He flipped his half-smoked cigarette onto the gravel and returned to the back door of the house.

Bill took a final drag from his cigarette, pitched it to the ground and continued on his rounds. He'd traveled less than twenty yards when he froze. Bolan knew with a certainty that he'd been made.

In one fluid movement the warrior got to one knee, took aim and fired a 3-round burst that ripped through Bill's throat. The man let his rifle drop, slumped to his knees and sprawled on the gravel without a sound.

The gravel was a dead giveaway. Better to get off it. The warrior crossed over the hedge and continued on until he was between two houses—the first and second ones south of the target house.

Through one of the side windows he could see Jimmy sitting at a table in the kitchen, having a drink from a bottle of whiskey. Yeah. He'd decided he wasn't going to make ten thousand pounds tonight.

The light in the house was dim, but it shone into the narrow space between the two houses. Bolan dropped low and crept along the foundation until he was beyond the window opening on the kitchen.

He'd seen nobody on this roof. It could be hell if there was a sniper up there.

He came to the front corner of the house. All that was going to be accomplished here tonight was to take out a few more of the Brigade. Neither Kathryn nor Finnerty were here. But the Executioner was, and he'd make his presence known when he was ready.

He returned to the rear. The man on the roof still sat there. He must have a little rank in the gang; he'd yelled down orders to Jimmy and Bill.

Bolan extended the front grip on the Beretta 93-R. He steadied his aim by resting his elbows on top of one of the cars parked in the yard and pulled the trigger.

The man on the peak of the roof snapped his head around, lost his purchase on the roof and began to slide. He slid down the steep slate, his hands clutching as if he hoped to grab something and stop before he fell. Then, tearing off a length of spouting in his last desperate grab, he plummeted from the roof, turning in the air as he came down. His head and face hit hard, and his AK-47 landed on top of him.

He was silent—so silent that no one had heard a thing.

The low brick wall in front of the target house rose in stages like stair steps along the sides of the structure until it reached six feet or so. Along the sides of the rear lot and across the back it was six feet high, and the top was studded with broken glass. He crossed the back of the house, the one with Jimmy in the kitchen, and reached the brick wall where it was only four feet high and smooth on top.

The time had come to break out another weapon. Bolan stashed the canvas bag at the bottom of the wall, on the south side, and slung the G-11 rifle over his shoulder. He shoved the knife and scabbard into his belt.

He dropped into the lot of the target house, alert for any sign of reaction. All was quiet, so he eased along the side of the house.

Bolan dropped beside one of the basement windows and peered through the glass, but he could see nothing. He pressed the frame, and it yielded a little but not much. It was a secure window frame. He pried at it with the tip of his knife. The soft wood gave enough to let him run the knife back and forth. Twisting the knife in the rotten frame, he was able to dislodge the latch.

Inside, the cellar was dark. The warrior stuck his head in to look and listen. Then, hearing and seeing nothing, he pushed his legs through the open window and dropped to the cellar floor.

Nothing. Silence.

Bolan stood on a solid floor in a room that had echoed with the sound of his drop but was now dead silent. He began to feel his way around the wall and discovered he was in the furnace room, which was dominated by a great iron furnace and a coal bin.

He worked his way around the room and found a wooden door, which he opened. The room beyond was as dark as the furnace room, even darker maybe because it had no window.

In this room, too, he worked his way around the walls until he came to a door, which yielded a hallway. He could make out a set of wooden stairs at the far end.

In a second Bolan was on the stairs, cautiously working his way upward toward the ground floor. The warrior reached the top and the door that had to lead into the main floor. He took the G-11 off his shoulder and held it ready as he slowly turned the knob and pushed the door.

The cellar door opened onto the kitchen. But there was no Jimmy here, swilling whiskey. This kitchen was dark.

Bolan stepped into the room. It was empty. He prowled the kitchen. They'd drunk whiskey here, and they'd smoked.

He looked into the backyard. Where no one had been before, three men stood smoking, guns slung over their shoulders. He guessed they'd been in the alley and had come in through the gate. Anyway, they were talking and smoking, and they hadn't yet noticed the body of the sniper who'd been on the roof.

Bolan went through the house and checked the front. Through the glass of the front door he could see a man standing just outside. The car was at the curb, and another man leaned against the driver's door, talking to the men inside.

He turned and went upstairs. A small lamp burned in a bedroom. He looked at the bed. The pillow was stained with blood.

Kathryn's, he supposed. He was all but sure of it.

"Hey! Danny!"

Bolan looked down from the bedroom window. They had discovered the body.

The warrior rushed back down the stairs and reached the door to the kitchen just as one of the gunners wrenched open the back door and ran into the house—on his way to alert the men out front. Bolan dropped him with a quick shot from the Beretta.

From the window he saw Jimmy bolt from the kitchen of the house next door and run to join the others standing over the body of the man from the roof.

Bolan checked the front again. The car had moved, but the man still stood at the door. Another subsonic 9 mm round knocked him over, and he sprawled on the front steps.

That alerted two men on the street. One of them raised his AK-47 and fired a burst into the air. An alarm.

They were smart enough not to approach the house, not to present themselves as targets to the man who had to be inside. They took cover behind a low brick wall in front of a house across the street, and there they waited.

Bolan shoved the Beretta into its leather and drew the Desert Eagle. The time for silence was over. Now he would generate a little terror of his own.

In a sense he didn't need to. The burst of fire at the front of the house had caused panic and confusion. Two gunners, AK-47s level in front of them, crashed into the kitchen and stumbled over the body of their companion. Their reaction was to let loose bursts of automatic fire—shooting at nothing, shooting out of panic.

The slugs tore through wood and plaster, ripping great ragged holes in the wall between the kitchen and the parlor. They swung their muzzles toward the hall.

Bolan was there, and ready. The Desert Eagle flashed and roared, and one of its huge slugs blew one gunman off his feet and against the other.

Jimmy was the second man. Addled with whiskey and with terror, he stumbled back to the kitchen door, at the same time wobbling the muzzle of his AK-47 back and forth, seeking a target.

He didn't find one. The target found him. A .44 bullet knocked him through the door, and he fell into the backyard.

The last gunman outside fired a burst that shattered the kitchen window and tore through a cabinet, smashing dishes. Then he sprinted through the gate and behind the protection of the brick wall along the alley.

Bolan ran for the front again. The car was back. It screeched to a stop at the curb in front of the house, and a man with an Uzi scrambled out. Then another, this one with a mini-Uzi.

Bolan unslung the G-11, and a quick burst cut down the two gunmen and punched through the car. The driver slumped over the wheel.

Mack Bolan knew where there were two more men—across the street behind a wall. He waited. They were smart. They didn't show themselves. Maybe they'd slipped away while he was at the back of the house.

For a minute or so he waited for another gunner to show himself. No one did. It was quiet. The battle of Casey Street was over.

CHAPTER TEN

Kathryn O'Connor lay on the floor in the back of a van. Her ribs were tightly taped, and her broken nose had been set and was covered by a dressing. Salve glistened on her split lips. She was groggy from pills the doctor had made her swallow. Even so, she was conscious of her unyielding steel handcuffs and the cold, hard leg irons on her ankles.

She didn't know where she was. On the road somewhere. The van sped away from Dublin, but she didn't know in what direction.

The pills invited her to sleep, and she drifted away.

In a car that followed the van, Timothy and Molly Finnerty sat in front, and Brian Connelly lay across the back seat.

"There's only one way to put it," Molly said bitterly. "Put male arrogance aside, you two. We've been driven out of Dublin. Driven out, goddamn it! Rationalize it any way you want to, but we've been driven out of Dublin."

"Shut up," Finnerty barked.

"Explain it some other way. The American has driven us out of Dublin."

"We've got nothin' left here, Tim," Connelly agreed, speaking in some pain from the back seat. "Nine men last night!"

"Worse than that," Molly went on. "Defections. Men are afraid to be involved with us."

"Not the good men," Finnerty grunted.

"What good men do you have in mind?" she asked. "Our best men are dead. The American has gone through our ranks like the avenging angel of God."

"You want out?" he asked belligerently. He glanced over the back seat. "You, Brian? You want out?"

"If I wanted out," Connelly replied resentfully, "I'd have stayed in the hospital and tried to recover from what the American did to me. If you want evidence of my loyalty, Tim, you go to hell. You've got all the evidence you're entitled to and all you're going to get."

Finnerty concentrated on the traffic and guided the car through a tight spot between two trucks. "Sorry, Brian."

"We're still ahead of the game, still in a position to shake the world," Connelly stated.

"How?" Molly asked.

"We've still got the girl," Connelly said. "What would have happened last night if somebody had shoved the girl up to a window and yelled, 'Go ahead and shoot, you son of a bitch!' What would have happened then?"

"I'd like to know," Finnerty muttered. "I'm not sure that wild man wouldn't have sacrificed her to whatever he thinks his cause is."

"He's obviously ready and willing to sacrifice himself," Molly pointed out.

"We've got to use the girl smart," Connelly advised. "We distract the American with her while we get back to the job at hand."

"Meaning?"

"Meaning, of course, the execution of the queen of the Brits. We don't need a horde of hooligans to do that. We've got the MILAN launchers. Two or three good men, every one of them worth a dozen of the kinds you thought you laid a trap with last night, can carry off that job...and we've won. We've won, by God!"

"I see the idea," Molly said. "We keep the American chasing after his girlfriend while we move her from place to place and the best of us go after Her British Majesty. Good, Brian! Damn good!"

"Let's keep our real purpose in mind," Connelly suggested wearily.

"THINGS HAVE CHANGED," Harrigan said to Bolan.

"Yes, definitely."

"Seriously. To start with, I've got another set of pictures of Kathryn."

He handed Bolan two Polaroid pictures. She'd received some sort of medical attention. Her nose was covered by a fat bandage. She held a newspaper in front of her—the *Irish Times*—in cuffed hands. Harrigan pointed out that if the paper was studied under a strong glass, someone could see that it was that morning's edition.

The front-page story was headlined War Against IRA! Casey Street HQ Attacked by Gang.

"If you read the story," Harrigan said, "you'll find references to 'public outrage' over the attack on an IRA house. There'll be another story in tomorrow's paper. A considerable quantity of cocaine was found in the house. Some prominent names in the IRA will be quoted as disavowing the group that used that house. The public outrage may subside then."

"Does the newspaper know about the kidnapping of Kathryn?" Bolan asked.

"No. We thought it best not to tell them that in the interest of her safety. Getting to the point, the chief point," Harrigan went on, "you're back in the good graces of the government, and I'm authorized to work with you again."

"I'm glad to hear it, Mike."

"It was finding the cocaine that did it. There was a hundred pounds of it in the house."

"They were running a protection racket, too. Shaking down all the small businessmen in the neighborhood around Paul's Lane."

"Someone beat their collector within an inch of his life yesterday afternoon," Harrigan casually mentioned.

"Someone would have killed him if he'd known more about him. He's the thug who beat Kathryn."

"Really? Anyway, you have just about run the Curran Brigade out of town. Which isn't to say you've killed it. They still have the MILAN launchers, and, frankly, I'm damn worried about what they mean to do with them."

"And they still have Kathryn."

"Right. And I've got to be brutally truthful with you. They're going to use her to distract you from the real problem. Nothing would suit Timothy Finnerty better than to have you running around Ireland looking for Kathryn O'Connor while he and his brutes mount an attempt to assassinate the queen."

Bolan nodded grimly. "They won't get away with that."

KATHRYN HAD NO IDEA where she was. It was somewhere two hours' drive from Dublin, she thought, but even the time she had to guess. She was in a comfortable house in a handsome, paneled bedroom with a stone fireplace and an adjoining bathroom. She sat on a big brass bed, propped against a pile of feather pillows. A woman who seemed kindly enough had taken her clothes and given her a short gray flannel robe to wear. The daily newspapers were piled on a small table by her bed. The woman had pointed to a shelf containing a score of books, suggesting she while away her time by reading.

She might have been a guest in a family home except for one thing—a heavy chain encircled her throat and was locked in place by a laminated padlock. The far end of the chain was locked to a thick steel ring set in the stone hearth, this, too, with a big laminated padlock. The chain was probably twenty feet long. She could go to the bathroom, she could sit in the tub and bathe, she could stand at the windows and look out. She could sit in an easy chair by the fireplace. She could go anywhere in the bedroom and bathroom, carrying her chain in one hand. Beyond the length of the chain she could not go.

The two windows of the bedroom opened on a courtyard, surrounded by the wings of the house. The van that had brought her here was parked there, as was the car the Finnertys and Connelly had come in.

This place was another Curran Brigade headquarters, and she was a prisoner in it.

MACK BOLAN OPENED the door of his small room in the modest hotel he'd chosen as a likely place for an out-of-work sailor or fisherman to stay in.

A man was sitting in the worn chair beside the room's sagging bed, and he watched the Beretta come out of leather, almost too fast for him to comprehend. And when it was out and the muzzle was leveled at his face, he smiled and said, "Nigel Kettering, Colonel MacKenzie. I'm with Scotland Yard, Special Branch. If you'll lower the Beretta just an inch or so, I can establish my bona fides."

In a minute the young man mentioned half a dozen details of Bolan's meeting with Brognola at Hendon and his subsequent meetings with men of the Special Branch—details that no one but an authorized agent of the Special Branch could know. Bolan shoved the Beretta back inside his jacket.

"I've read the papers," Nigel Kettering said. "You've done a remarkable job here. My original assignment was to support you with additional ammunition and so on if you need it. Now I've had a communication that asks us to undertake a somewhat modified assignment.''

''Let's have it.''

''Our request is that you focus on the MILAN launchers.''

''That seems to be the consensus.''

''To be frank with you, Colonel MacKenzie—and speaking in absolute confidence—the Royal Family has remained rather secluded the past three days since the attack on the British army lorry in Germany. So far the press and public have taken no particular notice, but—''

''But you can't risk their lives. You can't let them travel around as freely as before.''

''I'm given to understand,'' Kettering continued, ''that you're to be trusted with any and all information. When Her Majesty opened the Belgravia Garden Show, she traveled in a small car, and the Rolls-Royce traveled empty but for the driver. She switched cars only just outside the gate.''

Bolan nodded. ''Makes sense. Until we get Finnerty and his weapons.''

''Do you then agree, Colonel MacKenzie, that the MILAN launchers must be our chief target?''

''I agree.''

''There's not very much the Special Branch can do in Ireland. I assure you, though, that we do have certain . . . facilities. They've already been assigned to locating Miss O'Connor.''

Bolan nodded.

"So... how do you recommend we proceed in the matter of the MILAN launchers?"

"By setting a trap," Bolan replied.

HAL BROGNOLA SAT across a conference room table in Whitehall in London and faced four cabinet-level officers of the British government.

"I should hope you aren't suggesting," one of them said, "that we make Her Majesty the bait in a trap."

"I should hope not, either," Brognola replied, clenching his teeth on a big cigar. "Not Her Majesty, of course. But how about Her Majesty's car?"

"Anything pertaining to—"

"Why don't you hear the proposition?" Brognola interrupted.

Mack Bolan was a reluctant participant in the discussion. He was a doer, not a talker.

On the other hand, these people would listen. They knew he'd taken out Klaus Schimmel—and they knew who Klaus Schimmel was. They knew how much it meant to British interests to have had hundreds of pounds of Semtex blown up on a Dublin street. They knew what it meant to have had hundreds of pounds of cocaine intercepted and destroyed.

"Yes, of course," the man who seemed to represent the prime minister said. "We'll hear Colonel MacKenzie's proposal."

They all stared at him, and Bolan spoke quietly but firmly. "What they have in mind is to do one of two things. They either kill a member of the Royal Family—not necessarily the queen—or they so terrify you that you don't allow any member of the Royal Family to go out in public.''

''We won't allow that,'' a man in the uniform of a general of the British army said. ''They have all kinds of courage, the Royals. It will be difficult to convince them not to take unnecessary chances.''

''I suggest you announce something,'' Bolan stated. ''Tell the world that the queen will appear here or there on whatever day. Send the Rolls-Royce and send a policewoman instead of the queen.''

''Colonel MacKenzie is right,'' one of the cabinet men agreed. ''We have to lay a trap.''

BOLAN WAS the only one of the team being formed who had ever fired a MILAN launcher. Someone suggested bringing in an army officer, but it was agreed that the fewer agencies involved in the operation the better. Other team members said they would like to see a test of the missile so that they would know what they had to defend against.

A few hours later Bolan was aboard a Lynx helicopter, accompanied by Nigel Kettering and three other agents of the Special Branch. A MILAN launcher and two missiles were securely stowed in the rear. The helicopter flew in cloud and mist, with only an occasional glimpse of the green earth below.

The Lynx landed on a testing and firing range in Suffolk. The team was met by two uniformed police officers, one of whom related that a corner of the range had been set aside for them. And a car had been towed out, as requested.

The car was a junked Humber, a big, heavy car, once something of a luxury vehicle but now long past its years of service and towed here to serve as the target for a demonstration of the capabilities of the MILAN missile.

During the flight, Bolan had briefed Nigel Kettering on the operation of the launcher, so Kettering would serve as the second man on the firing team.

The day was cool, and a light drizzle fell from the ragged gray clouds. While Bolan and Kettering set up the MILAN launcher, the other agents walked to the Humber and inspected it.

"It's not armored," one of them said when they returned, "but it's a well-built, heavy automobile. At what range do you propose to fire, Colonel?"

"What would you like? A thousand yards?"

"What's the maximum?"

"A little over two thousand. We're looking at a stationary target, and I'm sure we'd have no trouble hitting it at two thousand. Moving, I'd feel better at fifteen hundred."

"We haven't been given two thousand yards of range," one of the uniformed policemen pointed out.

They walked back to about twelve hundred yards, Bolan carrying the launcher, each of the uniformed policemen carrying a missile. The warrior set up the launcher, and Kettering attached a missile unit as he'd been taught to do.

"Whatever you do, don't stand behind me," Bolan instructed. "When the launcher fires, it throws the tube back hard enough to flatten anyone behind. I'm going to fire in the direction of those trees to the left of the car, and while the missile's in flight I'll guide it over to hit the car. Ready?"

Everyone stood at a respectful distance to the sides. Bolan put his eye to the sight, which gave him a little magnification. He checked the car, then swung the launcher fifteen or twenty degrees to the left. "Fire!"

The men from the Special Branch tensed as a second or so passed before the missile ignited. Then it flamed, the tube flew to the rear and the rocket shot forward.

Bolan watched it fly. He saw the flares ignite on its tail. Slowly he swung the launcher to the right and watched the missile veer to the right as the aiming system followed the bright spots of the flares and sent the steering commands that moved the rudder in the stream of fire from the rocket. When the Humber was in the sight, he fixed the aiming point at the passenger compartment of the big car and until the final instant, he still had a view of the bright flares on the tail of the rocket.

The missile struck, penetrated and exploded. The big black car flew apart. No one inside could possibly have survived.

"THERE'S NO DEFENSE against that," one of the agents said as the helicopter flew back to London.

"That is, none except to capture or destroy the terrorists who have them."

"Yes, there is," Bolan replied.

"Indeed, Colonel?"

"Yes. The MILAN is a battlefield weapon meant to fight tanks. You saw how it had to be set up. You couldn't do that in the middle of London. Someone would see you setting up that very conspicuous weapon and would call the police. Something more. The scary part about the thing is its range. Someone could always throw a bomb at the queen's car. You're good at close-range protection. The new element introduced by the MILAN is that mile-long range."

"Yes," Kettering said grimly, "they could fire from a mile away."

"Where?" Bolan asked. "Where in the city of London could they get an aiming point from a mile away? Or half a mile? In the tangle of streets in this city the MILAN's range doesn't amount to so much. Where in the entire city could you sit down with a pair of binoculars and watch an automobile moving half a mile away? Buildings intervene. You don't have long views in London."

"Oh, we do, sir. We really do."

"Yes, but you know where they are. In the parks, along the river. Just keep the queen and her family away from those places. That is, keep her away when she's riding in one of the cars marked with the crest. Move her around in Fords, Vauxhalls or taxis. Where she's in danger is out on the motorways."

"Tall buildings?" one of the agents asked.

Bolan shook his head. "You can be sure they won't fire a MILAN from a tall building. That is, they won't if they know what they're doing. Even if they could get one up there, it was designed to fly a missile over reasonably flat terrain. It has lateral control but almost no vertical control."

"So we—"

"You have to set your trap outside the city."

"After what we saw this afternoon, I can't imagine how we'll ask anyone to drive the target car," Kettering said.

"We can handle that," a senior agent replied.

IT HAD ALREADY BEEN announced in the Court Calendar published in the *Times* that the queen would dedicate a new wing of the children's hospital at Canterbury. She would appear at 11:30 a.m., accompanied by Sarah, the duchess of York. An amendment to the Court Calendar announced that the duchess of York would accompany Her Majesty and that the Royal party would make a brief visit to Rochester Cathedral at 10:30 a.m. to view a new bronze plaque honoring the dukes of York.

To anyone who gave it thought, that meant that the queen and her young red-haired daughter-in-law would be driven from London to Canterbury on the motorway designated M2. There were other roads between London and Canterbury, but only on the M2 could they cover the miles between Rochester and Canterbury in the half hour or less they would have in which to do it.

The M2 passed through the outskirts of London and then through miles of open country. MILAN missile country.

Or almost. Though the country was open, it was populated. The M2 was something like an American interstate highway in the eastern states. Fields to either side. But businesses, too, and small farms with houses and outbuildings. And heavy traffic. To set up a missile launcher within fifteen hundred yards of the highway and not be noticed would be a difficult task.

Every foot of the M2 was examined in minute detail. Helicopters flew overhead, high-flying aircraft shot reconnaissance photographs, a score of vehicles, some of them vans carrying cameras, passed back and forth on the road. Before the queen's maroon Rolls-Royce passed through the gates of Buckingham Palace, a force of three hundred men was in place along the M2, watching and ready to spring a trap.

Working all night, photoanalysts had identified eight places where conditions seemed right to launch a missile against the Royal vehicle. Of those, they had identified three that were far more likely sites than the other five.

The three sites involved open vistas, a good view of the highway, so the missile shooter could see the traffic and identify the target. They involved remote fields where the nearest house was two or three hundred yards away. In each case there was a grove of trees or a stand of grain in a field to provide thin cover for the launcher and its crew. Each of the three sites also afforded an approach and later an escape over a country road.

Each of the three prime sites was put under surveillance by a team of fifty men. Smaller teams watched the less likely sites. Much of the force remained mobile, ready to move in helicopters and on the highway.

The helicopters were on the ground and a mile or so from the M2—kept out of sight so that they wouldn't scare away the quarry. Two choppers remained in the air at high altitudes and presumably out of sight from the ground. One was a command helicopter carrying high-ranking officers of the Special Branch. The other was a Lynx equipped as an assault helicopter. Bolan and Nigel Kettering were aboard that aircraft.

They scanned the ground through powerful binoculars, focusing on the fields on both sides of the highway. Bolan wore a headset and could hear the radio traffic on the command frequency.

Through his binoculars the warrior saw the queen and the duchess on the steps of the cathedral. They were obviously in no hurry, though he'd been told that the queen was always prompt about her appointments. She and the duchess were surrounded by clergy, and the street was filled with people. Then, abruptly, the royals entered the maroon Rolls-Royce, and it moved away.

"Moving. Heading for the flyover," came a voice over the command frequency.

"Transfer. Alert on the motorway. You have it."

"Alert Station One. You have it in three."

Station One was the first site chosen as particularly dangerous. Bolan swept his binoculars over the ground on both sides of the motorway. He saw nothing suspicious, nothing unusual. Everything looked exactly as it had for the past half hour.

"Passed Station One. Alert One-and-a-Half."

They had numbered the less-dangerous sites with fractions like this. Between 1 and 2 there was 1½ and 1⅔. The British could think of the most awkward ways of doing things.

Bolan looked at the maroon Rolls. It was preceded by two motorcycle policemen and a black Vauxhall and followed by a black Range Rover. The little convoy was rolling at sixty or seventy miles an hour, passing traffic that yielded to the left to let it pass.

"Alert Two."

"Two alert."

The warrior put down his binoculars for a moment. It was a warm summer morning and sweltering inside the chopper. He wiped his face on the sleeve of the rugged camouflage fatigues the Special Branch had provided. He was dressed like a soldier, as was Nigel Kettering. The Special Branch knew how to arm men, too. Kettering had a Beretta 92—the standard NATO 9 mm weapon—in a flap-covered holster on his web belt, and beside him on the floor of the chopper lay a Heckler & Koch G-11, just like the one they had provided Bolan with.

He put the binoculars to his eyes again. The maroon Rolls-Royce was past Station Two and rolling along a stretch of motorway not designated as dangerous.

But there was the flash! Unmistakable. Bolan yelled into his microphone, "Missile fired north of the highway! Missile fired! It's tracking!"

The maroon Rolls-Royce exploded in a storm of fire and flying steel and glass. The wreckage careered along the highway, skidding and turning out of control off the road and into the grass.

The Range Rover swerved and skidded to a stop. Cars and trucks veered off the highway.

The helicopter pilot didn't need to be told what to do. He put the aircraft into a sharp bank and a dive and went for the launcher.

"Hadn't figured on that," Kettering said bleakly. "Fired out of a shed or a barn. All they had to do was open the doors and—"

"The shed there, I'd guess." Bolan pointed at a small frame building.

"You got it."

The little building, painted white, was an equipment shed, Bolan judged, where a farmer kept his tractor and perhaps a small truck. It was twenty yards from a neat white frame house. Parked behind the shed was a dark blue van.

Bolan tapped the pilot on the shoulder and pointed at an open space beyond the van. The pilot nodded and headed for it.

"Here's where it hits the fan, Kettering."

"I've done this sort of thing before," Kettering pointed out. "That's why I was assigned to you."

The Executioner slid open the door, and as the chopper descended, its rotor kicking up leaves and sticks off the damp ground, he poised to jump. He left the aircraft, followed by Kettering, just as a burst of fire punched through the body of the chopper.

Bolan hit the ground firing. The burst had come from the shed, so he sent a dozen rounds from the G-11 through the wooden building.

Streams of lead chopped through the wood as the gunners inside tried to hit their assailant without aiming. They'd have to leave cover in order to direct their fire, so they tried instead to sweep the area behind the shed through the wall. Bolan and Kettering retreated behind the blue van and sent a couple of bursts into the building.

It was the chopper pilot who changed the situation. With slow and careful precision he lowered five tons of helicopter toward the shed. The skids came down on the peak of the roof, which sagged, then broke. The building collapsed. The pilot lifted off again without crushing the men in the shed.

The gunners weren't about to surrender, though. Scrambling out of the wreckage of the building, they swung around the muzzles of their AK-47s, looking for targets. One—not having spotted Bolan or Kettering behind the van—raised his assault rifle toward the belly of the Lynx.

Kettering cut him down with a sharp burp from his G-11, a 3-round burst that a practiced man could achieve with the lethal assault rifle.

One of the gunmen fired at the Briton, whom he had now spotted. Slugs ripped through the van. Bolan took that man out.

"I'd like to have a prisoner," Kettering muttered.

"You've got one."

The last terrorist threw down his rifle and raised his hands.

As Bolan and Kettering walked toward the gunman, the man sneered. "We got your bitch queen, anyway. How do you like that?"

Kettering dropped his rifle to the ground and drove a fist into the man's face.

AS HER MAJESTY walked into the children's hospital at Canterbury, smiling and nodding to the people who had come out to greet her, she was stopped for a moment by an agent who whispered a few words. The queen frowned for an instant, then quickly recovered and smiled again. She and the duchess of York had been in the Rolls-Royce for only about five minutes all told. At the edge of Rochester they had transferred into it from two Vauxhalls, and the vehicle had carried them to the cathedral. After their visit they had entered the Rolls again, only long enough to return to the outskirts of the town, where they had returned to the inconspicuous Vauxhalls. When the Rolls entered the M2, the two Vauxhalls were already on the A2, an ordinary highway a little to the north. They were a few minutes late at Canterbury.

No one had died in the wreckage of the maroon Rolls-Royce. It wasn't even one of the distinctive maroon limousines of the Royal stable. It was a decoy clone, built in a Scotland Yard laboratory-garage in Coventry. Radio-controlled, it was driven by a man in the Range Rover that followed behind it. With months of practice he had learned even to drive it through London traffic—a decoy limousine with wax dummies in its seats.

"Even so," Bolan said, "this didn't work out very well. They got off their shot and they hit a car. And though we captured another MILAN launcher, they've got at least one more."

TIMOTHY FINNERTY SWITCHED off the television and walked to the table where he picked up a cracker spread with cheese and popped it into his mouth.

"'An attempt on the life of the queen,'" he said solemnly. "You know what that means? It means we didn't kill her and we get as much hate as if we did."

Molly nodded. For the first time in a long time she was well into a bottle. "What'd he say?" She meant, what had the Irish prime minister said. She quoted him "'Our country doesn't stand for vicious terrorism. If any citizen of the Irish Republic doubts his duty right now, let me tell him what it is. It is to bring the attention of the constabulary, immediately, any information you have about these inhuman killers. They do not stand for Irish patriotism. They sully it. They mock it.' Tough damn talk, me boys. Tough damn talk."

Their host in this handsome country house was a tweedy man of sixty, a gentlemen farmer but the grandson of a man hanged by the British in 1916. He wore a great yellow-gray bushy mustache, and his face was flushed, his pale blue eyes bulgy and teary. With his tweed jacket he wore jodhpurs and riding boots, though he hadn't been astride a horse in ten years. His name was Colin O'Neill.

O'Neill loved port wine. The fortified alcohol had swollen his nose and given his face a permanent flush. He drank some now and sliced off a bit of Dutch cheese.

"Never mind the prime minister," O'Neill grunted. "If you'd succeeded in ridding the world of her Britannic Bitch, then what would they be sayin'? Let's not forget. What we have in mind is to make *you* prime minister, Timmy."

"Who the hell left all the cocaine in the house on Casey Street?" Brian Connelly asked sullenly. "Apart from the loss—"

"The newspaper story is devastating," Finnerty said. "I did it myself. I never dreamed the American would kill nine good men."

"Three more and a launcher," Connelly added.

"One of them prisoner," Molly put in. "Our name's on it, Tim. He'll talk, and our name's on it."

"All of which means nothing but redoubled effort," O'Neill said. "You're safe here. We can plan somethin' good. Let me work on it. I've got some experience, don't forget. Who else rid the world of Mountbatten?"

Molly's thought was that Colin O'Neill took too much credit for the assassination of Mountbatten, who had been blown up on his yacht.

"You don't stop just because you've had a failure," O'Neill declaimed. "You keep on. Always fighting. Always in the thick of it. Always ready. And we'll be ready. We've got some advantages."

"No sign of the American in that Canterbury operation," Finnerty said. "Maybe we've got him where we wanted him, running around Ireland looking for his girlfriend."

"Speaking of the girlfriend," O'Neill said. "Would you mind if I toyed with the girl a bit?"

"You'll be taking your chances with that," Molly told him. "If the American finds out and catches up with you, he'll—"

"I'd as soon you left her alone, Colin, if you don't mind," Finnerty said. "If we have to trade her for something later on, better to trade her in as fresh condition as possible, hmm?"

Colin O'Neill grinned.

CHAPTER ELEVEN

Sir Reginald Townley knew exactly who Mack Bolan was and what he did. To function as the Executioner Bolan had to trust a few people, most of them Americans but a few in other countries. In his special position in the Special Branch, Sir Reginald was a man who from time to time found it necessary to operate outside the rules; and he was a man who could appreciate Bolan's mission and methods.

"Now and then," Sir Reginald said grimly, "we have to act like the French."

Bolan knew what he meant by that. French security agencies were notorious for their brutal methods.

The man they had captured on the M2 lay on a gurney, tightly bound with heavy leather straps that totally immobilized him. He could hardly move a muscle. His left arm was strapped to a board that was clamped to a table. A needle was inserted in a bulging vein and taped in place. Through a plastic hose attached to the needle, they could inject him with anything they wanted. He looked very much like a condemned man waiting for execution by injection.

Sir Reginald Townley sucked hard on a cigarette that was burned down to a bare inch. His name, Reginald, suggested a fussy Englishman. Nothing could be farther from the truth. The man was tall and spare, rawboned he would have been called in America. His nose had been broken and lay off-center. His right eyebrow was torn in two by a scar, his lips were thin and bluish and his eyes were as cold and hard as any Bolan had ever seen. He'd been a paratrooper with the SAS and had been recruited for Scotland Yard, the Special Branch, only after he was too old for SAS duty.

He had a nickname. It was rarely used, but he had slapped Bolan on the shoulder and invited him to use it. Sir Reginald was called Sir Thud—or just Thud—though usually only behind his back. It referred to the time when a parachute had only partially opened and he had come down hard in a rice paddy in Thailand. The paddy had been wet and muddy, and he'd gone into the muck up to his armpits, which had saved his life. Even so, he'd come down with a thud and had been Sir Thud ever since.

They had tried normal interrogation of the captured man, and he had sneered at them. Even after he was strapped to the gurney he remained defiant. Thud had called in a doctor to administer the chemical that would make him talk. Bolan personally objected to chemical interrogation, but could not condemn the British, given the circumstances.

"You don't have to witness this," Townley said to Bolan.

"I've got a couple of questions of my own."

Townley bent over the man on the gurney. "All right, Patrick. One more. Will you answer my questions?"

"Go to hell!"

"Ah . . . Patrick," Townley said. "You're the one going there. But first we'll let you sample a little bit of heaven."

He nodded to the doctor, who shoved down a plunger with his thumb, and the chemical shot through the tube and needle and into the vein of the terrorist. The man stiffened. He seemed to try to fight off the effects of the powerful compound, but he couldn't. He relaxed. After a minute he lay loose inside his straps, his muscles no longer straining.

Townley had lighted another cigarette during that minute. "Doesn't always work," he muttered to Bolan quietly, "but let's see."

The man looked up as the big Englishman stood directly over him and stared into his eyes.

"What's your name, Patrick? What's your last name?"

"Boyle," the man replied in a dull, cool voice. "My name's Patrick Boyle."

"You're an ignorant, cowardly piece of work, aren't you, Boyle?"

"Yes."

Townley glanced at Bolan, who understood. He'd seen this kind of thing before. The drug had disrupted the man's will. He would agree to anything, but a questioner had to be careful. If you suggested to him that he'd come to England to murder the archbishop of Canterbury, he'd agree. If you suggested he'd come to train for the priesthood of the Church of England, he'd agree to that, too.

"It's important for me to find out who sent you to try to murder the queen, isn't it, Boyle?"

"Yes."

"Very important."

"Very important..."

"You want me to find out, don't you?"

"I...yes."

"You really want me to know."

"I want you to know."

"So who sent you? Who wants to murder the queen?"

"Tim..."

"Tim who?"

"Timothy Finnerty."

"Timothy Finnerty of the Curran Brigade?"

"Yes."

"It's important for me to find out where Timothy Finnerty is. Don't you think?"

"Yes...important."

"So where is he?"

"I don't know."

"When did you last see him?"

"A week ago, I think it was."

"Did he then order you to come to England and try to kill the queen?"

"No."

"How and when did you get those orders?"

"Tim called me on the telephone."

"When?"

"Yesterday."

"Where was he calling from?"

"He didn't tell me. I didn't ask."

Sir Reginald Townley stepped back, looked at Bolan and shook his head. "You want a go at him?"

Bolan nodded. He stepped closer to the gurney and looked down into the placid face of the drugged terrorist. "What kind of man is Timothy Finnerty?" he asked.

Patrick Boyle frowned for a moment. It was the kind of question that confused him in his state, and his mind wouldn't focus on it long enough to ponder an answer.

"Is Timothy Finnerty a great man?" Bolan asked.

"Yes. A great leader."

"Do you respect him? Would you do anything he told you?"

The terrorist nodded.

"What would happen if you didn't obey him?"

The terrorist shook his head. Again the question required him to match one fact with another and come to a conclusion, which he couldn't do.

"If you didn't carry out orders, would you be killed?"

"Yes."

"Who would kill you?"

"Whoever Tim told to do it."

"Tim himself?"

"No."

"Tim's a physical coward, isn't he?"

"Yes."

Townley interrupted. "Let me put that question another way. Patrick, is Tim a coward?"

"Yes."

"Does he ever go where there's danger?"

"No. Because...because he's the leader. We wouldn't want to risk him. Who would be the leader if—"

Townley nodded at the doctor, who pressed a little more of the chemical into the man on the gurney. When the terrorist began to string thoughts together and to assert himself, it was time to let him have another jolt.

"Kathryn O'Connor," Bolan said. "Do you know the name?"

"Yes."

"Where is she?"

"I don't know."

"When did you last see her?"

"Two days ago. No...three. I don't know."

"Where was she when you last saw her?"

"Casey Street. The house on Casey Street."

"Who beat her?"

"Brian. Brian Connelly."

"Did you see him do it?"

"Yes."

"Was it bad?"

"Bad."

"Where was she taken from there?"

"To a doctor. Tim took her to a doctor."

"What doctor?"

"Doctor Kelly."

FOG LAY ACROSS DUBLIN the next morning. When Bolan arrived at the modest house where Dr. Robert Kelly lived and practiced medicine, fog swirled over the pavement and between the buildings, giving the scene an unreal look.

Dressed as an Irish workman once more, Bolan walked through the street and checked the house. It hadn't been easy for a stranger to the city to find this street at dawn. Inspector Harrigan had offered to help him, but Bolan had said he'd rather pay this call on the good doctor all by himself. He might have to use tactics an inspector of the Irish Constabulary shouldn't witness.

Harrigan had put in a couple of phone calls and had determined that no Dr. Kelly had reported treating a young woman who had been the victim of a beating, which the law required him to do.

"He probably took it that her husband had beat her," Harrigan suggested. "Most doctors don't report those cases."

Bolan figured there was another reason—that this Dr. Kelly was in the employ of the IRA and never reported anything they didn't want reported. Sure. Gangs had their doctors. They produced a lot of business for them and paid them well.

It was possible, Bolan figured—not likely but just possible—that Kathryn was in this house. It was also possible that it was guarded by a terrorist or two. He'd make his approach accordingly.

There was no alley behind these houses. They sat on lots with space enough for small gardens. The doctor's neighbors had rows of vegetables growing between and behind their homes.

In the foggy dawn the street was silent and deserted. A few cars were parked on either side, but if anyone was inside one of them he'd be unable to see through the wet glass. It wasn't likely that anyone was watching the street from a window, even if the doctor's house was guarded.

Bolan walked between two houses and into the doctor's backyard, where he crouched and watched the rear of the house for a few minutes.

The windows were dark; the house was quiet. He stood and jogged to the rear porch, which creaked under his weight, and peered through the windows.

The window to the left opened onto a kitchen. He could see a table, a sink, a small refrigerator and cabinets. The window in the door opened onto a hallway. The window to the right of the door was covered by dark green paper window blinds.

Bolan checked the lock on that back door. It was simple and yielded in a moment to the blade of his knife.

A doctor, who would keep opiates and the like in his office, might have an alarm system guarding his house. Bolan decided to risk that. He opened the door, waited a moment, then stepped inside into the hallway.

He opened the door to the room concealed by window blinds, which was a sort of bedroom, furnished with a white-painted steel bed. Not a bedroom, really, though. It was a room where a patient could lie down and recover—or where a patient could be confined for a while.

Confined. Yeah. On impulse he opened a cabinet against the wall and found what he had suddenly suspected he would find—straps, chains. Dr. Kelly's patients didn't always leave when they wanted to.

Bolan continued to explore the house. Beyond the kitchen and the green-shaded room were two examining rooms, one on both sides of the hall. At the front of the house were the doctor's office and waiting room.

He reached the front door and looked out on the foggy street. Behind and to his right was a flight of stairs. The warrior drew his Beretta and cautiously climbed the stairs. They creaked, but he woke no one.

The house was configured much the same on the second floor—a center hall with rooms to either side.

Bolan guessed the room to the right and on the front would be the master bedroom. He eased the door open. It was the master bedroom, but no one slept in the brass double bed. The sheets and pillows were tossed wildly around. A window fan turned lazily in the front window, drawing damp air into the room.

He checked the room on the opposite side of the hall. It was a bedroom, with the bed neatly made.

In a third bedroom a middle-aged woman lay asleep, sprawled diagonally across a bed. The warrior stood there for a moment, looking at her, uncertain as to whether or not to wake her. Apparently she was the only person in the house. He closed the door and knocked.

"Huh? I'm asleep again as every good Christian is at such an hour."

Bolan opened the door.

"Who are you?"

Seeing that she didn't confront him with a pistol, he shoved the Beretta into its leather inside his jacket. "Where's the doctor?" he asked.

"Who needs him?" the woman asked. She scrambled to cover herself. "He's not here, anyway."

She threw her feet over the side of the bed and stood. Her nightgown covered her from shoulder to knee, and she stood with her hands on her hips, challenging him to answer. He guessed her age at about forty-five. She was a solid, muscular woman with light brown hair that hung disheveled to her shoulders. Her square-jawed face had been pretty once, though long weariness had marked it with discouragement.

"How did you get in here? You have somebody wounded downstairs? Or what?"

"Where's Dr. Kelly?" he repeated.

"Gone."

"Gone where?"

She rubbed her eyes, glanced around and saw her pack of cigarettes on the table by her bed. She picked it up, shook one out and lighted it with a paper match.

"I want to talk to the doctor."

"So do I," she said after she had drawn in smoke and blown it out.

The woman stared at him for a long moment, forming her judgment. Then she shrugged and said, "He left here in the middle of the night. Three in the morning, actually. I don't know where he went. He didn't tell me where he was going."

"Why did he leave?"

"How would I know? I heard the phone ringing. Next thing I know, I heard him rooting around in his room. I got up and went to see. He left."

"To take care of an emergency?"

She shook her head. "He took a bag of clothes, not a medical bag."

"Who are you? His wife?"

The woman sneered. "No, not me. He's not married. I'm his nurse, receptionist, housekeeper... I'm the one who's got to face the day's patients and tell them the doctor's gone and I don't know when he'll be back."

"Who called him?" Bolan demanded impatiently.

She shrugged.

"Timothy Finnerty?"

"I wouldn't be surprised."

"Was the policewoman here?"

"What policewoman?"

"Young woman. A blonde. Beaten, injured."

"She was here Monday and overnight. They took her away the next morning. Don't ask me where."

"She was chained to that bed downstairs," Bolan said.

"The doctor taped her broken ribs, set her broken nose and gave her something for pain. And, yes, she was handcuffed to the bed all night."

Bolan reached into a pocket. "I've got something here for Dr. Kelly. When he comes back, give him this." He handed her a .44 cartridge. "Tell him if he's still here when I come back, I'll give him another one. Through the heart."

KATHRYN O'CONNOR was wakened, not just by the gray light of dawn entering her room, but by the sound of a key in a lock. She sat up and was reminded by the jerk that a chain encircled her neck and kept her prisoner more than the locked door did.

She slept in the clothes they had given her, not daring to undress except for a bath each day. She tugged on her chain to gain slack, then rolled to the edge of the bed and off. She stood to face whoever was opening the door.

A man. She'd seen him from the window—a ruddy, country-squire fellow, wearing boots and riding breeches and a tweed jacket and carrying a riding crop with which he swatted his right boot. He had a big yellowish mustache and bulging pale blue eyes.

"This is my house," he said to her.

She was surprised to hear in his voice that he had been drinking, and she wondered if he had risen and taken a drink or had been drinking all night.

"Take off your clothes," he demanded.

She stood facing him, her right hand gripping her chain. She shook her head, not so much to say she wouldn't take off her clothes as to protest that she didn't understand.

"I said, take . . . off . . . your . . . clothes."

"Why?" she asked.

He raised his chin and sneered. "Look at yourself. If you eat, it's what I provide. If you sleep, it's in my bed. If you have a toilet to relieve yourself in, that's mine, too. I've come for my rent. So take off your clothes, girl, and be quick about it!"

What would he do if she didn't? She found out. She didn't move to undress, and he stepped forward abruptly and gave her a brutal backhand slash with the riding crop across her left hip. She began to unbutton her blouse.

Half-naked, Kathryn again grasped the chain that hung now between her bare breasts, as if in that chain she found some security against what this man threatened.

"The skirt, girl! And whatever else! Quick!"

The blouse and skirt were all. She pulled the skirt over her head and stood exposed—humiliated, angry and afraid.

Colin O'Neill sat down on a straight chair by the fireplace. "On your knees. Pull my boots."

Tugging the chain so that she could cross to the fireplace, she moved to where he pointed and knelt. He gave his right boot a shove down, then stuck his foot toward her face. She grasped the boot and pulled. It slid off. She put it aside and then grasped the other one and pulled on it.

"Timothy says he hasn't had you." O'Neill laughed. "Timothy's a fool. But Brian...now Brian's another kind of man. You're lucky I laid claim to you. On the bed now. On the bed."

She hadn't expected just this. She had expected something very different—and, in fact, from Brian Connelly. Anyway, she was ready.

O'Neill bent over to pull off his riding breeches. He poked her with the tip of the riding crop. "On your back now. Spread—"

He hadn't noticed that her right hand was under the mattress. By the time he was aware of what she was doing, it was too late. Suddenly she pulled from beneath the mattress the iron rod that had controlled the fireplace damper. She had searched the room for a weapon, had found this and had managed by an hour's grimy effort to wrench it loose from the damper in the chimney. It was a heavy rod, thicker than a poker, and she swung it at his head in a fast, violent backhand stroke.

The iron rod struck just above his eyes, crushing the skull and driving consciousness out of his brain. He dropped and lay facedown. She stood above him for a moment, then brought the bludgeon down hard on the base of his skull.

Colin O'Neill was dead. She didn't need to take his pulse to know that. Dragging her chain, she hurried into the bathroom to get a towel to put under his head to soak up the blood.

For a few minutes she sat on the edge of her bed, staring at the body. Then she decided. She opened the window. He was heavy, but he wasn't too heavy for her. She dragged him to the window and propped him against the wall. And then, with a grunting heave, she lifted him and shoved him through the window.

He fell to the courtyard below onto a wheelbarrow filled with fertilizer. She tossed his boots down on top of him, then closed the window. Finally, wiping up the rest of the blood, she rinsed out the towel in the bathroom, dressed and sat down to wait.

INSPECTOR MICHAEL HARRIGAN stood with his back planted firmly against the door of his office, his chin raised high, his eyes filled with apprehension and suspicion as he watched a blond young man crawl around the floor of his office.

The young man wore a pair of headphones attached to a box he carried on a strap around his neck, and at the end of a wire running from that box was a probe, which he kept poking here and there, under this and that, frowning and listening to whatever mysterious sounds he might hear in his earphones.

"All right," he said after a while. "Nothing more. Nothing more, that is, that I can find."

"Then stash all that stuff back into your briefcase," Harrigan said nervously. "I can't afford to have it supposed I let you in here for any reason, much less to check my office like this."

The young man nodded and began to disassemble his equipment and pack it into his briefcase.

"You have options with respect to that," he said, nodding toward a jewellike object lying in the middle of the green blotter on Harrigan's desk. "I suggest you don't do what you said you wanted to do. I would like to suggest a better idea."

The object, no bigger than one of the cubes of a pair of dice, caught the sunlight coming in through the inspector's window and glittered like a jewel. Actually it was worth almost as much as a gem its size. It was a cube of clear plastic. Inside it was an array of colorful electronic parts, all brightly colored. It was, in fact, a highly sophisticated radio transmitter. The young man had found it inside Harrigan's telephone.

Harrigan, when shown it, had said he wanted to hit it with a hammer.

It was dead now, cut off from its power source, which was the twelve volts in the telephone. It wasn't transmitting what they said in the office now, but it had transmitted everything said there for... Well, Harrigan couldn't guess for how long.

Every telephone conversation, everything said in the office—all of it had been transmitted out of the office.

The young man's name was Bruce Graham. He was an agent of the Special Branch, assigned to Dublin to the highly secret work of tracking down terrorists who constituted a threat to British safety, just as Nigel Kettering was. Although the Irish Constabulary extended cooperation from time to time, that had to remain a dark secret. An Irish government could fall if word got out that an Irish police agency was working hand-in-glove with the hated Special Branch.

"What we don't know, of course," Graham said, "is who received the signal from this transmitter. You have two choices as I see it. One is to destroy the transmitter, and the other is to reconnect it and use it as a means of transmitting false information to whoever planted it. I recommend the latter."

Harrigan glanced around his office. It had been his for eight years and it bore the stamp of his personality. His certificates, his plaque, his personal photos hung on the walls. The old leather chair had been scarred by him. *His* cigarette burns marked the desk. The rug was stained with coffee *he* had spilled.

And yet for a time this room hadn't been his. His privacy had been violated. That made him angry.

"If you reconnect it," Graham pointed out, "opportunities may arise to send out important disinformation."

Harrigan stood and stared at the evil glittering cube.

"Of course, we haven't much time to decide," Graham went on. "Its silence for the past ten minutes may be taken by whoever is listening as a visit by you to the bathroom. Whoever's listening likely knows you're in the office. If you're silent too long—"

"Reconnect the damn thing," Harrigan barked. "Then can you trace the damn signal? Can we find out who's listening?"

Graham shrugged. "Maybe. It's possible, but not certain."

FINNERTY GRABBED the chain around O'Connor's neck and jerked. She toppled against him and had to throw her arms around the man to keep from falling. He held the chain high so that it choked her.

"Goddamn you! You've done it now! It's murder, you bitch! Murder!"

She gagged but managed to speak. "Why don't you call the police, then?"

He dropped the chain and shoved her back onto her bed. For a long moment they confronted each other, their eyes burning with hate.

"You could have given him what he wanted," Finnerty muttered. "Was it so important? Your mother would have given it."

"You bastard."

Finnerty turned away from her and stalked across the room. "He wanted to kill you. I mean, Brian wanted to kill you. I should have let him."

"Why didn't you?"

"Even Molly. I hope you appreciate her. She thinks you're worth something. But she's alone now. After this we have to move again. You had it easy here. Comfortable."

"You're a fugitive," she said. "Made so by one man. Two weeks ago you were a big man. Now you're a fugitive, even from the Irish government, which has learned what you are and won't protect you any more. Even from the IRA—all but the worst of them. It's just a matter of time until one or another of them catches up with you."

"You and your American," Finnerty growled between clenched teeth. "You're a traitor! What's always damaged the cause . . . traitors."

She looked up at him and saw fanaticism in his eyes. Fanaticism . . . and fear, a combination that could make a man a killer. But not this man. He was timid. Others did his killing for him while he was somewhere else.

So why did they follow him? Because he was smarter than they were. In the end, when all was said and done, he was a leader—and few of them were. Few of them could articulate the cause. He made brilliant speeches.

But it was more than that—he was ruthless. He didn't do the killing he demanded, but he demanded it, without hesitation, without mercy—and so he had developed a reputation for dedication. Timothy Finnerty might be a physical coward, but he knew how to hit and where to hit—and there were plenty of men, always, with the courage to carry out his orders.

And, finally, he had managed to attach himself to "the cause." No Irishman would ever give that up— the cause—the ambition of driving the British out of Northern Ireland and uniting the Irish under one government.

Whether that government was one on which the Irish people agreed, by their votes in an honest election, wasn't important. Timothy Finnerty knew what was right. If no one agreed with him, still he knew what was right.

Which put him in a category with every terrorist in the world, no matter what the cause. She would do anything she could, including sacrificing her life, to stop him.

And she knew Mack would. He was her hope. Maybe her last hope.

CHAPTER TWELVE

Nigel Kettering sat with Mack Bolan in Dublin's Shelbourne Hotel. The warrior had decided to trust Sir Reginald Townley and Nigel Kettering—and no one else.

"The heart of our effort," Kettering told him, "must be on the attempt to assassinate a member of the Royal Family. Yours may be a little different."

"Doesn't have to be. I've gone after their arms, their explosives, their narcotics, which is the source of their money. In the end, all of it leads to their plot to kill the queen, and that in turn leads to their determination to govern Ireland themselves—and govern it their way. They're no different than any other terrorists."

"We've tripled the security around the Royal Family," Kettering said. "Even so—"

"Even so, you've got to eliminate the threat."

Kettering nodded. "Sir Reginald asked me to present a proposition to you."

"I'm listening."

"Kathryn O'Connor is a prisoner here, somewhere in Ireland. I swear to you we have no idea where. We're running down every lead. Think about this— where are they getting the MILAN launchers? The

Semtex? As many as a hundred thousand AK-47s? You killed Klaus Schimmel. Where was he getting that kind of stuff? Where are they getting the cocaine? The heroin?''

"I guess we know, or we've got pretty good ideas."

"We're thinking about a raid," Kettering said. "Sir Reginald's idea. It will be unofficial and where we can hurt them. I mean, where we can really hurt them. And when I say hurt them, I don't mean just hurt the Curran Brigade. I mean hurt the superterrorists, the men behind the terrorists. You'd be fighting a thousand miles from where Miss O'Connor is. She might very well die while you're gone—and maybe even as a consequence of what you do while you're gone. But this raid may do more to hurt terrorism than—''

"Don't work at justifying it," Bolan growled. "What's the deal?"

"If you're willing to take part, I've been asked to bring you back to Britain to discuss it with Sir Reginald."

"AN AIRBORNE OPERATION," Townley told Bolan. "If you don't mind, it's a chance for an old warrior to return to battle, maybe for the last time. I'm told by Hal Brognola that you have no fear of jumping and that you've done it many times. We may jump in, or we may use helicopters. And what we do may accomplish more to end terrorism in the world than anything else either of us will ever do in our lifetimes."

"I don't have to ask where."

"No, you don't. The Sublime Leader, hmm? We pop in on him, eliminate him if possible and wreak every kind of havoc we can on his self-proclaimed empire. Our purpose is to make it understood that supplying and encouraging terrorism costs more than it's worth."

"The British government's going for the throat?" Bolan asked dryly.

"An attempt to assassinate Her Majesty inspires all kinds of courage," Townley replied. "On the other hand, let it be understood that this is to be a clandestine operation that my government may choose to disavow if it's an embarrassing failure."

"Of course."

"It will be a small operation. Just you and me, plus Nigel Kettering and one or two other men who haven't yet volunteered. We'll go in heavily armed. Our purpose will be to do as much damage as we can, whether we get the Sublime Leader or not. If we don't get him, we'll scare him out of his wits. A few hours on the ground, then out."

"An opportunity I've been looking for for a long time," Bolan said.

FOUR HELICOPTERS CROSSED the coastline a little after midnight. They were RAF Pumas, but they were painted black and all insignia had been painted over. These were assault choppers, bigger and faster than the Lynx. Equipped with sophisticated ground-scanning radar coupled to their autopilot systems, they raced over the coastal hills and across the valley behind, never more than a hundred feet above the surface.

Two of them carried men and vehicles. The other two were heavily armed, one with missiles and machine guns, the other with two 20 mm cannons and machine guns. All four were equipped with electronic countermeasures devices meant to confuse radar systems on the ground or on overflying aircraft.

Mack Bolan sat in a special seat just behind and between the two pilots in the lead chopper. Of all the men on this mission, he was the only one who had been in this part of Africa before.

Reconnaissance photos taken only a few days before indicated that the Sublime Leader had installed a dozen new radar-controlled antiaircraft batteries around his fertilizer factory at Aoudella. The high-altitude reconnaissance planes had detected the searching beams of those missile batteries. The radar had, in fact, locked on, though no missile had been fired. It had been as if the Sublime Leader had beamed up a warning—yes, we're down here and capable of bringing you down, so don't come back.

The purpose of the mission was to leave those missile batteries nothing to protect.

A fertilizer factory. Sure. Fertilizer, with a sideline of pharmaceuticals, poison gas, nerve gas, the poor man's atom bomb. The Iraqi army had used poison gas against Iran. The world had recent evidence of what chemical warfare could do.

A new terrorist weapon.

The flight of helicopters swept over another low range of hills, barely clearing the tops. The birds pulled in their wheels and flew a little over two hundred miles per hour. Crossing over a village, they were there and gone before anyone really woke or could possibly identify them.

Bolan tapped the pilot on the shoulder and pointed at a faint glow of lights on the horizon to the northeast.

"Aoudella?" the pilot asked.

"Right place for it, about."

"Odd they'd light it that way, don't you think?"

Bolan nodded. "I bet you it's a field of lights and maybe some fake buildings, saying Bomb Here."

"If we fly high enough to find out, their radar will see us," the pilot told him.

"Right. Stay down on the deck. Let's look for a road."

"What's that to the right, Colonel?"

Bolan peered out the right window. "Quadag," he replied. "And if that's for sure what it is, it tells me where we are exactly."

"Want to go look?"

He frowned and considered for a moment. "Yeah."

The leader swept into a shallow right bank and flew toward the dim yellow lights a few miles to the south.

"Sorry we can't fly quiet, Colonel. That's one thing these birds can't do."

Bolan scanned the land below, obscured by the darkness and only vaguely visible by the light of a half moon. He had reviewed the maps and the recon photos, but he recognized nothing. He identified the lights to the south as the village of Quadag only because he knew that was what it had to be.

But he'd know Quadag if he was on the ground. It wasn't the first time he'd been in the area.

Sir Reginald came forward. "Why the deviation from course?" he asked.

"If those lights are Quadag, then we know exactly where we are and what road goes to Aoudella," Bolan said.

Sir Reginald nodded at the bright glow on the horizon to the left. "And that?"

"A decoy."

The Englishman frowned at the glow for a moment, then nodded. "I agree."

Bolan tapped the pilot on the shoulder once again. "Tell the others to hold back. Why show them four of us?"

The pilot spoke into his microphone and ordered the other choppers to reduce speed and stay away from the village.

The pilot lowered his ship until it was flying no more than fifty feet above the ground, the blast from its rotor stirring up dust.

"Make a pass over the town and buzz out," Bolan ordered.

The pilot nodded.

The lights ahead were two pole-mounted electric lights in the town square, powered by a diesel-powered generator that chugged all night every night to keep the lights burning—the pride of Quadag, a village that kept its central square lighted all night. Facing the square were a low mud-brick mosque and a school—also the pride of the village.

It *was* Quadag. His quick glimpse as they swept over confirmed it. He knew the land around here. Not the way he knew some parts of the world, but well enough for this mission.

He pointed to the north and east. The pilot turned and flew that way, calling the other three choppers after him. After another five minutes or so, Bolan gave a quick thumbs-down sign, and the pilot extended his wheels and began the descent.

A second chopper landed. The remaining two, the gunships, hovered overhead, according to their standard operating procedures, ready to blast anything that threatened the ships on the ground.

In the darkness, under the dim moonlight, Bolan, Sir Reginald Townley and a volunteer from SAS jumped down from the lead helicopter. The copilot unstrapped and wheeled their motorcycles to the door, then helped them to unload them.

The dirt bikes were rugged, high-powered machines with deep-tread tires. Each bike was equipped with oversize saddlebags of stiff plastic in which each man carried his extra weapons, ammo and explosives. Straps bound weapons to the bikes. These weren't sport motorcycles—these had been modified as weapons of war.

Nigel Kettering and two volunteers from the SAS unloaded from the second chopper, and they reviewed signals. The helicopters would withdraw across the border but would be within a hundred miles. When the team needed them, they'd return. But not to this site. Once the presence of the team was known, it would be assumed they'd be picked up where they'd been dropped off. Bolan, Sir Reginald and the pilots reviewed map coordinates. Everyone understood where the team was to go when the job was finished.

Bolan had already explained the roads and the land to every member of the team. He took a minute now to review everything, to be sure each man knew where he was in this alien desert and would know how to reach the pickup point if he was the only survivor.

It was understood. The members of the team mounted their motorcycles and followed Bolan on an unpaved road toward Aoudella.

THE SUBLIME LEADER, Modu Ballem, lay on a divan, cushioned by a score of soft, fat cushions. He was stark naked, as he always was after about eight in the evening and until ten the next morning. Clothes, he said, didn't become him. Clothes, others said secretly, never daring to say it except to closest confidants, might have covered his corpulence and inadequacy.

He was attended by six girls, three African, three European. The Europeans attended him for two years, on contract. Each one, having served her term, left him after pledging secrecy and never again wanted for money. Some took cash payment. Some were set up in business, such as the importation of narcotics into certain nations in Europe or in the Western Hemisphere. The African girls were slaves he bought in the markets the Western world didn't believe continued to exist. None of them was older than eighteen.

When word reached him that one of the coastal radar stations had detected incoming aircraft, flying at a speed that suggested helicopters, Ballem ordered his air force to take to the sky and find the helicopters.

It was a mistake. His powerful jet fighters took off, flew around, looked for intruders, detected none and returned to base, their fuel exhausted. At that moment his enemies might have struck, while his air force was on the ground.

His enemies slipped in under his cover.

When the clandestine strike force landed near the village of Quadag, Ballem was satisfied that the earlier reports had been nervous mistakes. He was fascinated with what one of his newest slaves could do and with how the Europeans reacted to what they saw.

And then interruption.

"Sublime Leader, your forgiveness."

"Granted."

"A penetration of our airspace. Of our borders, sir. Helicopters, almost certainly, well inside our sacred frontiers."

"Establish a Stage One Alert," Ballem ordered.

"Established."

SIX MEN ON BIKES roared up the road toward Aoudella. So far there was no suggestion of opposition. They had forty miles to travel along a road that varied between being entirely unpaved and paved with a little loose gravel to prevent wheels from sinking deep into the loose sand.

It was a long way from Ireland and from where he might do anything to help Kathryn—yet Bolan knew he could do more to save her, and more to save the world from the kind of terror-mongers who held her, by staging this attack on Modu Ballem, than anything else he could do.

He had to remind himself of that constantly as he guided the bucking, roaring bike over the wretched road. The Sublime Leader. Terrorist. As the world, horrified, withdrew its support from the terrorist movements, however called, a few egomaniacs like Ballem fed them everything he could—arms, explosives, narcotics, money and, before long, surely, chemical weapons.

Why? Because there was a firm kinship. Because they were all egomaniacs.

Bolan and his companions rode without lights and encountered no traffic—there was none on the roads between dusk and dawn.

But patrols, maybe.

Abruptly, out of the northeast, the overpowering roar of fighter jets shook the earth as the aircraft rocketed overhead. Like fools. What could anyone see on this dark ground, at that speed, from that altitude?

Even if the choppers were still in the air, on their way south and across the frontier, the jets wouldn't find them.

The members of the team wore camouflage combat fatigues, combat boots and fiberglass motorcycle helmets. Each man was an arsenal, carrying the weapons he favored.

Bolan sported the Desert Eagle and a Heckler & Koch G-11. The silenced Beretta had no place on this mission. Instead, he carried extra magazines for the other two weapons. Grenades hung from his straps.

Townley toted a G-11, but like a tradition-bound British officer, he carried a Webley revolver on his hip.

Nigel Kettering knew weapons, Bolan had learned. He'd chosen an Ingram submachine gun. It was perhaps appropriate for a diminutive man—short and compact. For a pistol he carried the standard NATO weapon, the 9 mm Beretta 92.

The three volunteer soldiers from the SAS carried two Uzis and one M-16.

It would have been ironic to bring along a MILAN launcher, and they had discussed it, but had decided it was too unwieldy for this operation. Strapped to the bikes, however, were four LAW 80 rocket launchers. To add to the team's firepower, Bolan and one of the volunteer soldiers were carrying—again, strapped to the bikes—two MM-1 projectile launchers. The saddlebags on the motorcycles carried extra ammo, but mostly MM-1 projectiles.

Bolan knew his way to Aoudella. He didn't know the roads well, but he knew that tracking the glow of light on the horizon would lead them only to what he judged was a decoy, not to Ballem's fertilizer factory on the outskirts of the city.

He knew the general layout of the town. The fertilizer factory was on the northwest side, the palace in the center. When Ballem was in residence, the palace was surrounded by "revolutionary guards." Revolutionary—the rationalizing word for half of the vicious crimes committed in the world since 1917.

The bikes weren't quiet. Their engines roared through the night, but it was a noise the population was accustomed to. The revolutionary guards liked motorcycles, too. They rode them through the countryside, committing "revolutionary" crimes, and the people of towns and villages cowered in their homes and hoped not to be visited.

Six bikes sped through grubby, dusty little towns. Dogs barked but people didn't awaken.

AOUDELLA SLEPT. Only the Sublime Leader, who never slept before dawn, lay on his back, sipped brandy and writhed under the efforts of the slave girl who'd been trained to make him writhe.

An officer entered. "Your forgiveness, Most Holy."

"Granted."

"Unauthorized motorcycles on the road from the southwest."

Modu Ballem sat up. "You disturb me to tell me about motorcycles? Drunks riding motorcycles around the roads in the middle of the night? I withdraw my forgiveness."

The officer dropped to his knees.

"Send out a squad. My orders are that they are to shoot these motorcyclists. Go!"

The man scrambled to his feet and ran from the room.

Ballem lay back and stared at the ceiling. He glanced at the waiting girl. "Distractions," he said. "The burdens of office. I don't know if I will be able to regain my concentration or not."

THE OFFICER DID MORE than send out a squad in an armored car. He telephoned the "fertilizer" factory and reported the presence on the south road of several unauthorized motorcycles.

The chief of security for the factory was a German by the name of Heinrich Kroll. He was an iron-hard athlete, carrying not an ounce of surplus flesh on his tall frame. He carried himself ramrod straight and spoke in the clipped tones he supposed his father had used as an officer of the Waffen SS.

He put down the telephone and turned to the assistant with whom he was sharing a bottle of brandy. "Suspicious vehicles approaching the town," he announced.

"Maybe we should call an alert," the assistant suggested.

"Try to get the workers out of bed in the middle of the night?" Kroll sneered. "Forget it. Anyway, what good could they do?"

Kroll rose from the table just the same. He slugged down the last of the brandy in his glass, then strapped a wide leather belt around his middle. The belt held the Walther P-38 his father had carried during World War II. He picked up a mini-Uzi.

"Come, Fritz," he said. "We'll check the perimeter."

AOUDELLA WAS an ancient city surrounded by a crumbling wall. For centuries it had slept in the dry sunshine, forgotten. Its modern-day population was only half what it had been a thousand years before when it was an important trading town at the crossroads of caravan routes, famous for its oasis and feared for its garrison of soldiers that guarded the town but also raided the country for two hundred miles in every direction. It had been famed, too, for its slave market, which officially closed only in 1937.

Until recently no one lived in Aoudella—no one, that is, of wealth or power or ambition. Everybody who was anybody lived along the coast. Ninety percent of the country's population lived within sight of the sea. That is, until recently...

Everyone knew the Sublime Leader's reason for locating his "fertilizer" plant at Aoudella. Anyone who wanted to attack it would have to fly over hundreds of miles of desert, giving his radar time to lock on, his missile batteries time to arm and fire.

Everyone also knew, but no one discussed, his reason for moving there himself. He was afraid, afraid of an attack from the sea, of an attempt to kidnap him, of an attempt to assassinate him. He had refurbished the old emir's place at Aoudella—how lavishly no one knew—and spent most of his time there.

The old palace, with its thick, high walls and labyrinth of rooms, was easy to defend, easy to hide in.

Modu Ballem's best and most-trusted guards were deployed in and around the palace. Even the factory wasn't as well protected.

The decoy factory, with its bright lights, lay to the northwest of the city and to the northwest of the real factory, and probably a mile or so away from the real factory. Bolan wasn't sure about that. The factory had been built since he was here, and the decoy had been put up within the past month.

In any case, the bright lights glowing in the distance silhouetted the town, which in silhouette looked like a low, jagged hill.

Riding the lead motorcycle, Bolan felt the bike bounce high off a tremendous bump, and when it came down he found himself riding on blacktop. Modu Ballem had ordered the roads paved for a couple of miles to prevent traffic from raising the huge clouds of dust that had been a condition of life in old Aoudella.

He glanced around. A couple of the other riders were skidding around after hitting the edge of the pavement. But all of them were righting their bikes. None were down. Bolan twisted in more power and sped toward the town.

First evidence of the armored car was a stuttering flash of orange light—a machine gun opening fire. Fortunately the blacktop was gritty with windblown sand, and Bolan was able to twist his bike into a sideways skid and throw it off the road and into soft sand. He came to an abrupt stop with the bike down on its side, his leg thrown up over and out of harm's way.

One of the men behind him wasn't so lucky. A bike shot past Bolan and into the face of the machine-gun fire. The rider fell off and went bouncing and sliding along the pavement. The bike went straight ahead and crashed into the armored car.

The men in the vehicle weren't aiming. They were simply sweeping the road with bursts of machine-gun fire—the tactic of ill-trained soldiers who supposed a machine gun worked like a scythe and mowed down everything within its range.

But the noise and muzzle-flash of the machine gun had alerted the rest of the riders, who did what Bolan had done. They were off the road on both sides and were on their bellies in the dark.

Someone fired a burst at the armored car, which was futile. It was a heavily armored vehicle. The machine gun was firing from a turret that was also equipped with a small cannon. It wasn't a tracked vehicle. It rode on big tires and could attain high speeds on roads, but the tires were solid rubber and couldn't be flattened by rifle fire.

But they had a weapon for it.

One of the LAW rocket launchers was strapped to Nigel Kettering's bike. He recognized the need for it and shortly came crawling forward, dragging it with him. "You do it," he grunted to Bolan. "You've fired one before. I've been briefed but have never actually done it."

It was a British weapon, a one-shot rocket launcher that was to be fired and cast aside. At short range it was as effective as the MILAN launcher. You had to aim, though—aim once and for all, because the rocket burned in the launch tube and then flew straight with no way to adjust its course to the target.

In fact, under the tube was a spotting rifle, allowing the shootist to test his aim. Bolan wouldn't need that feature. The armored car was close.

The revolutionary guards inside the vehicle were probably undecided about what to do next. Had they knocked some drunken motorcyclists off their bikes and terrified them? Or had soldiers deployed from the motorcycles that seemed to have skidded off the road?

The machine gun fired a couple of tentative bursts, slugs ricocheting off the blacktop and whining away into the night.

"REPORT, YOU IDIOT!" Kroll screamed.

He heard the roar of machine-gun fire from the highway south of Aoudella, but his radio, tuned to the Sublime Leader's security frequency, remained silent.

"What the hell are they doing?" he yelled at his assistant. "The first goddamn rule is to report your situation! Report! Report! What the hell's going on?"

But there would be no report from the armored car. Bolan had crawled to the edge of the pavement, aimed at point-blank range and squeezed the trigger. The rocket had shrieked out of the tube and flown fast at the vehicle. The armor-piercing warhead, designed to disable a heavy tank, had shot through the armor of the personnel carrier, the warhead exploding inside. The armored car erupted in a fiery blast of heat and smoke.

MODU BALLEM HEARD the explosion. He rolled away from the girl and off his divan. "Get my military uniform!" he yelled, "and get Kroll on the telephone!"

He spoke with Heinrich Kroll as two valets helped him into his khaki uniform, the one in which he was most often photographed, resplendent in medals, sashes, gold braid and ribbons. He stood with his arms apart as they buckled his belt, the one that held his scabbard and sword, plus the Colt .45 that was his side arm.

"Defend the factory!" he yelled at Kroll. "I will defend the palace! Muster the guard!"

Kroll turned to his assistant and shrugged. "Wake up the workers."

The assistant had already done it. A hundred dark-visaged, bearded sons of desert warriors, men who had borne weapons since they were old enough to walk, were milling inside the factory fence, heavily armed with automatic weapons and ready to fire on anyone reckless enough to approach.

Half of the Sublime Leader's own guards were men like these. The other half were footloose European mercenaries. He strode into a courtyard in the center of the palace and made a speech, telling them the city was under attack by "imperialist pirate raiders" and urging them to fight bravely for "all we hold dear."

THE MAN who had been knocked off his motorcycle had been, in fact, knocked off, not shot off. He was badly bruised and cut by skidding and flopping on the pavement, and his left ankle was at least sprained.

Bolan and Kettering helped mount him behind one of the two remaining volunteer soldiers, and the team moved on.

No one had escaped alive from the armored car. They rode around it where it sat in the middle of the road, filled with dull red flame, billowing smoke.

Someone in Aoudella or at the factory had the presence of mind to switch off the lights on the decoy factory. Darkness descended on the whole area, relieved only a little by moonlight.

A few dim yellow lights burned in the old town. More burned in the area just outside the wall, where followers of the Sublime Leader had built villas for themselves. The cluster of villas around the walls gave Aoudella a sort of suburb, a place where palm trees grew over small green lawns—watered with water trucked in by tanker. The tile-roofed houses there had a scandalous reputation in the town as places where every impiety was indulged—wine was drunk, women went about improperly dressed, and even the most important prayers often remained unsaid.

The ancient gates that had once blocked the road where it passed through the walls had fallen down two centuries or more earlier. Bolan rode through, and the rest of the bikers followed.

The streets of the old town were a jumble—narrow, twisting, some of them blocked by litter and all of them dark. Bolan maneuvered by keeping an eye on the higher bulk of the palace. He worked his way constantly to the left until the palace was to his right, then looked for streets running north. He made as much speed as he dared, with the bike twisting and skidding, dodging the shadows of crates and carts abandoned in the streets.

The five motorcycles, throttled back, made less noise. Bolan led. Sir Reginald Townley brought up the rear, constantly glancing back to look for anyone who might take off after them. They rode without lights, negotiating an obstacle course in the dark.

The old town seemed not to notice, except on one street where suddenly as they passed, a man in a kef-fiyeh stepped into the street and opened fire with a pistol. Townley tossed a concussion grenade, almost casually, and it blew the man off his feet.

"THE ENEMY IS in the streets!" Modu Ballem screamed into the telephone. "The palace is surrounded! Send me half your force immediately!"

"Very well, Sublime Leader," Kroll replied. He hung up the telephone and shook his head at his assistant. "The bastard wants half the troops. To hell with him. I think maybe we *are* about to be attacked. Check deployment. Make sure everybody's where everybody's supposed to be. And turn on the lights."

From a window in a room at the palace, Modu Ballem heard the explosion of the concussion grenade tossed by Townley.

"Artillery!" he yelled.

"A grenade," a guard replied. "I request permission to send two squads out to find out how many men are at large in the streets and how they are equipped."

"And leave the palace undefended?" Ballem asked, his voice shrill with mixed scorn and disbelief. "Never! Every man stays here! Every man fights to the death against the invader!"

"Two squads," the guard pressed with barely controlled patience.

"Two squads less to defend the palace. It's unthinkable. You will order every man to take his assigned station on the walls and defend the palace."

"And your person," the desert warrior added.

"And my person!" the divine leader shrieked.

CHAPTER THIRTEEN

Bolan had ridden into a blocked street and had no choice but to turn around. He switched on his headlight for a moment so that the other riders would see him coming. He swerved among them and out into the street from which he'd come.

Suddenly the sky to the north brightened. Someone had turned on the lights in the factory compound.

Someone at the mission's first objective, the chemical weapons factory just outside the northwest corner of Aoudella, had lit a beacon for them, and the glow relieved the blackness of the narrow, winding streets.

The Executioner twisted in more power and shot the bike between heaps of empty crates discarded in front of stands that sold food during the day. At a corner he skidded on some garbage, but he kept the bike up and moving, entering what looked to be a street that might run diagonally to the corner of the town.

The street wasn't straight, but it did wind northwest, and in another two minutes Bolan rode through a gap in the crumbling old town wall and onto a dusty open plain.

No villas lay on this side of Aoudella. The wealthy didn't build their homes so close to the factory. The land was flat and rocky. All that distinguished the road from the land on either side of it was that it was clear of rocks. The factory was a mile or so ahead.

Bolan could see immediately that the factory was defended. It was surrounded by a high fence topped with coils of razor wire. Stone blockhouses stood at intervals along the walls and at the corners. He took binoculars from one of his saddlebags and scanned the perimeter fence. The towers were equipped with machine guns—and the surface-to-air missile batteries. He could make out four of them, which were outside the fence. Probably there were others on the north side.

Behind the fence lay a low stone wall manned by desert warriors. He'd seen their kind before. A quick look showed him twenty men. There would be a hundred, maybe more.

Townley came up beside Bolan. "I'm afraid we're not going to surprise them. They've turned on the lights and called out the guard."

"I guess we have to see how good they are."

The man who had injured his ankle south of the town was ordered to stay with the cycles and keep watch on them. He had an Uzi and plenty of ammo, plus a dozen MU-50 grenades.

The five remaining members of the team unloaded their saddlebags. Besides their automatic rifles, pistols and grenades, each man carried a part of the team's heavy weapons—the remaining three LAW 80 rocket launchers and the two MM-1 projectile launchers.

They spread out on the east side of the road and walked toward the factory, conscious that they were almost certainly being watched.

As they closed the distance to the chemical factory, more details of the layout became apparent. The factory consisted of a group of small prefabricated steel buildings, each separated from all the others by about fifty feet. In the center of the compound stood a tall tangle of tanks and pipes, similar to a cracking tower at an oil refinery. A high plume of steam drifted from the top of it. On the west and north perimeters and against the fence were six or eight storage tanks.

When the team had walked half the distance to the factory, Bolan signaled a stop and he took time to have another look through his binoculars. A few European men were walking purposefully around the compound, carrying what looked like kits of tools.

Thud Townley, too, was looking through binoculars. "They're shutting down," he announced.

"What?"

"I'd guess they're expecting trouble, so they're shutting down the chemical operations. Too dangerous to have the factory running while there's shooting."

"Germans?" Bolan asked.

"That's what our intelligence reports indicate. The factory was built by a German company and is being run by German technicians. East German. They're supposed to train the locals to operate the machinery, but so far it's being run by Germans. When they finish what they're doing, they'll pick up their weapons and become part of the defense."

"They must have spotted us," Bolan said.

"I should think they have. They're waiting until... well, what was it the American chap is supposed to have said at the Battle of Bunker Hill? 'Don't fire until you see the whites of their eyes,' wasn't it?"

"Let's move," Bolan said. "I figure we're in for some kind of nasty surprise."

The surprise came a minute or so later when they had advanced about hundred yards. They heard the whump and whoosh of a mortar. Seconds later the shell burst in front of them. It was a phosphorous round, hurling deadly white fire over a ten-yard radius. The round fell short, but it wouldn't take the enemy forever to adjust the range.

Bolan turned and signaled to Kettering, who was carrying one of the LAW rocket launchers. Bolan himself was carrying an MM-1, but they weren't yet within its effective range. He gestured to Kettering to hand him the LAW.

Another mortar round sang through the air. It, too, fell short, but by less than the first.

"What have you got in mind?" Townley asked as Bolan dropped to his knees and aimed the rocket launcher.

"I'm going to find out what happens if I blow a hole in one of the tanks in that tower. If some of the chemicals get loose, they'll have something to worry about."

"So might we," Townley replied.

"Look at the steam. Look at the smoke off the phosphorous rounds. Not much wind, but what there is is blowing east to west. Whatever this shot shakes loose, it's not coming this way and it's not going into the town."

Another mortar round fell, this one behind them and closer still.

"Shoot then." Townley shrugged. "It's either that or we run like hell."

Bolan sighted carefully. They had only three LAWs left, and he couldn't afford to waste a rocket. He didn't have much time, either. He aimed at the base of the tower, where the tanks were concentrated, and fired.

The rocket roared out of the tube. The rocket burned out very quickly, and the missile then flew like a shell. Bolan tossed aside the burned-out launcher tube and grabbed his binoculars to have a better look at where the missile hit and what it did.

The armor-piercing warhead punched through the glass-lined steel tank and exploded inside. The tank ruptured all around, and the chemical inside spewed out on the force of the explosion, spraying the buildings and ground, and the men, for fifty feet around. A fog of fumes immediately rose off the chemical and began to drift westward. Men scrambled from their positions and ran in panic.

The blown-open tank was connected to half a dozen pipes, and all of them were torn loose. Liquids gushed from the pipes. As the liquids mixed, small explosions flared on the ground and smoke drifted across the factory compound.

Bolan signaled the team forward, and they closed the distance between them and the fence. The mortar had been silenced for a minute or so by panic and confusion. Now it was fired again. The round burst far behind the advancing team. Someone saw and adjusted, and the phosphorous bursts fell closer.

Automatic rifle fire began to spatter the ground, too. The gunners were now unsure of where their attackers were, so the fire wasn't yet dangerous. But it would be, as soon as the first gunner spotted the team and directed the fire.

A hundred yards from the fence, Bolan stopped. Now they were close enough to shower the compound with shells from the MM-1s.

He and Townley were carrying the two MM-1s. Both men knelt, loaded and cocked the weapons. Kettering and two volunteers searched for targets and opened fire with their assault rifles.

Townley loaded his MM-1 with six smoke projectiles and six tear gas. He fired first, aiming at the east side of the factory so that his smoke and gas would drift across the factory compound.

The projectiles burst in a violent cluster, and a huge cloud of mixed smoke and tear gas drifted as the Briton had planned. The mortar stopped firing, and the rifle fire diminished to a few scattered bursts.

Bolan had loaded his MM-1 with twelve explosive projectiles. He fired six toward a steel prefab building to the right of the factory gate and six toward one on the left.

The explosive rounds blew the buildings apart. The one on the left simply collapsed. The one on the right collapsed, too, but something in the wreckage burst into flame, producing a smoky orange fire that billowed upward. The lights went out, but the bright orange fire in the wrecked building lit the targets.

Townley had reloaded his MM-1 with explosive rounds, and now he let fly all twelve in rapid succession. They landed in the middle of the compound in the tangle of pipes and tanks that made up the tower, which collapsed and spewed out more chemicals.

The assault team witnessed a general retreat from the factory. Engines roared; two big trucks sped out the far side and off into the darkness. Men—some of them choking and vomiting—stumbled across the ground, running as best they could to get away from the attack and, more, to get away from the frightening fog of smoke and fumes that drifted and seemed almost to pursue them.

HEINRICH KROLL HADN'T yet retreated. He stood in the middle of the north end of the compound, where the trucks had roared away, and cursed and waved his Uzi at his panicked troops. His own damn Germans had stolen the trucks. Technicians. Well, they'd better not go home. He'd see that word of their cowardly defection reached Berlin.

The factory was wrecked, of course. The distilling and fractionizing tower lay in ruins, completing its own destruction by leaking its corrosive chemicals, which were rapidly eating the precious metals of some of its components.

Explosive fire kept coming in, blasting apart buildings that hadn't been built to take such punishment. When some of the storage tanks burst, the destruction would be complete.

He didn't think he'd been attacked by a large force. Commandos, that was all. And if the damn Sublime Leader had only sent out a small force from the palace, they could have attacked the commandos from the rear, and right now Kroll could be wiping them up instead of being in retreat.

He glanced around one final time. Damn! A year's work, hundreds of millions, gone in five minutes.

Well, he wasn't about to be stuck here for the end. His Range Rover was parked behind the building that had been his headquarters. He had used his Uzi to shoot down one son of a bitch who'd gone near it.

He didn't know where his assistant was, and he wasn't going to wait to find out. Kroll got into the Range Rover and drove off into the desert north of the factory.

BOLAN AND TOWNLEY had halted their attack for a few minutes. There was no point in slaughtering men who were struggling to retreat. They waited until they saw no more figures scrambling around the compound. Then they moved forward slowly, firing occasional shots from the MM-1s, blasting one building after another, setting bright new fires.

"I'm not sure what those fumes are," Bolan said to Townley, "but I don't see any point in going in there and finding out. Let's keep upwind."

The Briton nodded. "Don't want to leave any full tanks, though."

"Try puncturing them with rifle fire," Bolan suggested.

It worked. The tanks were made of thin, glass-lined steel. Slugs from the M-16 and the G-11s punched through them, and chemicals poured out of the holes. One tank burst into flame; the heat ruptured another one.

Then they set to work on the SAM batteries. There turned out to be six of them, including two they couldn't see until they reached the north side of the factory.

The batteries were sophisticated new equipment of Czech manufacture. Their radar was capable of locking onto a high-flying aircraft in seconds, and the missiles, once fired, locked on, too, and followed a maneuvering aircraft.

Grenades blew the radar and computers to pieces. Shots from the MM-1s wrecked the firing mechanisms. The missiles fell to the rocky ground where two exploded.

A surprisingly fierce and protracted explosion of one of the buildings inside the factory fence told the attackers where the supply of missiles had been stored.

The work was finished. The Sublime Leader's chemical weapons plant was history.

The assault team raced back to the motorcycles and prepared to leave the scene.

"We've got two choices," Bolan announced. "We can ride out of here and go for the choppers, or we can try an assault on the palace."

"I never like to leave a job half-finished, sir," Reilly, the man with the injured ankle, said. "Besides, I might be able to get a little closer to this operation."

Bolan and Townley agreed it would be a mistake to reenter the city the way they had come out—through the northwest corner. Moving on the ground here, they were silhouetted against the light of the factory fires. Besides, if they took off to the east or west, someone watching might think they'd done all they had come to do and were leaving the area.

There was no real road around the walls of Aoudella, only a sort of track. It was enough for the dirt bikes. They made a circuit to the east, holding down their speed so that the roar of their engines wouldn't be as loud.

The old town loomed above them as a jumble of dark shadows. Again they could make out the higher bulk of the palace and could see lights in the windows.

Twice, as they worked their way south along the track outside the eastern wall, they saw the glaring headlights of big cars—Mercedes from the look of them—speeding north on a road half a mile to the east. Someone was abandoning Aoudella—maybe the Sublime Leader.

No. The Sublime Leader was in the palace. Standing at a window, he watched the fires burn in the chemical factory. He was calmer now, as if he had accepted the loss. He'd put aside the sword that would have hung awkwardly at his side, impeding anything he tried to do. He had tossed away his heavy cap, which had a steel lining like a helmet. Though still glittering in medals and ribbons, he wasn't as gaudy as before. His right hand continued to run nervously over the Colt .45 that hung on his hip.

He spoke to the desert warrior who commanded his guard. "It was a commando raid. Fifty of them, maybe. No more. And that Teutonic idiot Kroll, with 250 men, couldn't fight them off." He shrugged. "Well, transfer of the plant to our control and ownership hadn't been completed." He smiled. "You understand what that means? It means we haven't paid for it!" He pounded his right first into the palm of his left hand. "And we won't!"

The gimlet-eyed, dark-visaged desert fighter nodded. Not a trace of a smile showed on his face.

"Probably they're on their way back to the helicopters," Ballem said. "But keep alert! We could be the target of a secondary attack before they leave the country."

"'Secondary,'" the desert warrior mused. "Could they regard *you* as secondary?"

Modu Ballem chuckled. "A serious mistake. What's more important than I? What has ever been?"

BOLAN SPOTTED a breach in the wall. It wasn't a gate; it was a place where the centuries-old wall had crumbled, leaving a gap. The warrior stopped while he and Townley studied the opening and considered.

Trap? Not likely.

Bolan nodded at the Briton, dismounted and walked up to the gap and through it. The walls of the palace were fifty yards away.

The palace was old, built in an era when a wall of mud brick was a good defense, a formidable obstacle against raiders armed with bows and arrows, spears and swords. It was a jumble of buildings put up over the centuries without a plan. Some of the buildings were falling down like the wall. Some had been restored.

Bolan's problem wasn't with the wall. It was in finding the defenders, then finding the Sublime Leader. The guards could be anywhere, and they were undoubtedly armed with deadly modern infantry weapons.

Townley joined Bolan. "We've got plenty of projectiles left for the launchers," he said. "We could lob in some grenades."

Bolan shook his head. "Ballem has servants. We don't want to kill them."

"Mmm."

"We've got no choice but to go in," Bolan said.

"Right. We'll have to leave Reilly to guard the bikes as before."

Five men moved inside the wall. They carried their assault rifles and the MM-1 projectile launchers, and they left two LAW launchers and some grenades with Reilly. Cursing, the injured Reilly sat down among the motorcycles to wait.

Directly behind the gap in the wall, a small stone building lay in ruins. Bolan and Townley led their men to the left, south. Ahead of them and in a corner of the wall stood a tall old round tower, which would afford men on top a field of fire over a third of the palace compound—as it had undoubtedly once done for archers. They approached it cautiously, then spread out along the bottom of the wall.

Covered by the others, Bolan trotted out of the shadow of the wall and tried the heavy wooden door. He pushed, and it swung back.

The interior of the structure was dark and smelled stale and foul. The warrior closed the door behind him and switched on a flashlight. Cupping his hand around the lens, he allowed only a little light to escape, not enough to be seen from outside, not enough to leave him blind when he switched it off again.

The room had likely been a guardroom. Stone steps spiraled up around the wall, but they had crumbled, and access to the upper part of the tower was by a crude wooden ladder that had been made by nailing boards together.

Bolan opened the door. "I'm going to climb up," he called softly to Townley. "Cover me down here."

Back inside, he switched on his light again and climbed the rickety ladder to a point where the stone steps were intact. From there he climbed a few steps and emerged in another room much like the first.

Again stone steps led upward in a spiral around the walls. This set hadn't crumbled, and he began to climb again, being careful that the stones didn't break under his weight.

There was no railing at the edge of the steps, which were about two feet wide. From the second floor they circled upward about twenty-five feet until they passed through a hole in a wooden floor.

The warrior reached the top. When he passed through the hole in the floor, he was out under the sky.

The wooden floor was weak and dangerous, and it splintered when he put a foot down on it. It rested, though, on a stone ledge that ran around the tower, and this gave Bolan a place to stand.

Okay. From up here he could do a real recon.

The tower wasn't the tallest structure in the palace compound. Near the west wall stood another tower, much like the one he was on. He knelt behind the stone parapet and watched the other structure intently.

He could see men on top of the tower and what looked like machine guns. Sure. If they were smart, the guards would mount machine guns up there, which would cover not just the entire western half of the palace compound, but also two big gaps in the wall. Men positioned up there could pitch grenades, too.

The biggest building inside the walls was an H-shaped structure, part of it four stories high, part three. A portion of the roof was flat, a portion sloped. Guards stood around on the flat parts. The western leg of the H looked crumbled, but the eastern leg was solid, and he could see lights in the windows.

The space between the two legs at the bottom of the H was a courtyard in which two Mercedes limousines were parked. They were guarded.

He could see across the roof of the central building—it was, in fact, the palace proper—to the northwest corner of the compound. There, on the roof of a square building, sat a small helicopter.

The warrior was distracted by the sound of an engine. He turned and saw headlights. A Range Rover drove along the streets of Aoudella and proceeded through a wide gap in the south wall. It pulled up beside the two limousines, and a man got out. The guards let him pass into the palace.

"THERE ISN'T A WAY to get inside quietly," Bolan said. "There are guards in the courtyard and on the roof. I figure, too, they patrol. I don't know why we haven't seen any."

"We could take out the chaps on top of the tower for a beginning," Townley suggested.

"I've got another idea. The fact that there's a chopper and two limousines inside the walls makes me think that the Sublime Leader is still here. I want to take out that chopper."

"And the limos?" Kettering asked.

"And the limos," Bolan agreed. "Let's coordinate. Thud and I will go get the chopper. You stay here with these two men. Get in position. When you hear us fire on the chopper, you fire on the limos."

HEINRICH KROLL HAD DRIVEN into the desert some distance, then swung around west and had come into Aoudella from the south. On the way he'd overtaken three desert men who had fled from the factory. He had shot them.

Kroll didn't think the commandos had left the country yet. He'd seen no sign of the helicopters they must have used to fly in. He had been out in the quiet, open countryside, and a flight of twenty or thirty helicopters wouldn't have missed his attention.

He didn't think they'd bother to attack the palace. He judged they'd go for the air base at Exyeh. The presidential 707 was there, with eight MiGs and two Mirage fighters. Or they'd go for the radar and SAM installations that defended the base, leaving it vulnerable to air attack.

In any case, nothing more had happened in Aoudella, and he meant to take advantage of the quiet here and make good his escape.

IN HIS OFFICE in the middle of the palace, Modu Ballem sat behind his desk, a mini-Uzi within easy reach. The desert warrior who commanded his guard sat in a leather-covered chair and stared at him.

The telephone rang. Ballem answered and received a brief message.

"So," he said to his chief of security. "Kroll has returned. It's my will that he die as soon as he enters this room. No, on second thought, let's hear a few words from him. Then he dies. One of us shoots him.

It makes no difference who. I will do it if the opportunity presents itself. You do it if you must.''

The taciturn guard nodded.

They waited. Minutes passed, and Kroll didn't appear. The Sublime Leader telephoned the gate. Yes, they were sure it had been Kroll. No, he had said nothing about why he had returned.

"The helicopter!" Ballem screamed. "He came back to steal my helicopter! To escape in my helicopter!"

Grabbing the Uzi, the Sublime Leader raced for the door.

RETURNING ALONG the wall, Bolan and Townley had taken a moment to step out and report to Reilly. He'd seen no patrols.

The two men spotted one as soon as they crossed through the wall again—five swarthy men in varied and ragged clothes, carrying AK-47s and walking south along the wall of the palace.

They made poor guards. They carried a powerful flashlight with which they probed the holes and crannies in the jumble of buildings, giving a glaring warning to any intruders. Also, they laughed and grunted as they made their rounds. Maybe they didn't take their work seriously. Maybe they thought their AK-47s made them invincible.

Bolan and Townley watched them swagger by. They could have taken all five of them out with a single grenade, but they weren't ready yet to alarm the entire palace guard force—some of whom were bound to be better soldiers than these.

The Executioner and the Englishman slipped north along the inside of the old wall, climbing over heaps of debris. They passed a long, low building—a sort of shed but built of stone, maybe once a stable—between the wall and the palace. Safe in the shadows, the men examined the helicopter that sat atop the square building at the north end of the palace H.

It was a Bell helicopter, small, handy, easy to fly— but a two-man aircraft. That was all it would carry— a pilot and one passenger.

"My heart revolts at having to destroy a pretty little bird like that," Townley whispered.

Bolan had no such qualm. It was the escape vehicle for the Sublime Leader, no doubt, who was the secondary target. They had taken out the primary target. Now...

HEINRICH KROLL had trotted through the palace, out across a narrow strip of courtyard, into the old granary and up the stairs to the roof, which had been reinforced to take the weight of the helicopter.

The pilot was waiting.

"The Sublime Leader orders you to fly me to the coast," Kroll said.

"No, sir," the pilot replied. He was an Icelander, a rogue pilot wanted by the law for using his skills to carry heroin across Europe. "My orders are to—"

The pilot's eyes flared with fear as he saw the muzzle of the Walther pressed close to his chest.

A 9 mm slug blasted into his chest. The pilot fell.

Standing fifty feet east of the building, Bolan and Townley heard the shot but hadn't seen what happened. Expecting the shot to draw the attention of guards, they slipped between the wall and the building in the northeast corner and crouched in deep shadow.

In the shadow of the tower Bolan had climbed earlier, Nigel Kettering heard the shot, too. He and the two volunteer soldiers had been waiting for a signal for them to attack the limousines in the courtyard. They had hidden themselves at the base of the tower because the five guards Bolan and Townley had seen minutes before had swaggered on along the palace wall and now stood at the southeast corner, still laughing and smoking.

Kettering wasn't sure what the single shot meant, but he supposed it would be a good idea to make a distraction for Bolan and Townley. Something was happening, and that was the least he could do.

With the hand signals every soldier knew, Kettering ordered one of the volunteers to make ready to pitch a grenade. He pulled one loose from his belt, nodded at the soldier and simultaneously they threw two MU-50s.

The five guards looked down curiously at the little steel objects rolling toward them on the cobblestones. No smoke issued from the fuses, and until the last second they didn't recognize the objects as grenades.

Then the two orbs exploded, blasting out a storm of steel pellets at high and deadly velocity. Taking scores of hits, the five guards fell to the ground and didn't move.

Kettering was already on the run toward the limousines. Gripping his Ingram 10, he fired a burst of .45 rounds into the engine of the nearer limousine. The car rocked under the impact of that torrent of steel, and vital parts were blown off the engine.

One of the soldiers, kneeling, did the same to the other limousine with his Uzi, and both cars were disabled.

But their guards weren't, and they weren't fools like those who had died at the corner of the palace. Taking immediate cover behind the bodies of the big Mercedes limousines, they opened fire with their AK-47s.

Slugs from two rifles hit Nigel Kettering at the same time. He staggered back and fell, his chest and throat torn apart and spewing blood.

The kneeling soldier kept up a steady barrage, forcing the guards to keep their cover. The other pitched a grenade, then a second, then a third.

The first bomb struck the body of a Mercedes and fell back on the courtyard. It exploded, and its pellets served only to scar the limousine. The second bounced off the hood and fell beyond. Its blast drove pellets into the guards behind the cars, killing two and wounding two. The third hit the roof of a limousine and fell among the dead and wounded, finishing them off.

Now the guards on the palace roof began to fire down. They weren't sure where the attack had come from, and the two soldiers were able to duck back behind the stone tower before they were hit.

THE SOUND of the firefight at the front of the palace came to the Sublime Leader as he ran across the open ground between his residence and the granary.

"They're in the palace!" he shrieked at his chief of security.

The desert man brushed past him and into the granary, bounding up the steps toward the roof.

On the roof Heinrich Kroll sat at the controls of the little helicopter. He'd just pressed the starter button, and the engine had caught and begun to run, roughly at first, soon to smooth out.

Expecting interference, Kroll had left the canopy in its slid-back position. He was ready with the Walther. The instant the desert warrior popped up through the trapdoor, Kroll shot him square in the forehead.

The man fell backward, knocking Modu Ballem off the lower steps.

"Kroll, you fool! It carries two! You and me!"

But by the time Ballem reached the trapdoor, the helicopter was lifting off. It was eight or ten feet above the roof and had begun to bank to the east.

Ballem took careful aim with his mini-Uzi and emptied the magazine at the fleeing aircraft. Twenty-five slugs missed, but a few grazed the frame and the plexiglas bubble.

Mack Bolan didn't miss. A stream of 4.7 mm rounds from the G-11 ripped through the bottom of the chopper and tore through Kroll. The chopper cleared the northeast corner of the wall and crashed in the street just beyond, flames shooting into the air.

Modu Ballem squatted in a corner of the granary, sweating heavily while he shoved another clip into his machine pistol. He strode to a window and looked out, but saw no one. He heard gunfire from the roof and some at the south end of the palace.

Ballem left the granary through a door on the northwest corner, which put him on the ground just inside the biggest breach in the old wall. He glanced to his left. His guards still manned the stone tower inside the west wall.

He had only one choice. He could leave the palace compound through the breach in the wall—if he could reach the building in the northeast corner. It was a garage, which housed a four-wheel drive truck, an oil field wagon. A machine gun was mounted in the rear, and there was a bag of grenades between the front seats.

Out on the streets . . . who was loyal? Maybe no one now. Better to make a break for the garage. Better to dash for the coast, or to the air base. Ballem checked one more time and sprinted for the garage.

No one noticed. Bolan and Townley had moved inside the palace and were working their way through the long corridors. Gunfire was slacking off. Something else was going on. The people of the palace had begun to loot it.

The two men met no opposition. The only armed man they saw threw down his weapon, grinned nervously and ran.

MODU BALLEM REACHED the garage.

The truck was there. He checked the arms. Yes. The machine gun stood on a mount in the rear, and the grenades were where he had remembered. Two AK-47s lay on the floor of the front seat.

He started the engine, and, creeping forward, he eased the truck out and drove for the breach in the wall. In a minute he was on the street outside.

Bolan and Townley had reached the south end of the palace. Through the front door they could see the crippled limousines, saw the bodies of the guards.

They had left one of the MM-1s with Nigel Kettering, and just now the surviving soldiers had begun to lob explosive projectiles at the stone tower. When Modu Ballem saw the flash of machine gun fire from the tower, he saw that the guards were trying to find and to stop the succession of projectiles that had begun to explode on the tower walls and work their way higher as the aimers found the range.

He left the headlights off and drove east, as quietly as possible, circling the wreckage of the helicopter where dying flames flickered around the clearly visible body of Heinrich Kroll.

He turned south and drove along the outside of the palace wall, conscious that firing inside was dying away. The presidential guard was fleeing, or surrendering. Cowards. Animals...

Reilly heard the approaching truck, then he spotted it. He didn't know who it was, what it was, and was prepared to let it pass. He got up and stepped inside the breach in the wall to be out of sight.

Ballem saw him and stopped at the breach. He zeroed in on the motorcycles. So!

He reached into the bag between the seats and pulled out a grenade. The soldier was just beyond the breach, but the shrapnel would do its job.

He pitched the grenade, but threw it too far. The orb struck the ground twenty-five or thirty feet beyond Reilly and rolled ten more feet before it exploded, during which time Reilly had thrown himself to the ground.

Damn it! If the son of a bitch wanted trouble, trouble he could have. Reilly scrambled up and fired a burst through the breach in the wall.

Ballem floored the accelerator, and the truck rushed forward. He hadn't planned on this at all. His purpose was to reach the highway and put distance between himself and Aoudella. He didn't need a firefight with soldiers at the palace wall.

But he had made a mistake. A big mistake.

Reilly hobbled out through the hole, his ankle stabbed with pain at his every step. He grabbed a LAW launcher, aimed a missile at the retreating truck and fired at short range. The missile tore into the rear of the truck, through its gasoline tank and exploded.

The body of the Sublime Leader, president-for-life, Holy Receptor of the Divine Will, flew twenty feet into the air and fell back into the churning gasoline fire.

CHAPTER FOURTEEN

Kathryn O'Connor turned uncomfortably in the tangled sheet and under the tangled cotton blanket on her cot. Tim had promised discomfort as the least part of her penalty for killing O'Neill, and she was miserably uncomfortable and had been uncomfortable for several days.

She was confined in a cellar room again, where at night there was no light at all, and she lay in darkness so complete that after many hours it overwhelmed the reason even of a brave and controlled person such as herself. During the day she could make out the limits of her cell—for a dungeon cell was what it was, almost. The place had been the coal bin for the big old iron furnace she could see beyond the wooden door. The furnace had been converted to oil—the cellar smelled of oil. A little daylight entered the bin through the boarded-over window above her head. A little more entered the furnace room through the dirty glass of a tiny window on the far side of the furnace. The floor was grimy with the dust left from coal that hadn't been here for years. She was grimy with the stuff. It was on her skin as much as on her clothes.

She had no access to a toilet. A chamber pot sat in a corner at the foot of her cot. They left a paper milk carton of water with her all the time, but she had to drink that; she couldn't wash with it.

They did feed her. The doctor came in to see her from time to time. He had retaped her ribs three times and had told her they were healing nicely. The swelling had gone down on her face. Her nose was almost normal. She was a lucky girl, the doctor had said, then laughed.

The lucky girl wore handcuffs and leg irons. The chain between her leg irons was locked to a five-foot chain that was in turn locked around the bed. She could shuffle over to the chamber pot, and that was about it.

The day before yesterday...she didn't know what day it was. Maybe it had been the day before that. Anyway, Tim had taken more Polaroid pictures of her to send to somebody. Maybe to Mack.

She had no idea where she was. She guessed it might be somewhere in county Tipperary, but that was only a guess.

Sometimes Tim came down to see her, sometimes Molly. So far the threatening Brian Connelly hadn't come, but Molly told her—as though Molly took some kind of pleasure in saying it—that Brian wanted to kill her.

They had made sure she had no weapon. They had examined the bin thoroughly to be certain there was nothing she could break loose and use to tamper with her irons or injure a jailer.

Hour after lonely hour, during the dim, short light, she had examined every inch of the space she could reach to the end of her chain. There was nothing.

Kathryn had lost hope.

SEVEN HOURS after he left Aoudella, Mack Bolan was back in Dublin. He didn't trust Inspector Michael Harrigan anymore and didn't intend to see him. But a confidential message waiting for Sir Thud Townley at the Special Branch said the Irish Constabulary had received a new set of Polaroid pictures of Kathryn O'Connor and that Colonel MacKenzie might want to see them.

He went to headquarters. He might as well.

"They aren't entirely intelligent, our Curran Brigaders," Harrigan began when Bolan had shaken his hand and sat down.

"How's that?"

"They've sent us more Polaroid pictures." He passed them to Bolan, four of them. "Have a look. Then I'll tell you what I mean."

Bolan looked at the pictures. Her face was black with some kind of dirt, and her unwashed hair was tangled. She held a newspaper weakly in handcuffed hands. Her lips were parted, her chin was low and her eyes sagged in hopeless fatigue.

"The demand is greater," Harrigan said. "They want your surrender. But never mind that. They're not too smart. They've tipped their hand."

"How?"

"I know where they are, roughly. In a little while we'll be able to track them down, surround their hiding place and rescue Kathryn."

"I'm listening," Bolan grunted.

They had ridden the dirt bikes back to the southern border, carrying the body of Nigel Kettering across the back of the Executioner's bike. The choppers had flown them to the carrier. Bolan and Townley had been flown from the carrier to London in a pair of jet fighters. He'd slept a little during the flight and a little during the helicopter ride to Dublin, but Mack Bolan was tired. His patience wasn't long.

"Polaroid cameras," Inspector Harrigan said. "How much do you know about them? Did you know the film is extremely fine-grain?"

"If I had known that, what would I know?"

"You'd know that a Polaroid picture can be enlarged very big and still the image remains distinct. It lends itself to computer enhancement."

Bolan tossed the photos back onto Harrigan's desk. "Go on."

Harrigan took an eight-by-ten sheet from a folder and handed it over. It was an enlargement of the top of the newspaper Kathryn was holding. Even the small print was legible.

"The *Irish Times* again," Harrigan told him. "Only not the newspaper sold in Dublin. Like every major newspaper, the *Irish Times* runs several editions every day. The earlier editions go on trucks and trains out to the countryside. And it publishes county editions, meaning editions containing local advertising and

meant for circulation only in one county. If you know
how to read the code printed just under the line under
the headline, you can tell what edition that paper was.
That newspaper was an early edition with a local in-
sert for county Tipperary."

"Tipperary... that covers a lot of territory, doesn't
it?"

"Yes, and, of course, it could have been carried to
Tipperary by someone. But it's a lead. County Tipperary. Now, what else can we learn from these Polaroids?"

"Spit it out, Mike."

"She's black. I'm betting she's covered with coal
dust. Notice that she's lighter around her eyes. She's
rubbed her eyes, and the moisture around her eyes—
her tears—has washed the dust off. Also, notice the
lighter skin on her left wrist. She's holding up the
newspaper, and her handcuff has slipped up her arm,
uncovering skin not blackened with dust. We don't
have coal mines in Tipperary, so she's not in a mine. I
wish she were. It would make her easier to find. But,
no, she's in the coal bin of a building or house that's
heated, or once was heated, with coal."

"How many thousands of houses?" Bolan asked.

"Look at the picture I've marked with a 3. She's
sitting on a coat. An enlargement of the floor area
shows a few chunks of coal on the floor. Look at the
wood. Chips of coal stuck in the cracks. A coal bin.
But empty. I'd guess the house was converted to oil
heat years ago. Otherwise there'd be a lot more coal in
the bin—and maybe no room for a prisoner."

"Could be that they're getting a fresh load of coal in the fall," Bolan suggested.

Harrigan shook his head. "How many home owners end the heating season with an empty coal bin or an empty oil tank? People stop firing the furnace when the weather turns warm, not when they use up their supply of coal.

"We've been doing our detective work," Harrigan went on. "In county Tipperary there are just three companies that do oil-to-coal conversions. We've got from them a list of all the conversions they've done in the past five years. That cuts our list to about 150 houses."

Bolan raised a skeptical eyebrow.

"Dividing the list among towns, among constabulary offices, we've handed each office no more than ten houses to check. The reports are coming in. It's easier than you might think. Six of the places on the list have turned out to be churches. Others are the homes of elderly, conservative people, well-known in their communities. We'll get it down to no more than a dozen before long—houses a little remote, where the local people don't know the occupants very well, where maybe some strangers have been observed lately. In small Irish towns people know one another's business. That's why I wouldn't want to live in one of them. It's also good for my kind of work."

"So finally—"

"So finally we'll choose a house or two," Harrigan said, "and we'll raid."

"And get her killed."

"Please...we know a little something about our business. Anyway, I thought you would probably want to come with us to the most likely place."

THE MOST LIKELY PLACE was a small brick house on the edge of the town of Thurles, a little north of Holycross Abbey. They were met at dusk by the local constable, an aging man with a great white mustache who talked to them about the house he identified as the likely hideout of a gang of terrorists.

"It was the home of a fine family by the name of McGillicuddy. A greengrocer, he was. Honorable man. But the wife died and the children left for America. He moved to Cork to be closer to his last remaining child, a daughter. The house has been with an estate agent for five years or so. Been leased to this one and that one, not all of them very respectable people. One couple who moved in wasn't a couple. They weren't married."

"Who lives there now?" Harrigan asked.

"I'd have said nobody a week ago. Then some fellows arrived and took the house on a month's rental. Paid in advance, according to the agent. There've been four cars there. I mean, never more than two at a time. A man and a woman seem to be the chief occupants. Man with a beard. The woman's red-haired, and not very respectable lookin'."

"The Finnertys," Harrigan said to Bolan.

"What's that?" the constable cried. "You mean we've got Timothy Finnerty in our midst? Him and his gang of cutthroats?"

Harrigan nodded.

The constable pondered the news for a moment, the corners of his mouth turning down until his face was set in an unhappy grimace. "All right," he said then. "Let me show you the layout."

The solid little house, built of brick, beams and stucco, was set on a roomy lot where the greengrocer had tended a garden that was now overgrown with weeds. A frame garage stood behind the house. Everything was a little run-down. The house wasn't yet ramshackle, but it had the look of a place no one had cared about for several years.

A fuel oil tank stood on a stand between the house and driveway. It was plain, though, that a nearby cellar window had been where a coal chute was thrust through and coal was shoveled into a bin below.

If Harrigan's guess was right, Kathryn was in that coal bin.

And it wasn't just a guess. Harrigan and his men had done careful detective work. After all, she was one of their own, a detective of the Irish Constabulary. They were very likely right. She was in there.

She was in there, and Timothy Finnerty had far rather kill her than allow her to be rescued.

Harrigan had agreed to allow Bolan to enter the house first to do what he had to do, his own special way. The constabulary had helped outfit him for this mission—with the black clothes he favored for night work, a black turtleneck sweater, black pants, black boots. He carried the Desert Eagle on his hip, the silenced Beretta under his arm. He was also equipped with a rope, a knife and a flashlight.

Harrigan and his team of five men would stand back and wait while the warrior tried to get Kathryn out. They wouldn't ask questions if they found, when it was over, that some of the Curran Brigade hadn't survived.

Clouds obscured the moon if there was one, so the night was dark. Bolan approached the house from behind through the garden of a neighbor whose lot backed up on this one.

The house was dark. Not a single light shone.

He checked the garage, which contained a car. The warrior squatted by the car and let the air out of the rear tires, cutting off that avenue of escape.

The weeds in the garden and others growing along the driveway provided a little cover. He moved cautiously, figuring someone was watching from the windows.

But it was so dark that a man in black clothes could move unseen across this kind of ground. He knew he could. He'd done it countless times. People staring into the dark soon grew tired of it. They couldn't keep it up. Their eyes stopped focusing. The man moving in the dark had an advantage.

Up to a point. It was an advantage that would quickly disappear as soon as he tried to enter the house.

He checked the cellar window. The opening had been cut through the stone foundation precisely to let a steel coal chute run from a truck and through the opening—so coal could be shoveled onto the chute to run down into the cellar bin.

The window was too narrow for a man's shoulders. He couldn't climb in.

Where else could he get in?

He looked at the roof. He could go up the beech tree, lower himself onto the roof and enter the house through an upstairs window. Other than that there were doors front and back, first-floor windows all around. And whatever he did, he had to do it quietly. He had to have total surprise when he hit Kathryn's keepers.

He slipped around to the beech tree.

"MacKenzie!"

He swung around. Harrigan stood there, waiting.

"I thought you'd decide to climb the tree," Harrigan said quietly. "What if we coordinate? We make a racket outside just as you go in through a window. We might confuse—"

"And we might not," Bolan interrupted. "And if we didn't, they'd kill her in a second."

"Suppose we shot the house full of tear gas? We've got breathing apparatus you can wear."

Bolan shook his head.

"All right, I've got one more idea. Suppose a car comes around the curve yonder and crashes into a tree? It gets their attention, but it doesn't look like an assault."

"Go on."

"What I'll do is run a car up against a tree and set off a grenade under the hood. If you didn't happen to be watching, you'd take that for a wreck."

"That's a deal," Bolan agreed. "Keep an eye on the roof. When I'm ready to go in, I'll give you four quick blinks with the flashlight."

A minute later Bolan was in the tree, crawling out on one of the lower limbs toward the roof of the house. A minute after that he'd put his feet down gently on the roof. The rafters had creaked but not loud enough for anyone in the house to have heard.

The roof was steeply pitched. The surface was asphalt shingles.

He looped his rope around the vent pipe from the plumbing and slid down toward the eave on the south side. When he reached the leaf-choked eavestrough he leaned over and looked down to locate a window.

He was directly above one.

Long since trained to go down a rope, feet up or feet down, Bolan went down feet up. With the rope looped around him, he hung with one hand free and peered through the window.

The room inside was absolutely dark. He decided to take a chance. With the muzzle of the silenced Beretta, he tapped the glass lightly. No reaction.

He took another chance, cupping the lens of the flashlight inside his hand and shining a little light into the room. Still, nothing. No reaction.

He could see that he was looking into a bedroom. In the short moment of light the warrior gave himself, he saw a bed and a dresser. He tried the window, but it was locked.

He stared into the darkness of the road, wondering if Harrigan had his car ready. There was one way to find out.

He pointed the flashlight toward the road and blinked it four times. The explosion was a sharp crack, followed by a secondary explosion and the whump of escaping flame. In that moment of noise Bolan shoved the muzzle of the Beretta through the window. The roar of the grenade, plus the ripping and banging of torn metal and breaking auto glass, covered the crash of window glass.

The Executioner reached through, turned the latch and raised the window. Once inside, he used the light for a moment to fix his bearings. Then he threw himself across the room and pressed against the wall beside the door. No one came to investigate. No one opened the door.

He switched on the flashlight again and explored the room. On the nightstand by the bed were Polaroid pictures of Kathryn. She was injured, bleeding, chained...

This *was* where she was being held. He stared at the pictures. There would be no quarter given. Now there was no question.

The warrior eased the door open and stepped into the hall, which was dimly lighted with glare from the fire across the road. Maybe they were at the windows downstairs, looking at the accident.

But he checked the upstairs rooms before he went down, covering his back. A bathroom. Two more bedrooms. Nobody.

But the house was obviously occupied. The beds were jumbled; half-empty glasses sat on the bedside table in the biggest bedroom; the ashtrays were full.

He went to the stairs, lay prone on the floor and looked into the hallway below. Still nobody.

Convinced now that the house had been abandoned, the warrior descended the stairs, pistol up and ready. Living room, dining room, kitchen—nobody.

The Executioner found the door to the cellar and jerked it open. A dark, smelly hole. That was where they had confined her. He could smell fuel oil and coal dust.

He switched on the flashlight and started down the wooden stairs. Suddenly he stood in a glare of white light. Someone had switched on an array of brilliant lights, most of them on stands, and they burned into the soldier.

Bolan threw himself to the right, crashing through the stair rail, hurling his body against the wall four feet away. He struck hard and fell hard, but that was what saved him from the burst of slugs that ripped through the stairs and pounded into the stone wall behind him.

He rolled over, firing two shots toward the lights. The .44 Magnum slugs cracked through the cast-iron body of an old furnace.

Another burst of assault rifle fire smashed into the wall to Bolan's right and ricocheted, whining and chipping stone. There was only one man, apparently, behind the big furnace.

"I know you'd show up sooner or later." Bolan guessed. "Connelly?"

"Let's see just how good you are."

"Is she still in the coal bin? Alive?"

"Walk in and see."

"If you get past me, you're still dead. I'm not alone."

"More alone than you think," Connelly taunted.

As he kept Connelly talking, Bolan studied the situation. The .44 slugs had shattered some of the cast iron of the furnace, but they hadn't punched through and out the back of the thing. He couldn't get to Connelly as long as he was back there. On the other hand, Connelly couldn't get to him either without stepping out to take aim.

Actually, that wasn't entirely so. How long would it take him to figure out that his ricochets had a good chance of getting Bolan if only he lowered his aim?

"I volunteered to stay down here and get you," Connelly said.

"Brave man."

"You've led a charmed life, American. Maybe that's because you've never met Brian Connelly before. That is, you didn't meet him before you mangled his face and gave him a reason to kill you."

"I hadn't heard that you ever needed a reason."

"Ha!"

Keep him talking. The more he talked, the less he thought.

By now Harrigan had to have heard the firing inside the house. Where was he?

What had Connelly said? "You're more alone than you think."

Okay. So that was how it was. He had to keep the man talking.

"Did you have her before you killed her?" Bolan asked. That question was bound to get some sort of a response.

"I didn't kill her, if it makes you feel any better. And you don't know *anything,* American. You're into something you don't understand at all."

Bolan put that in the back of his mind. What did Connelly mean by that?

In the forefront of his mind was something very different. The answer.

The cords from the lights on stands ran one way to a multiple-outlet box that lay on the floor by the furnace. And from that box a heavy cord ran to the entrance box, to the box where electricity came into the house.

The warrior leveled the Desert Eagle on the entrance box and fired. The box exploded in multiple flashes of blue fire, and all the lights went out. Only Bolan had a flashlight.

"Smart!" Connelly yelled. "Smart, you son of a bitch!"

Bolan crawled fast toward the furnace, so as not to be where he figured Connelly would let loose a long burst.

He was right. The cellar lit up for a moment in the yellow glare of that burst. The slugs spattered around Bolan's former position.

Connelly had sense enough to move. Firing at the point where his muzzle-flash had come from would be futile.

Bolan heard the distinctive sound of a fresh magazine being shoved into an automatic weapon. The Executioner was ready for Connelly now. Shoving the flashlight against his chest, he switched it on. Then, covering the lens in his hand, he thrust it out to his left and rolled it across the floor.

Connelly was visible for a moment in the flash from his muzzle. Long enough to take aim.

The Desert Eagle boomed, and the cellar was brightly lighted for an instant in that commanding muzzle-flash. Bolan didn't see Connelly fall, but he heard his weapon clatter on the stone floor.

The warrior picked up his flashlight and shone the beam into the coal bin. Cot, chamber pot, chain. She was gone.

NO ONE WAS OUTSIDE.

What had Connelly said? That he was more alone than he thought.

Across the road the shattered car still burned. No emergency assistance had arrived yet.

Bolan circled around the next house to the north and crossed the road. He moved under cover of the persistent darkness and approached the burning car.

He all but stumbled over Mike Harrigan's body. The detective lay facedown, shot in the back of the head. A gangland execution. A terrorist execution.

Bolan glanced around, his every sense acute. He heard a low moan. Lying a dozen yards from Harrigan was the local constable. Bolan knelt over him.

The old constable's handsome mustache was red with his blood. "They called us traitors," he mumbled. "Ireland's constant problem, they said. Informers. They're...beasts! Do something, American! At least get the word..."

KATHRYN SAT in the back seat of the low, sleek Ford. Her handcuffs were tied to a rope around her waist, and she still wore the leg irons. She was gagged, her mouth full of dry cloth, bound in place by a strip tied tightly around her jaw.

She had seen what had happened. All of them had seen. Brian Connelly had been left to kill Colonel MacKenzie, and when the front door of the house opened, it had been MacKenzie, not Connelly, who stepped out.

Finnerty had stomped on the accelerator, and the Ford had sped quietly and smoothly away, beyond interference by a man on foot, no matter how brave he might be.

"Brian..." Molly whispered.

"A good man," Finnerty said.

"Good! How good could he have been?"

"If the word from Aoudella is true... If Ballem is really dead—"

"Then we concentrate on what we have to do," Molly interrupted. "Damn the cocaine and heroin! Damn all the AK-47s in the world! We've got one clear job to do!"

"Rid the world of Her Britannic Majesty," Finnerty muttered.

"Or her heir. We've got all we need. A few more brave men. Two more MILAN launchers. We—"

"Let's not forget that the money that bought them came from the enterprises you're so ready to condemn," Finnerty chided.

"But the damn enterprises have accomplished their purpose. I sold my body on the street while it served my purpose, and when it didn't anymore, I concentrated on what counted!"

Timothy Finnerty fixed his eyes for a moment on the woman he had married—not even glancing at the road ahead for that moment. He had married her for her strength. Whore she was—for sure—but tough, shrewd and devoted to the cause.

It had been Molly who had put her Walther PPK to the back of Harrigan's head and executed an informer. He himself had shot the constable, and he knew he had left him alive. He couldn't steel himself to fire the second shot—if for no other reason than to have to hear Molly's scorn over his needing a second shot.

"Purpose," Molly grunted.

"Molly, I—"

"I married you," she said, "because you're a born leader. You're a coward, Tim. You'll run from danger. Sometimes you're not too smart, but you make a good appearance, and you make a pretty speech. Connelly followed you for the same reason. He was a better man than you, but he was smart enough to know he couldn't inspire devoted followers the way you do." She paused and shrugged. "You're the Adolf Hitler of our cause, Tim."

"*Molly!*"

"Are you shocked?" she asked scornfully. "Every leader of a real cause—what the Establishment likes to call a terrorist cause—is like Hitler to one extent or another. *He* knew how to lead! He knew how to put a cause ahead of everything! The late, lamented Modu Ballem had Hitler's charisma but not his courage or intelligence. And you, Tim, have all the charisma. You have part of the rest of it. And I married you because I can supply what you lack."

Finnerty shook his head, not to negate what she had said but to express his confusion over the many ideas she had included in what she had just said.

"So let's clean up everything and get to the main cause," Molly suggested.

Finnerty wasn't sure exactly what that meant, but he nodded.

"The first thing we do is get rid of that piece of garbage in the backseat. A quick shot to the head and leave her in the ditch."

"*No!*"

"What do you mean, 'no'? She's outlived her usefulness, Tim. Back there she was bait to bring the American into the trap we set for him, and he escaped the trap and got away. So what good is she now?"

"Molly, we will not kill her," Finnerty grated with unusual firmness.

"What do you plan to do—carry her around for the next ten years?"

"Molly—"

"What the hell's the deal?"

"I have my reasons," he said glumly.

"Do you think it would be entirely inappropriate to tell your wife what your reasons are? Was there some kind of relationship between you two sometime in the past?"

"Molly—"

"*No!* Not 'Molly.' Not 'Molly go away and don't ask questions.' No, by God! Just why can't we dispose of the informer in the backseat?"

The woman withdrew a pistol from her handbag. "Why, Timothy?" she asked coldly.

Finnerty stared at the road ahead. "Because she's my sister."

CHAPTER FIFTEEN

"I understand it now," Bolan said. "I had time to think it through on my way back here."

He was in a room in a motel a short distance from Heathrow Airport. Hal Brognola had just arrived on the Concorde, and Sir Reginald Townley had joined them for a talk about what had happened and what was to come next.

"Somebody in Mike Harrigan's office was watching and listening while he was doing his detective work to find Finnerty. That same somebody saw me there. Whoever it was called Finnerty and warned him."

"So why do you suppose they killed Inspector Harrigan?" Brognola asked.

"I'd guess there were no more than two or three guys in the office who had the intel and could have warned Finnerty," Bolan said. "Mike would have figured out which one it was."

"Somebody else will figure it out, too," Brognola grunted. "The traitor was with you in Thurles. What's more, he picked the other men who went out from Dublin. All of them were traitors. When they went back to Dublin—"

"I doubt if any of them went back," Bolan said. "They were IRA. The way they see it, they killed two informers, which made them heroes. They've gone over entirely now and are sitting this morning in some IRA house being saluted for their service to the cause.''

Brognola chewed on his cigar. ''The raid at Aoudella has raised a noisy stink at the United Nations. Some of the delegates have called it a CIA operation and complained that we destroyed a fertilizer factory and brutally murdered the president of a Third World country.''

''The 'Sublime Leader' committed suicide,'' Townley commented dryly.

Brognola nodded. ''So where's Finnerty? And where's Kathryn O'Connor? And what's next?''

''Kathryn is . . . dead,'' Bolan said. ''She's got to be by now.''

Townley reached for the pot and refilled his cup. ''The Special Branch has a very considerable file on Timothy Finnerty. I doubt Kathryn is dead. I'm not sure I can tell you why, but I do doubt it. No, I think he'll keep her with him, and I think what's left of the Curran Brigade will fix its attention one hundred percent on its goal of assassinating a member of the Royal Family.''

''How many Brigaders are left?'' Brognola asked.

''A good many. Timothy Finnerty has a strange appeal for fanatics. Extremists. The very worst of the IRA. You've destroyed a good part of their arms and almost broken off their narcotics trade, but Finnerty still has men who'll follow him to the death. Uh, *their* deaths, that is. And he has some money, no doubt.

The elimination of Modu Ballem cut off his future supply of narcotics, arms and money, but he has some left. He's still a dangerous man."

"So what's the next move?" Bolan asked. "We can't sit around and wait for something to happen."

"I'm afraid that's all we can do," Townley replied. "He's in hiding again, and until he makes a move, we don't know where to go after him. However, I do have one suggestion, something I saw in Finnerty's file. You might go to Boston..."

BOLAN CROSSED the Atlantic with Brognola on the Concorde. Sequestered in the big Fed's briefcase were photocopies of much of the Finnerty file maintained by Scotland Yard. During the flight he and Bolan discussed the information in the file.

"He withheld something from us," Brognola told Bolan. "I can tell by the page numbers. I don't know what it could be."

"He doesn't trust us."

Brognola shrugged. "Maybe. Anyway, there's enough intel here to make it possible for you to try what he suggested. If you want to."

"Apart from what Finnerty's done to Kathryn, he made it personal when he killed Mike Harrigan. Mike was a friend. I'd started to suspect Mike himself was the traitor, and I was wrong. He was a good, brave man and Finnerty killed him. I'm going to stop Finnerty, no matter what it takes."

Sir Reginald Townley had told Bolan and Brognola that the Curran Brigade had an American branch. Originally the organization had been a fundraising operation exclusively, soliciting donations from Irish Americans who sympathized with the goal of uniting all the counties of Ireland under one Irish government.

But contributions had dried up, according to Townley's intel, when word got back to the States that the Brigade had degenerated into nothing more than a terrorist gang. After that the Boston office of the Curran Brigade became exactly what Finnerty's offices in Ireland had become—centers for drug trafficking, with sidelines in other rackets.

The Brigade, as it was known in Boston, had intruded on the turf of the Palombo family, which had objected strongly. The Palombos had responded in their traditional way, with guns, and the Brigade had reacted in *its* traditional way, with bombs. Two Palombo capos and Virgil Palombo had been blown apart.

Now the Brigade reigned supreme—where it wanted to. The organization didn't try to take over Boston. It only demanded to be left alone—by everybody.

The head man of the Boston Brigade was John Finnerty, known as Black Jack Finnerty—Timothy's younger brother.

Black Jack's job was to collect money and send it to Tim. He skimmed a lot of it—according to Townley's intel—and was the wealthy man his brother was not.

If the Boston Brigade could be broken up, Timothy Finnerty would be left almost entirely without money now that his drug smuggling business in Ireland had been ruined. If he didn't succeed in assassinating someone important on his next attempt, he might not be able to afford the weapons for the next try. MILAN launchers didn't come cheap on the black market.

Townley's intel said that the Irish community in Boston rejected the Brigade as a gang of thugs. It also said that a hard-core of Boston Irish, including many recent immigrants, adhered to the IRA in general and to Timothy Finnerty's Curran Brigade as a band of romantic warrior heroes.

The first problem would be to make contact.

THE EXECUTIONER had long experience in making contact. The people he was looking for didn't hide themselves.

Harvard was as good a place as any. Around the periphery of the campus the dealers in everything worked the streets. The students...sure. The college boys were into drugs as much as anybody else.

None of the dealers knew where the stuff came from, or where the money went. They sold the narcotics, kept their share of the profits and turned the rest over to the collectors. There was no point in trying to find out from them who was really behind the operations. The police knew that. And they couldn't take them all off the streets. Once they were out of circulation, the jailed dealers would be replaced within hours.

Bolan stood on a street corner, observing the action, looking for the Brigade connection.

"Lookin' for somethin'?"

He'd noticed the thin girl in skimpy shorts and halter but hadn't figured her for a dealer. "Well, maybe. Could be. Got somethin'?"

"Only the best. Only genuine. You can't do better around here."

Bolan glanced around. Somebody might be watching. She could be a decoy. Short of that, she might be a girl with a habit, sent out to risk approaching the guy who might be a narc, until the safety of the situation was established.

"Been had," he said. "More than once. Bought what wasn't the real stuff."

The young woman looked at the big man skeptically. "Forget it. Only wanted to sell you fifteen minutes of my time in a nice room."

Bolan closed his hand around her arm. "No, you didn't. I know what you're selling, and we can make a deal. But what I want to know is, how can I be sure it's any good?"

Frightened, she stared at his hand, winced at the grip with which he held her. "I—"

He was alert for anybody who'd seen him grab her. That would bring the guys who protected her, for sure. If anybody protected her.

"I'm no narc," he told her. "You won't get trouble. Or maybe you do have trouble, and if you do, I'm your way out of it."

"You're nuts."

"You got a habit?" he asked.

"What do you care?"

"So the answer's yes. What is it? Coke?"

She nodded.

"Suppose I tell you where you can get it for a dollar a pop," he said.

"You're out of your mind!"

Bolan shook his head. "One dollar. No questions asked. Whenever you need it until you can kick the habit. No arrest. No criminal record."

What the warrior was talking about was a program Hal Brognola had established. It was a pilot project, for witnesses chiefly, but also available to others in need. Justice would supply whatever it took to maintain the habit at one dollar a pop—no questions, no preaching—until the addicts were able to be convinced to get off the stuff.

The dollar-a-pop program freed men and women from their dependence on gang suppliers. This girl, for example. If she could sustain her habit for a dollar a pop, why would she stick with the people who enslaved her for her daily fix?

"Hey..." the girl whispered. "What are you? Some kind of religious nut? What do I have to do? They'll come after me."

"Who'll come after you?"

"I'm not going to say. Why should I throw away my life for some kind of cockamamy idea you—"

"The deal is this," Bolan said firmly. "You can come down off your habit. You can keep it. Either way, you become a member of a federal program. You leave Boston. Yeah, they'd come after you here and maybe get you sooner or later. So we move you to some other city. Where'd you like to go?''

The weak, teary-eyed young woman peered up into Bolan's strong, calm face—and was perhaps encouraged by what she saw there. "Frisco. I always wanted to live in Frisco."

SOCIAL CLUB. It was just a neighborhood bar, but they called it a social club, as if no one but members could come in—which wasn't true. It was a place where men got together and drank and watched the Red Sox games on television.

Right now, tonight, the Sox were playing the Yankees. Guys at the bar stared at the television set above the shelves of bottles. Guys at tables divided their attention between the Red Sox and the women who sat with them.

An Irish bar in Boston. Friendly, and not friendly. The intrusion of Bolan—much as he looked like some of the men in the bar—interrupted conversations, suspended enthusiasm for the Red Sox and generated an atmosphere of suspicious hostility.

They knew their neighborhood, and they didn't like strangers.

"Monahan," Bolan said to the bartender, mimicking as best he could the accents he had heard in Dublin. "Newly in from the old sod. And what is it a man drinks in a good, friendly bar in Boston?''

"Whiskey," the bartender replied. "And what kind will you be havin'?"

"Well, my favorite's Old Bushmills. So you have it on this side of the water?"

Everyone who heard relaxed visibly.

"Old Bushmills," the bartender replied. "And sure. On the rocks?"

"Rocks? What would be 'on the rocks'?"

"Over ice," the bartender told him.

"Ice? You'd pour good whiskey on ice?" Bolan managed to inject just enough horror into his tone.

The bartender grinned as he poured a shot of the Irish whiskey into a small water glass. The warrior tossed back the shot of the fiery liquid. The bar watched and approved. Everyone went back to what they'd been doing before.

The bartender stood by with the bottle, and with Bolan's nod he poured another shot into the glass. Bolan tossed back the second shot. "Well," he said, "we're lucky to be where we are."

"You think so?"

"I mean, the Brits have run wild the last week or so. Somebody murdered Brian Connelly even."

"I don't think I know the name," the bartender said.

"The man was very close to Timothy Finnerty. His right-hand man, some said. Murdered by the Brits. Help from informers. Damn..."

"Finnerty. I've heard the name."

"Every son of the old sod has heard the name."

"You a friend of his?" the bartender asked.

"Well . . . an admirer, let's say."

"I hear that some admire him, some don't."

Bolan grinned. "Some are loyal to the cause. Some are not."

"Monahan, you say?' And where are you livin'?"

"At the Holiday Inn on Broadway," Bolan replied. "Temporarily. I'm not staying in this country long."

"Back across?"

"Yes."

"And why so short a trip, may I ask?"

"I brought some merchandise with me. When I'm rid of it, I'll be going home."

HE FIGURED they'd come, and found them waiting for him when he returned to the Holiday Inn.

"Monahan?"

They caught up with him as he was about to enter the elevator, two husky men in T-shirts and baseball caps.

"What can I do for you guys?"

"You dropped a name in a bar a little while ago. You know what you're talkin' about? Or don't you?"

"I used the name Finnerty," he said. "I figured somebody'd come calling."

The elevator door opened, and the two men pushed in, shoving Bolan in ahead of them. He let them get away with it.

"What do you know about Finnerty?"

"I know he's in deep trouble," Bolan replied. "He's lost everything, just about. Everybody's down on him. He's a fugitive."

"So what's it to you?"

"I know where there's some merchandise. It was supposed to be for Timothy Finnerty, but right now Timothy Finnerty couldn't pay the price of a case of whiskey. So I thought I'd come to Boston and see Jack, see if *he* wants it."

"What merchandise is this, and where is it?"

Bolan shook his head. "Who are you? Why do I tell you guys anything?"

The bigger of the two men grabbed Bolan by the shoulders of his jacket and shoved him hard against the wall of the elevator. The warrior drove his knee upward into the man's crotch, crushing his testicles. The bully moaned, sagged and fainted.

The other man went for a gun and found himself looking cross-eyed at the barrel of Bolan's Beretta 93-R, which was pressed against his nose.

The elevator door opened. The Executioner stepped out and let it close behind him. He ran to the stairs and down to the ground floor of the hotel.

A Honda bike waited for him in the parking lot, chained to a light pole. He'd rented the vehicle, figuring it would come in handy in Boston.

The two big guys came out of the Holiday Inn through a side door—one bent over and staggering, the other supporting him. They got into a Chevrolet and sped out of the lot—shadowed by Bolan.

They weren't hard to follow. The man who'd tried to pull the gun was driving, and driving conservatively. Traffic was heavy, and the bike was the perfect way to tail the Chevrolet. It was nimble in traffic, and inconspicuous.

Anyway, they didn't have far to go. The Chevrolet pulled up to the curb in front of a concrete-block building bearing an illuminated sign that read The Limerick Club.

Bolan drove by, then turned and went back to have a closer look. He saw that the place was a private club, with a sign on the door saying Members Only!

It was the kind of thing you saw everywhere, in run-down neighborhoods usually—the private clubs where the local wise guys congregated. In New York the capos called them hunting and fishing clubs. In Boston the Brophys put Irish names on the clubs and painted green shamrocks on the signs. The Palombos gave theirs Italian names. Whatever anybody called them, they were for the wise guys, the animals that preyed on the city.

And the two bullies had come here to report to…Jack Finnerty? Maybe. Or maybe somebody close to Finnerty. The Executioner would have liked to hear the conversation inside when these two made their excuses to the guy who'd sent them to the Holiday Inn.

A person didn't have to stand on the street and watch very long to figure out what was going on in the Limerick Club.

No women were allowed—no women except those who were selling their bodies. That was what the girl on the street in Cambridge had told him—that the Finnertys used women, just used them.

The girls who went in wore shorts so skimpy that their bottoms showed. They were nobody's wives, nobody's girlfriends. They were what the girl in Cambridge had said—bodies for hire. And she hoped they got enough from the Micks—her word—to make it worthwhile.

The Finnertys were also dealing drugs right out of their club. Cars pulled up, and money and merchandise changed hands right there on the street.

More couldn't be seen from the street, but more was going on. Bolan had witnessed the whole scene before too many times and knew very well what went down inside that little concrete-block building.

BLACK JACK FINNERTY presided over the Limerick Club like some kind of long-ago Irish king—or like some New York Mafia godfather.

He was like his brother in many ways. A man who saw the two would see the family resemblance. Black Jack wore a black beard like his elder brother, and his grin was toothy. But he wasn't as heavyset as Timothy.

He sat in a back room, apart from the bar that filled most of the building. A deep, leather-covered couch dominated the smoky, hot room, which was his office, actually. He leaned back very comfortably into a corner of the couch and fondled the breasts of a young woman who sprawled over him. He smoked a cigar, and a glass of whiskey was within easy reach.

"What the hell do you think you're doing?" he asked angrily when the two henchmen interrupted his leisure.

"The son of a bitch damn near killed Greg—kicked him in the balls," one man said, "and pulled a gun on me. He's no fool and no pushover."

Jack Finnerty shook his head. "Nobody's a pushover when you send two pushovers to handle him. Who the hell is the guy? What's he want?"

"Says he's got a load of merchandise that Tim couldn't pay for. Wants to know if you want it."

"What did you do, try to muscle him?"

"Well . . ."

"Greg, you're lucky your balls are still hanging between your legs. What the hell is this? I send you two to find out somethin', and you try to muscle the guy!"

"The guy—"

"Never mind! You get outside and watch for him. If he shows, run back in here and give the word. Don't try to do him yourselves. Obviously he's better than any six of you. Now, *out!*"

THE EXECUTIONER was carrying the Beretta and the Desert Eagle, more than enough to do the job he had in mind. Right now the problem was how to get into the Limerick Club.

He'd parked the bike down the street, and now he stood in the shadows across the street and watched the traffic around the club. The still-suffering heavyweight who'd taken the shot to the crotch in the elevator left the club and took up a station on the sidewalk. He was joined by his confederate.

Okay. It figured. They were the only two who'd had a look at the guy who might show up and kick the hell out of somebody else. So put them out front to look for him. The move made sense. The boss inside didn't know who the warrior was and wasn't ready for what was about to fall on his head.

Bolan watched the two hardmen across the street. The man who'd taken the knee in the scrotum was still in pain. He walked back and forth, gingerly exercising. He figured the pain would go away...and it could start any time.

A car pulled up, and a dealer lounging in front of the club walked over to the vehicle. He had business to do.

The guy who'd tried to pull the gun spoke to his companion, then went inside, followed by the dealer, who'd wrapped up his business.

Bolan walked across the street. "How ya feelin'?" he asked the bully.

The guy stepped back toward the door, spreading his arms wide, holding his palms toward the warrior in a gesture of surrender.

"Who's in there?" Bolan asked. "Finnerty himself?"

The man nodded.

"Want to take a message to him?"

Another nod.

"Okay. First thing, I've got a little object I want you to take in to him." He handed the man a .44 Magnum cartridge. "You know what this means?"

The bully nodded a third time. "Yeah. I heard what this means."

"Okay. So carry the message. Tell Jack Finnerty I'm out here, waiting for him. Tell him he's got two choices—come out and face me, or get the hell back across the Atlantic. Starting tonight. It's midnight. I give him four hours to make it plain he's pulling out."

"I get ya."

BOLAN FIGURED it wasn't safe to sleep in his room in the Holiday Inn. Jack Finnerty would react one of two ways—he'd retreat, or he'd attack. If he didn't attack, at the very least he'd check his chances. He'd send a team to see if the tough guy went to his room to sleep.

Somebody had left a Cadillac unlocked in the parking lot. Bolan got into the back seat, made himself reasonably comfortable and settled down to wait.

They came at 3:00 a.m., three guys in a Ford. Bolan watched as they cracked the lock on the back door of the hotel and entered. He had no doubt about where they were going, what they'd do—go to his room, take him out if he was there.

He was waiting when they came back out. He'd used the silenced Beretta to put a bullet hole through the windshield, squarely in front of the driver, where it would have exploded his head if he'd been behind the wheel. No one had heard the pop of the subsonic round, but the hole was unmistakable. The warning was dramatic.

It was enough. The wise guys abandoned the Ford and ran.

THE HIT TEAM had left what they considered a warning—a trashed room, searched, overturned, with a warning note left in the bathroom: Not afraid. War. Jack.

Well, maybe... He'd see.

It was safe to sleep in the bed now. Bolan jammed a wedge in the door and slept with the Beretta in his hand, but dawn came quietly.

He showered quickly and shaved, then spent a few minutes restoring the room. No point in making the poor little maid do that. He called down for coffee and ham and eggs.

The warrior knew he had to wait for the next move. And there would be one unless they figured he'd pulled out of here. As a smart man would.

But he had a hunch that he should stay put, that something would come here—something he'd miss if he left.

Before he finished his coffee that something came. The knock on the door was firm but not strong. At first he supposed it was the maid come to make up the room. Even so, he had the Beretta in his right hand when he opened the door.

"Good morning."

His visitor was an elderly woman. In her seventies, he guessed. Her face was deeply wrinkled, and she blinked at him through thick bifocals, but she stood erect, confidently balanced, and she wore the clothes of a middle-aged woman—a light gray linen jacket over a white silk blouse and a pair of dark blue slacks. She'd caught sight of his pistol before he slipped it behind his back, but apparently she wasn't surprised or alarmed by it.

"Good morning," Bolan said. "What can I do for you?"

"My name's Mrs. Desmond O'Connor," she said. "I'm Kathryn's mother."

SHE AGREED to Bolan's suggestion that he order another pot of coffee.

"I'm a surprise to you, hmm?" she asked when he'd put down the phone.

Bolan nodded. He'd offered her the only chair in the room, and he sat on the unmade bed.

"You needn't tell me where Kathryn is," she said. "I know."

"I've done—"

"Yes, I'm sure you have. But don't you wonder how I knew who you are and why I've come to see you?"

"I'm curious about both," he admitted.

"You identified yourself to Jack by sending the big cartridge. You told him you're the same man who's been fightin' Tim in Ireland."

"But you said you're Kathryn's mother. What's your relationship with the Finnerty brothers?"

"They're my sons," she said. "Tim and Jack are Kathryn's half brothers."

Bolan frowned hard, skeptical. "She's been injured. Her brother hurt her, or allowed her to be hurt, and she's being kept in chains."

The woman nodded. "Timothy's a strange man. Still, I don't think he'd kill her."

Bolan shook his head. "I don't have much confidence."

"The way it was," Mrs. O'Connor went on, "was that himself—I mean Finnerty, the boys' father—was a hard man, a violent man. Killed a policeman, he did. So they hanged him for it. That was in 1939. I was left with three children to raise—a daughter, the eldest, and the two boys. I did the only thing I knew to do. I went out on the street and sold myself. But I was very lucky. Not so soon, but after about ten years, I met the late Mr. O'Connor. Desmond. He knew what I was, but he asked me to marry him. So I did, and we had a daughter, Kathryn. She's the best of my children. I suppose the good things in her come from her father."

"When did you come to America?" he asked.

"When Jack came. I was a widow for the second time. Timothy married a bad woman. I didn't want to be with him. Bad things are going to come from him. *Have* come from him."

Bolan nodded. "So why have you come to see me?"

"Jack sent me to tell you that Tim will kill Kathryn if you don't leave Jack alone. I'm not supposed to tell you I don't believe that. I'm supposed to say my piece—what Jack wants me to say—and leave. But I'm tellin' you something different. I'm tellin' you, go back. Go back to Ireland. I've heard them talkin' on the phone, Jack and Tim. Somethin' bad is gonna happen. Somethin' awful!''

"Do you know what?"

"Somethin' they say will bring about a revolution in Ireland. Listen to me! My sons are bad men. I'm not proud of those two. But Jack's just a petty criminal here in Boston. That's all he is, my younger son. And if you stop him from doin' what he does, someone else will do it.'' She shook her head emphatically. "But Timothy is somethin' worse. He's makin' ready to commit some horrible crime. You've got to stop him."

"Why are you telling me this?"

"For Kathryn," Mrs. O'Connor said solemnly, "and for Ireland. I love my daughter and my country. And something horrible is going to happen to both of them."

"Take a message back to Jack, then, will you?"

She nodded.

"Tell him I'll see him later."

CHAPTER SIXTEEN

Kathryn couldn't figure out Molly. Sometimes she thought the woman was determined to kill her, no matter what Tim said. Other times Molly was kind to her, bringing her extra food or a glass of whiskey, and still other times she observed Molly studying her closely, with intent curiosity in her eyes.

They had moved to Belfast. Ulster—Northern Ireland—was home to the real fanatics. Finnerty had a hard-core following, a little band of cold men who were ready to do anything he said. They treated Finnerty with deferential respect, as if he were a hero.

They had weapons and money, and they were planning a major move. They came to the house to talk. She could see them from her window, hear them through the door of the room where she was confined.

Kathryn wasn't locked in a coal bin anymore, and she suspected she had Molly to thank for that. They were in a modest, soot-stained brick house on a soot-stained Belfast street. She was locked in a bedroom at the back of the house, and because the Curran Brigaders came to the house through the alley and in the back door, she could watch their comings and goings. Sometimes her brother walked out to greet them in the walled backyard, and she saw them pay their respect to him—everything but kiss his hand. Because they talked loud, with arrogant confidence, she could hear something of what they said.

That was how she had found out that they were scheming something big. But there was nothing she could do about it.

Kathryn still wore handcuffs and leg irons, and her leg irons were chained to a steam pipe. She could get close enough to the window to look out, but not close enough to touch the glass or break it. She'd been given two dishpans of water, and soap, and allowed to wash the coal dust off her skin, and Molly had taken away her soiled clothes. For two days she'd been naked until Molly returned with a pair of tattered blue jeans and a man's vest undershirt—what she'd worn since.

Kathryn had lost count of the days, but it was about two weeks now since she'd had free use of her arms and legs. Her muscles were cramped; her wrists and ankles were bruised. She stumbled around the room a little, jerking on her leg irons. She tried to discipline herself to do what exercises she could, but most of the time she just lay on the bed, staring at the ceiling, or sat looking out the window.

Waiting.

Waiting for what? She didn't know.

FINNERTY SAT at the kitchen table, sucking hard on a cigarette, gulping whiskey. Molly stood at the sink, also smoking, also drinking, but feeling both critical and a little worried about the way her husband was letting the Brigaders see him pour down whiskey. If he ever lost the confidence of these men, he was history.

If the three Brigaders sitting at the kitchen table with him noticed that he was drinking a good deal of whiskey, they showed no sign of it. They nauseated Molly, these Belfast types, the way they treated Tim as if he were a man who could do no wrong.

And he played them like musical instruments. He used them. He *was* smarter than they were, and he dominated them. But it was a dangerous game, she thought.

"Okay," he was saying to them now. "We have to do what we can with what we've got. I suppose you read in the papers or saw on the telly that the so-called Sublime Leader was murdered by the Brits. Understand what that means to us, gentlemen. In the past three months we received ten thousand AK-47s from him. On credit. We were paying him off by handling his cocaine and heroin for him—making a profit of our own, besides. Now, no more weapons. No more 'merchandise.' We'll find other sources in time, but until we do we have to live on what we've got in hand."

"We've got plenty enough for what we've got to do," said one of the three, a man older than Finnerty, with white hair falling over a flushed forehead. "Except for the MILAN launchers. We've got but two left—and four rockets. I wish we had more. They're our artillery. If we offered enough money, could we—"

Finnerty interrupted him with a shake of his head. "We paid a fortune for each one we had. A *fortune*. But even if we offered a fortune now, we couldn't buy any more. The word's out. Anybody who sells us one is apt to suffer what the Sublime Leader suffered. At the hands of the SAS."

"We've got enough," another man said. "All we need is the opportunity."

"It will have to be done across the water," Finnerty replied. "I hardly need tell you that Her Britannic Majesty isn't coming on a state visit to Ireland."

"What if we got Charlie instead?" the third man asked.

"He's not coming to Ireland, either."

"Ah, well . . ."

Finnerty shoved his glass toward Molly and with a curt nod ordered more whiskey. When she poured him a short one, his eyes flashed, so she poured more.

"One of our MILAN launchers is in Scotland," Finnerty told his men. "The other's in Cork. That one has got to go across. We mount the attack with two of them."

"What attack, Tim?"

"I don't know yet for sure. We'll find the opportunity. Her Majesty or His Highness, one or the other. Her if we can, him if we can't. Now . . . we've got to get our best men in place in England with the best of our weapons. We've lost a lot. Men and weapons. We can't afford to lose more. I want you to get across the water. You know how to do it—how to get men and weapons across the Irish Sea. We'll set up our rendezvous there, and a system of communications. And when the time comes, which it will within the next few days, we'll move together and do what we have to do."

The white-haired man raised his glass. "It will be glorious!" he cried.

Finnerty and the others drank his toast, but Finnerty hadn't finished issuing orders, and he went on. "No more than a small part of everything in any one boat," he warned. "Men. Weapons. We may lose a boat or two. The Brits are on top-stage alert. Don't let them destroy much by sinking one boat. There's only one boat we can't afford to lose—the one carrying the MILAN launcher."

"Another one, too, Tim," the white-haired man said.

"Oh? Which one is that?"

"The one carrying yourself, Timothy Finnerty. We can't afford to lose you. That's for sure."

"A DAMN QUICK TRIP of it," Sir Reginald Townley said. He'd met Bolan at the gate as he came off the Concorde at Heathrow Airport. "Damn quick. Didn't like Boston?"

"I was confronted with— Well, you know."

"I know...?"

"The page you tore out of the file you gave to Hal and me. The family relationship."

"Sorry about that, old boy. I wasn't sure how you'd react to it."

"Kathryn's mother lives in Boston. The mother of the Finnerty brothers. And she came to see me. Jack sent her to warn me off if I didn't want Kathryn killed. The old lady chose to tell me something else—that Tim Finnerty is about to launch a major operation. She overheard a telephone conversation between Tim and Jack. And she says she loves Kathryn and Ireland more than her two sons. She urged me to rush back over here. It's about to hit the fan, she said.''

"I'm getting some hints of that myself," Townley admitted.

"The old problem?"

"Right, the old problem," the Englishman said. "For the Irish, anyway. They talk too much, and we British have formed a long habit of listening."

Townley had used his authority as a top-ranking officer of Scotland Yard to take Bolan around passport and customs checks so that the return of "Colonel MacKenzie" to London would be as little noticed as possible—and so his weapons could come through without trouble.

It was an odd morning in London—blue sky, bright sunshine, a moderate wind. A driver waited at Townley's car. He sped out of the airport toward London.

"Detective work falls into two main branches," the Englishman said as the car left the boundary of the airport and entered the motorway. "Computer work. And we've got some damn good computer work going. We've got a computerized model of Her Majesty's activities and itinerary for the next month—together, in fact, with the same for the other Royals. We're matching that intel with what we pick up about the activities of various known IRA terrorists. It's very technical, that kind of thing.''

''So what's the second main branch of detective work?'' Bolan asked.

''Let me save the answer for a moment. Right now we've got something damn ominous. In the past twenty-four hours there's been a significant exodus of Irish terrorists from their usual haunts. Men we keep an eye on are in motion. Where are they going? What for? I like what your old lady in Boston told you. I like it very much. It fits the pattern we see developing.''

''I didn't think she was lying.''

''The second element of detective work,'' Townley went on, ''is to go out and get the bastards. How'd you like to ride with me on a patrol boat tonight in the Irish Sea? They're coming across. That's almost certain. It's time to go hunting. Soldiers who don't reach the battlefield don't fight. Or, better put, terrorists who don't reach England don't commit murder here.'' Townley's face darkened. ''It's gloves-off time.''

SOMEONE REMOVED the blindfold from her eyes and untied the gag. Kathryn blinked and spit out the dry rag from her mouth.

''Keep very quiet, little girl,'' Finnerty muttered, ''and you'll be okay.''

Molly had her by the arm and urged her forward. Kathryn stumbled across the plank and onto the boat.

It was a fishing boat and stank of fish—fresh fish, rotten fish, a decade of fish blood and fish guts spilled on its decks.

More than that, it was a modest fishing boat. Sure. An inconspicuous fishing boat. She read the name painted on a board mounted just below the windows of the cabin. *Dundrum*.

As Kathryn shuffled into the cabin, she noticed the twin .50-caliber machine guns mounted on the rear.

A modest fishing boat.

MACK BOLAN and Sir Reginald Townley boarded a black-painted, heavily armed patrol boat on the waterfront at Blackpool. Their small jet had landed at Woodvale, and they had been transferred to Blackpool by helicopter.

The patrol boat belonged to MI5, and its crew were trained intelligence officers. If something awkward happened, this crew would keep it quiet, no matter what.

There was no point in going to sea until it was dark. The boats that ran illegal whiskey, narcotics, arms, illegal aliens, and whatever else across the Irish Sea didn't move in daylight. They waited until the night fishing fleets were out—ninety-five percent honest fishermen eking out a living in an overfished sea—and hid themselves among those hundreds of little boats.

"It's a big sea," the skipper of the patrol boat grunted, "and we'll be in international waters. Wouldn't want to make a mistake."

The boat wasn't named, or even numbered. Among the crew it was called the *Mountbatten,* for the World War II hero viciously murdered, with his grandchildren, by the IRA.

IN THE HEADQUARTERS of the Irish Constabulary in Dublin, a black crepe ribbon hung on the door of the office that had belonged to Inspector Michael Harrigan. Down the hall was the office of the man who had been his superior—Inspector Supervisor Duncan Rafferty.

Rafferty was on the telephone. "Just put the word out," he said. "Every channel of communication. Whatever you can do. Let the docks know. That goddamn murdering patrol boat's at sea. The one they call the *Mountbatten*."

THE PATROL BOAT WAS a night hunter. Its supersensitive radar scanned the night sea. Townley explained the radar to Bolan.

"Look at the blips. You know what they see? Diesel engines. Not the wooden hulls. The steel of the engines and power train. That's what reflects the signal. Look here. See how much bigger this blip is? That means he carries something more than engine and so on. What? Maybe guns. More reflecting steel."

The warrior stared at the green spots glowing on the face of the radar screen. His first thought was that he'd seen far more sophisticated radar and that Townley's enthusiasm was misplaced. His second thought was that these guys, using this radar, had run down a thousand gun-running fishing boats over the past couple of years and that nothing was wrong in placing confidence in an operation that had been a success.

He heard and felt the acceleration of the diesels. The skipper was going to check out the boat that had generated a larger radar blip.

ON BOARD the *Dundrum,* where Kathryn O'Connor sat chained in the cabin, a strange, intense man talked with Timothy Finnerty.

"The decoy is among the fishermen," he said.

"Never underestimate the murderous English," Finnerty warned. "They didn't build a world empire by being easily deceived."

"Barbarians..." muttered the intense man, who was the captain.

"We're outsmarting them," Finnerty said. "We're going to win this battle."

Kathryn's eyes had adapted to the dim light in the cabin, which was only the faint orange glow off the compass and other instruments clustered around the wheel, but it was enough to enable her to make out the faces of Tim and the captain—the faces of zealots, fervent, agitated, and yet somehow oddly at peace in their complete certainty about what they were doing.

From their conversation she understood the plan for the night. What the captain had referred to as a decoy was a boat set up to make a big radar echo. Thin steel plates had been hung over its sides and propped against its cabin.

It carried no contraband—no arms, no narcotics, no wanted men. If the British patrol boat stopped it and searched it, the searchers would find nothing. In fact, they wouldn't even find the steel plates, which would be cut loose and dropped into the water at the last moment. The British would be left wondering how this boat had produced so emphatic a blip on their radar screen.

As a decoy it had two purposes. Its primary purpose was to lure the patrol boat away from this boat, the one carrying Timothy Finnerty to England. Its second purpose was to lure the patrol boat within the range of several heavily armed boats.

The decision about whether or not to open fire would depend on how far away the *Dundrum* was. If it was at a safe distance, the attack would be made. But the attack wouldn't be risked until the *Dundrum* was clearly safe.

ABOARD THE PATROL BOAT Bolan stood beside the captain and watched the green smears on the radar scope.

"Painting a lot of traffic," the captain said.

Paint was the word they used for the smears of phosphorescent green caused by a radar reflection. The smears brightened with each sweep of the beam, then faded almost completely before they were reinforced again by another pass of the rotating beam.

One smear in the middle of a lot of other smears was clearly brighter than the others. The boat either had a steel hull or was carrying a load of weapons.

"We'll go for him," the captain declared. "Got to remember, though, that he could be a decoy."

The captain pressed a button and a horn sounded on the boat. Men raced from the cabin and took their action stations.

The *Mountbatten* was equipped with two .50-caliber machine guns in two tub mounts on either side aft. The crew were all officers of the Special Branch, and all of them were armed with their choice of weapons.

Bolan and Townley carried H&K G-11 caseless assault rifles. Besides that, Townley had brought aboard ten German-made Armbrust projectile launchers. These shoulder-fired weapons were loaded at the factory, could fire only once and were thrown away after firing. They were loaded either with armor-piercing rounds or fragmentation rounds. These bore fragmentation rounds.

The *Mountbatten* was fast and quiet. Steering by radar, the helmsman slipped the boat among the fishing boats and headed toward the one that was making the big smear on the screen.

Although the fishing boats looked clustered on the screen, they were, in fact, a minimum of fifty yards apart. A supplementary short-range radar with a screen just above the wheel allowed the helmsman to avoid hitting anything.

Most of the fishing boats were lighted. The little rowboats bobbing on the waves were lighted with gasoline lanterns that cast a bright greenish-white glow over the water.

Not all of the boats were lighted, but since none of them had painted a bright smear, the *Mountbatten* ignored them and went for the boat that might be carrying arms.

"THE MURDERIN' BASTARDS are fast," the captain of the *Dundrum* said to Timothy Finnerty. "They're going to be on the decoy in five minutes." The captain was getting radio reports from the fishing boats being passed by the patrol boat.

"What's his course?" Finnerty asked, nodding toward the decoy, which was within sight and no more than a hundred yards away.

"About one-twenty degrees."

"We're running parallel, then." Finnerty glanced at the compass. "Why not turn to, say, one-eighty and make more distance between us and him?"

"We've kept to this course so as to look like just another boat in the fishing fleet," the captain pointed out.

"We don't look like a fishing boat," Finnerty replied. "We're dark. Why not turn on the lights and change course?"

"Well, that'd give our people a chance to shoot up the Brit patrol boat."

"Do it," Finnerty ordered.

STANDING ON THE BRIDGE of the *Mountbatten,* Bolan saw the sudden appearance of lights on one of the boats that had been running dark. "Why'd he do that?" he asked as he picked up a pair of powerful binoculars to have a look at the suddenly lighted boat.

"For a reason, for damn sure," Townley replied. "Maybe he's the one we ought to go after."

"We're within minutes of intercepting the bandit, sir," the captain said. "After we check him out, we can return and chase down that one. He can't make anything near our speed."

"Dundrum," Bolan said, reading the name on the boat.

"He'll be easy to find," the captain told them. "He's turned south, and he'll be out of the group by the time we're ready to go for him. Our radar will pick him up."

"There's a woman on board," Bolan said.

"Not terribly unusual," the captain replied. "Some of the fishermen's wives and daughters go out with them."

"I want that boat," Bolan said grimly. "I have a feeling about it."

"We'll get him."

Fewer of the boats around them now were running with lights. The bandit lay straight ahead, gleaming now on the scope of their short-range radar.

"Look at this, Captain," the helmsman said.

Bolan, too, looked at the scope. As they watched, the bandit target dimmed. It didn't shine on the screen as it had done for the past quarter hour. It dimmed and suddenly looked the same as the other boats around.

"What the hell is going on?" Townley growled.

"He's a decoy," the captain said. "He was carrying steel plates—radar reflectors—and he's thrown them overboard."

"Turn and go after the *Dundrum*," Bolan ordered.

"Right. Left to one-eight-zero," the captain said briskly to the helmsman.

The helmsman used the throttles as well as the wheel to swing the patrol boat around. Then the night erupted in torrents of gunfire. Machine guns on at least four boats, including the bandit, opened up on the *Mountbatten*. Streams of steel-jacketed slugs ripped into the hull and superstructure. Splinters flew; a crewman fell.

The patrol boat returned fire. The twin .50s on the rear fired streams of tracers across the water, and one attacking boat was immediately silenced. But the gunfire pouring into the patrol boat didn't diminish. Other boats were joining the attack.

A gunner on the *Mountbatten*'s rear deck fired an illuminating rocket, which burst above the attackers and began to fall slowly, lighting the attacking vessels in a bright white glare.

Townley shoved two Armbrusts toward Bolan and pointed to the left. The Executioner put the launcher to his shoulder, took aim on the nearest boat to their left and fired. A cloud of plastic flakes flew out the rear as the projectile burst from the tube.

The round struck the cabin of the attacking boat and burst through the thin wood before it detonated. More than two pounds of explosives filled the cabin and sprayed the rear deck with a hellstorm of high-velocity shrapnel. In the light from the descending flare the warrior saw the attacker's machine gunner literally ripped to pieces. The cabin fell apart, and he could see the man at the wheel—collapsed over it, a bloody mass of torn flesh.

Bolan had another Armbrust at his shoulder, and just before he fired he watched as Townley's first round exploded on another boat. The effect was equally devastating.

Another star shell burst overhead, preserving the illumination. The attacking boats were turning away—the Executioner could see their helmsmen frantically twisting their wheels—but their machine gunners kept firing. Two men lay dead on the *Mountbatten,* and two more lay wounded. Bolan hadn't realized that the bridge was armored until he felt the shock of heavy artillery impacting and realized it wasn't punching through.

The boat that had lured them there, the decoy, was among Bolan's targets. There was no machine gun on board, but assault rifle fire was coming from half a dozen flashing, spitting muzzles.

Bolan fired his second Armbrust at the vessel. The projectile glanced off the rail, splintering a gaping hole, but didn't explode. Like the first projectile the warrior had fired, this one exploded in the cabin. Townley's second shot blew the boat to pieces.

The Executioner chose a boat that was still firing .50-caliber rounds at the patrol boat and let it have his third fragmentation round. This one hit the machine-gun mount itself, engulfing the gunner. When the thin smoke cleared, nothing of the gunner could be seen.

Five boats were out of commission. Now they had to be careful about identifying targets. They didn't want to fire on innocent fishermen.

Others had fired, but since their gunners had had the sense to cease firing so as to avoid being targets, it was impossible to distinguish them from the other boats that were innocent.

Half a dozen boats were flying white flags. One fisherman stood atop his cabin and waved a big white cloth. In a moment he fell, shot down by a burst from one of the retreating boats.

"Now for the *Dundrum*," Bolan said to the captain.

The captain shook his head. "We took fire from at least six heavy machine guns, and we've got big holes in the hull and are taking on water. We've got a ruptured fuel tank and are leaking fuel oil fast. Besides, we've got wounded who have to get to hospital. I'm afraid we'll have to make for home as fast as we can . . . and hope we make it."

JUST BEFORE DAWN the *Dundrum* slipped quietly into Colwyn Bay where a van was waiting at the dock. Four people left the boat, which immediately departed. Obviously the fishing boat had delivered someone from Ireland. No one who saw it cared. The curiosity of two men was piqued by one thing, but they were busy and didn't bother to report it to the local police station for another hour.

"Odd thing," one of them said to the constable in the station. "A girl came off the boat. In irons, she was. She could hardly walk for the chains on her legs. They hurried her along, and she kind of stumbled. Odd, don't you think?"

The constable thought it odd enough to telephone Scotland Yard.

CHAPTER SEVENTEEN

"I knew he wouldn't kill her," Townley said to Bolan. "Anyway, I thought he wouldn't. But there's no point in searching for a dark green van."

"He's smart enough to have transferred into some other kind of vehicle within the hour."

"Anyway, we know he's in England now, or Wales, which means he's about to make his move. So the focus turns to the other part of our detective work—the computer matching of moves by the Royal Family with moves by terrorists."

"Anything promising?"

"As a matter of fact, yes. But I've got something else here. A wire from Hal Brognola. It's in code. Can you read it?"

Bolan studied the wire for a few minutes, using a pencil to turn the numbers and symbols into words. He had memorized the code a long time ago. It was private, between him and the big Fed.

Thought you would be interested to know that John Finnerty is being held without bail on charge of possession of 2.5 kilos cocaine, 3.2 of uncut heroin. Picked up by narcs on a tip. Between you and me in strictest confidence, I'm almost sure somebody planted the stuff on him. He screams that's so, but, of course, no one believes it. Expect he'll do 20 years minimum, maybe 30. I had nothing to do with it, did you? Hope it doesn't interfere with what you're doing in U.K.

Bolan handed the deciphered message to Townley. "I have a pretty good idea who fingered him," he said. "He'll never guess."

"I wonder if Tim Finnerty knows?"

TIM FINNERTY KNEW. The word had reached him from Belfast.

"I understand it. It's a trade they want. Brother for sister."

"Forget it," Molly said. "You haven't got time to think about it. When you're president or prime minister, you can negotiate with the Americans from a position of strength. But you'll never be president or prime minister if you screw up this job. This is your last chance, my boy. If you don't get Her Britannic Majesty this time—or at least His Royal Highness—you're lost, gone and forgotten."

Finnerty glanced at Kathryn. "She's not just my sister now. She's a negotiating chip."

"I'd supposed she always was."

Kathryn sat on a couch. Still wearing handcuffs and leg irons, she was also held by a short chain padlocked to her ankle and to the frame of the couch.

They sat in a mobile home parked in a field on the Salisbury Plain, not many miles from Stonehenge.

Kathryn knew why they were there. The queen was coming to a horse show that was opening the next day and would last the rest of the week. It was one of those occasions when the queen traveled in a private capacity as a horse owner and breeder. While she was there, they'd try to assassinate her.

And if they succeeded—maybe even if they didn't—everything Mike Harrigan had feared, that Mack had come to Ireland to try to prevent, that *she* had dedicated herself to preventing . . . would happen.

Ireland would suffer. What would the British do if IRA terrorists murdered the queen? What *could* they do? Something ruthless.

And here she sat in chains. She could do nothing. Molly was never more than a few feet from her, unless Tim or one of his men was there to watch her. If she screamed, one of them would knock her senseless. Maybe even kill her.

She could do nothing. She'd never guessed a person could know such frustration, could be so completely helpless, so totally without hope.

TOWNLEY SHOWED Bolan a detailed map, also a recent aerial photograph of the area. The village was called Chippenbridge. Half a mile beyond the village stood a wooden grandstand, a complex of barns and stables and a show ring for horses.

"They've put up striped tents since that photograph was taken," Townley told him. "They'll be serving caviar and champagne, not to mention whiskey and beer, roast beef and Yorkshire pudding, and many other good things.''

"Quite a social occasion, I gather.''

"It's not a race, you understand,'' he explained. "They show horses, they sell them. They're race-horses, mostly, but they don't race them at the Chippenbridge Show. There's an auction of horses, but many are traded at private sale. Horsemen come from all over the world to see the horses and buy and sell. It's not a public occasion exactly. You have to have an invitation to get in. Several thousand invitations are issued, but for every person who receives one, ten others wish they could have one.''

"And the queen mingles with the crowd?'' Bolan asked.

"Well, in a sense she does. Obviously she can't mingle with a crowd as you and I could do. She's surrounded by security people who severely limit the number of people who can approach her. Those who are allowed to get near her are well known to her and to her security officers—or they've been discreetly searched before they approach.''

"You're confident someone with a bomb couldn't get near enough to harm her?''

"That's what we've feared for a long time. Explosives. I may say, Mack, we have that aspect of things pretty well under control. We've taken some pretty sophisticated measures.''

"So it comes back to the MILAN launchers.''

"It does. Precisely. Obviously we can use several roads to bring her to the show, and we can put decoy cars on the roads as we did before. But we don't know how many MILAN launchers the Brigade has, and we don't now how big the attack will be. Judging from the number of IRA terrorists moving around this weekend, we have to think it'll be a concerted attack, probably from several directions at once, and possibly with a variety of weapons."

"Maybe the queen should cancel her appearance at this horse show."

"She can't cancel every public appearance," Townley replied. "She must open Parliament, appear on horseback at the Trooping of the Color and, well, there are scores of appearances she has to make. If she can be frightened out of those appearances, effectively the monarchy has been destroyed. She's not willing to allow that to happen, and neither are we."

"Then there's a lot of highway to protect," Bolan said dryly.

"I may as well be frank about something. The cost of all this concentrated security is becoming a burden. I want to protect Her Majesty. I also want to get Timothy Finnerty."

"So do I," Bolan replied.

"GOOD WORK," Finnerty praised. "I knew I could count on you."

He stood beside a horse trailer. It was nothing unusual, just a trailer designed to be towed behind a small van and carry one horse. The three Brigaders—Belfast men—who'd been in Chippenbridge for two weeks had modified the trailer, but the modification was absolutely unnoticeable.

Their work had consisted of raising the floor of the trailer by just twelve inches. Between this false floor—on which the horse would stand—and the bottom of the trailer was a compartment twelve inches deep and as long and wide as the trailer.

Room for a folded MILAN launcher and its missiles. Room also for AK-47s and plenty of ammo loaded in magazines. Room for pistols and grenades.

As Finnerty watched, the three Belfast men showed him how they had trained the horse to walk up the ramp into the trailer. The horse would also back out. They had worked with him for the past three days until the horse had no fear or hesitation.

To gain access to the weapons under the false floor, they had to unload the horse. They could have installed doors in the compartment, but that would have been a tip-off to an experienced security officer. It would have revealed the false floor and the secret compartment.

No. Better that the horse had to back out. His standing on the false floor would also discourage any attempt to check the floor. What security officer would want to crawl between the legs of a horse to check a floor for a trapdoor?

Even if one did, he wouldn't find a trapdoor. There wasn't one. The whole floor pulled out.

"The van and trailer will be absolutely clean," one of the Belfast men said. "Not a weapon in the van or on one of us. We can go through any security check they set up."

"Lucky Kevin knows horses," Finnerty said.

"Y'owe me three hundred pounds, incidentally," the youngest of the Belfast men said. "I had to pay three hundred more than you allowed to buy the horse."

"You need so good a horse?" Finnerty asked.

Kevin stroked the horse affectionately. "You can't go to the Chippenbridge Show with a nag in your trailer. Even the Special Branch knows that much about horses. Anyway, he's an investment. When all is over we can sell him. He doesn't race anymore, but he stands at stud, and he earns his keep and then some."

"You've got your spot picked?" Finnerty asked.

"As good as there is," the oldest Belfast man replied. "We may get a second chance if the first doesn't work. If Her Majesty doesn't pass us comin' to Chippenbridge, maybe she'll pass us on her way out. If she doesn't come this way, maybe she'll go back to London this way."

"The way I want her going back to London is in a body bag," Finnerty growled.

"WHAT'S MY ROLE in this operation?" Bolan asked.

"Quite an independent one, I think," Townley replied. "Everything's tightly organized. Every unit has its assignment. Every man in each unit has his. I believe, though—and have always believed—that every well-organized operation should have what I call some wild cards. I can't play that role myself. Unhappily I've been given overall operational command and will have to stick close to my communications center. But I've given six men wild-card assignments. They're to go where they want, check into anything that looks suspicious and act independently whenever they think they must. You interested?"

"Count me in."

"The other six chaps are veterans of the SAS. All of you will have special passwords, and I'll ask you to carry radios so you can keep in touch with me. I'll brief all of you on communications procedures. Don't want you to get shot by regular units, you know."

THE CHIPPENBRIDGE SHOW opened the next morning, Monday. All Sunday afternoon and all night, trucks and vans had rolled through the village and to the grounds, carrying hundreds of horses to the stables and barns. Green-and-white striped tents went up overnight, and dawn arrivals found champagne breakfasts ready to be served by white-jacketed waiters.

The weather was fine. High clouds cruised overhead, and every Englishman knew that fast-moving clouds could mean a radical change in weather within half an hour. But as the sun rose higher it brought unaccustomed warmth to the Salisbury Plain, relieved by a strong breeze.

The queen was expected a little after noon. There was excitement about that, but that excitement was only part of a general air of excitement and anticipation.

As the morning wore on, the crowd grew. Soon they were elbowing one another. More vans and trailers arrived and had to park along the roads and lead their horses into the grounds.

Every tenth man and maybe every twentieth woman on the grounds was a security officer. They were noticeable only for their subtle lack of interest in the horses. Of all the people on the grounds, they were the only ones who could walk by a beautiful mare or a handsome stallion with hardly a glance. Their eyes were on the crowd. Almost no one noticed when now and again they quietly led someone away. Besides suspected terrorists, they picked up a variety of men and women wanted on other charges. Prison vans parked almost out of sight behind the stables slowly filled with complaining prisoners, and from time to time a van moved away, carrying prisoners to London.

MACK BOLAN RODE a motorcycle, which gave him the mobility he needed for his wild-card role in the operation.

The bike was equipped with a radio that beeped a constant signal, which was a locator for Townley and his staff in their mobile headquarters in a big truck. More important, the beep identified bike and rider for the regulars covering the roads and ground, also for the choppers overhead. In addition to the radio, Bolan had a tiny Handie-Talkie.

He figured the attack on the queen—if there was one—would happen some miles from the horse show. He explored the roads, scanning the roadsides with eyes experienced in finding enemies in the bush or in the fields.

THE QUEEN HAD FLOWN from Windsor to Blackbushe Airport by helicopter. There she changed to the maroon Rolls-Royce. A few minutes after noon the royal automobile, covered from the air and on all sides by security forces, sped west toward Chippenbridge.

The queen was accompanied by her husband, the Duke of Edinburgh. They wore tweed jackets, riding breeches and boots. The duke wore a flat tweed cap. He wasn't quite as much interested in horses as she was, but he was caught up in her enthusiasm for one of her favorite occasions, and they chatted and laughed and were, as far as their driver and bodyguard could see, unconcerned about the threat of assassination.

THE VILLAGE of Warbury was aware of the Chippenbridge Show, some ten miles away, but only one man in the village had received an invitation—an aged country gentleman who in years past had never missed the big horse show but this year considered himself too feeble to go elbowing through a crowd. No one from Warbury was attending the show.

A rumor had circulated that Her Majesty might drive through the village on her way to Chippenbridge. No one was standing around on the street waiting, just the same. Everyone in Warbury had business on a Monday. Everyone was attending to business. Including the rector of Warbury Church.

Dr. Edward Gaitling, the rector, shuffled down the center aisle—shuffled because he was sixty-seven years old and in failing health. He'd read a funeral service in midmorning and had accompanied the grieving family to a cemetery at the edge of town—the graveyard around the church being filled—and had been fatigued by the experience.

Already tired from that, he'd just now had to watch while security agents poked around in his church, looking for God alone knows what. They were gone. He'd assured them he'd telephone them if any strangers entered the church that afternoon. He carried the card with their number in his pocket.

He found comfort in this church, which he'd served these many years. He found comfort, that is, beyond the comfort of religion. He found comfort in the old stones, in the quiet moldiness of the little building. Part of the church was nearly a thousand years old. He enjoyed showing visitors the corner where archaeologists had positively identified stones laid during the reign of King William Rufus, who had died in the year 1100. Most of the church was of later origin, of course—including some lamentable eighteenth-century work that really marred the building.

Dr. Gaitling wanted to kneel and say a short prayer, but his aching knees suggested to him that he had best say his prayer standing. And so he did. He closed his eyes and recited in his mind an old prayer he had enjoyed for fifty years.

The words of that prayer were the last thoughts that ever passed through the reverend doctor's mind. He wasn't conscious, not even for an instant, of the violent blow struck against his head with a steel bar.

The man who had killed the rector didn't let him fall to the floor. He caught him as he toppled and quickly jerked his black coat up over his head to soak up the blood so that it wouldn't fall and stain the stones. Another man entered the church from the side and helped the murderer carry the lifeless body to the east side.

The weapon that had killed the rector was a crowbar. The murderer now wedged it in the crack under the stone top of a tomb. He pried, and the flat lid of sandstone yielded. The other man grabbed the lid, and together they slid it toward one end of the sandstone box.

They had removed two skeletons the previous night. The old bones, with some powdery fragments of what had apparently once been fabric, were in a big plastic trash bag now hidden in the corner of a garage. The tomb contained something more important.

A MILAN launcher and rockets, and two AK-47s. The men removed these weapons and replaced them with the body of the rector. He'd like that, one of them observed, being put to rest in this fine old tomb in his own church.

Timothy Finnerty stood beside a telephone booth on a street corner in the village of Chippenbridge. It was a workaday village, like Warbury, and most people were about their business, not much interested in the horse show at the grounds outside of town.

Finnerty checked the time, then stepped inside the booth and dialed a number.

"Tim?"

"Right."

"Okay. We've got her. They just turned onto Salisbury Road."

Finnerty hung up and dialed another number.

"Mr. Finnerty?"

"Right. The operation's yours. You have ten minutes."

The Irishman stepped out on the street again and lit a cigarette. The boy who'd answered the phone would now get on his bicycle and pedal to Warbury Church. If the team there had done its job, they'd be ready.

He mounted his own bicycle. He'd return to the caravan on the hill outside the town. Molly would be anxious to know what was happening. So, for that matter, would Kathryn.

The field command post had moved closer to Chippenbridge. Though it was supposed to be inconspicuous, the big truck was obviously no ordinary vehicle. The dish antennae on the roof were a tip-off.

Bolan parked his motorcycle beside the truck.

"Colonel MacKenzie? Sir Reginald's expecting you."

Inside, Townley had a huge aerial photograph spread out on a trestle table. The main roads had been marked with colored pens. So had some features of the landscape.

"This is the route chosen for Her Majesty's approach to the horse show." He pointed to a pink line drawn over one of the roads. "Local people call it Salisbury Road. We chose it because the countryside is so open on both sides. We've stationed men in these groves of trees. Farmhouses and barns are covered. The road goes through just one village—Shrewbury. We have soldiers, police and plainclothes operatives there. The village of Warbury is on this intersecting road, almost a mile from the route. Even so, we've got men on the streets there."

Bolan studied the big photo. "What's the scale?" he asked.

"Roughly five inches to the mile."

The warrior picked up a ruler and placed it on the photo, with the five-inch mark on the road the queen was about to take. The end of the ruler and the ten-inch mark signified roughly the range of a MILAN launcher. He ran the ruler across the picture, keeping the five-inch mark on the road.

"We've given special attention to the upper floors of houses and barns," Townley informed him. "Figured they'd want to put the launcher up as high as possible to get the range."

Bolan shook his head. "The MILAN doesn't need high places to fire from. In fact, it works better over level terrain. The rocket flies straight, not in an arced trajectory, and is set to fly about two feet above the sightline. If the launcher tripod is set on the ground, the rocket flies only two to four feet above the ground along a flat line to the limit of its range."

"A mile, you say? But what's the really effective range?"

"A mile."

Townley nodded, but it was obvious that he was skeptical that the MILAN could be fired accurately a full mile.

The telephone buzzed. While Townley picked it up and listened, Bolan continued to study the map.

"In ten minutes she'll be passing this intersection," the Briton said, pointing to the intersection between the queen's route and the side road to Warbury. "In twenty minutes she'll be on the grounds at the horse show."

"I'll go for a ride and be back in twenty minutes."

THE MOTORCYCLE WAS no dirt bike like he'd had at Aoudella. It was a fast, heavy BMW, too glitzy for his taste in bikes, but fast. He roared onto Salisbury Road and sped west.

As Townley had said, the land was all open. Except for groves of trees and farm buildings, which were covered, the only real hiding place within the range of the MILAN was the village of Warbury. The Briton said he had it covered, but his mistaken notion about the effective range of the MILAN and his idea it should be fired from a high place caused Bolan to wonder just how well he had covered this village almost a mile from the road.

The beeper signal from the bike cleared a way for him along a road now thoroughly covered by security forces. He swung north at the intersection and rushed toward Warbury.

ATTACHED TO THE CHURCH on its south side was a venerable little stone house, the rectory. The windows of the building had afforded Dr. Gaitling a restful view over fields and groves, to what locals called Salisbury Road, and beyond across more fields until, in the hazy distance, he had some days seen the spire of the church at Weyminster.

Dr. Gaitling had, in fact, situated his desk to face a pair of glass doors that opened from the study onto a little rose garden he had tended just outside, to give him, as he had said often, a pleasant short-range view as well as a pleasant long-range one.

The MILAN launcher sat on the study floor, facing those glass doors. The man who had murdered Dr. Gaitling lay beside it, studying the road through the sight. He shook his head, and the two men lifted the launcher and moved it a little closer to the doors. The second man moved to open the doors, but the murderer shook his head. They wouldn't open them until the last moment.

The body of Dr. Gaitling's housekeeper lay in the cellar.

The boy who had ridden his bicycle to the church to bring the word from Finnerty was in the church. In the past half hour two people had come in and asked if he had seen the rector. The boy had replied he believed the rector had gone down to Salisbury Road to see the queen pass by.

A third man had ignored the boy, who was a stranger in town, and had looked around the church and then started through the short passage to the rectory. The boy had shot him with a silenced pistol. His body was in a closet.

The rectory was perfect. Lying on the floor again and watching the road through the sight on the launcher, the gunner was pleased with the open view. Only one large tree interrupted the otherwise unobstructed vista. He could see two miles of road. If he should by some chance miss with the first rocket, there would be time to launch a second.

BOLAN RODE into Warbury. A uniformed policewoman stepped into the street and raised her arm.

"Can I help you, sir?"

"Are you receiving my beeper signal?" he asked.

She looked confused. "Beeper, sir?"

Bolan pulled his little Handie-Talkie from his jacket pocket. "Reginald, this is Mack. You've got an officer in Warbury who doesn't seem to have the word."

"Let him listen," Townley's voice boomed from the little radio. "This is Sir Reginald Townley speaking. Who's in command there?"

"Inspector Bradley," the policewoman replied.

"Well, where is he?"

"In his car, I believe."

"Give that man on the cycle every cooperation. And tell Bradley if he's not in the center of town, that's damn well where he should be—where he's conspicuous and on top of everything. Tell him to contact me immediately. Uh, Mack, Her Majesty should be coming in sight from where you are. About now."

Bolan gunned the bike and took off, leaving the policewoman standing in the street. On his way up the road he'd done as much recon of the village as he could. If there was anything going on here, the most likely place was the church. It had big windows facing south, and it would probably be little visited on a weekday afternoon.

He roared up to the door, swung off the bike and strode into the handsome little church.

Not quite abandoned on a Monday afternoon. A youth stood near the altar, looking at him as he walked in. A youth of . . . what? Eighteen?

"You the only one here?" Bolan asked.

The youth nodded. "The rector went down to Salisbury Road to see the queen pass by."

Bolan was instantly alert. How had the rector known the queen would use Salisbury Road? That was a secret Townley had kept from everyone until the last possible minute.

"What makes him think the queen's coming along Salisbury Road?" Bolan said.

The youth's chin jerked up, as if the question alarmed him. Then he recovered himself and shrugged.

Bolan glanced around the church. The queen would be in sight from here about now, Thud had said.

The launcher wasn't in the church. "Where's the rectory?" Bolan asked.

The youth's eyes widened, and he shook his head. "Don't know."

Bolan spotted the oak door that had to lead into the rectory and trotted toward it. And he knew what would happen. He'd guessed, and he also sensed it. Halfway to the door he dived to the floor. A bullet whipped past him and slammed into a stone pillar.

Bolan rolled onto his back and fired a round from the silenced Beretta. The youth sprawled on the floor, but the warrior didn't have time to check for vital signs.

He got to his feet, jerked the door open and ran through the short passage into the rectory.

The door into the study was open, and there it was. The MILAN launcher.

THE GUNNER WHO HAD murdered Dr. Gaitling was tracking the maroon Rolls-Royce in the telescopic sight. He had to let it pass far enough down the road so that the oak tree wasn't in his line of fire. A few more seconds...

He felt a presence and looked up from the sight to see. What he saw was the Executioner.

A subsonic 9 mm round blasted into his head at the base of the skull, but in the convulsion of death he pulled the trigger and fired the rocket. The ejected tube flew back across the room and crashed into a glass-fronted bookcase.

The second man was raising his AK-47 toward Bolan when a round punched through his forehead. The warrior threw himself onto the floor and pressed his eye to the sight of the launcher.

He could see the rocket, could see the sighting flares burning on the tail. The missile was obediently following whatever course the sighting system ordered, and since the launcher had spun around as the murderer rolled away from it, the rocket was flying toward Salisbury Road and at this instant toward one of the police cars preceding the maroon Rolls-Royce.

The cars were spaced maybe fifty yards apart. Bolan shoved the launcher around so that the sight aimed at the gap between two police cars.

As the cars raced along the road, he moved the launcher and kept the missile on course toward that gap, hoping the cars would remain spaced, that a motorcycle wouldn't dash into the gap just as the rocket arrived, that no vehicle would be parked where the rocket had to hit.

He raised the sight, thinking maybe he could make the missile fly above the convoy. But the MILAN system didn't work well on the vertical plane. He had no choice but to let the missile fly through the gap he had chosen.

It did, roaring between the two cars, trailing fire and smoke and its control wire, startling the men in the second vehicle. It plowed into the field a hundred yards from the road and exploded spectacularly.

CHAPTER EIGHTEEN

The church filled with people. The first in were two women, who screamed when they saw the youth, his shirt soaked with blood pouring from a shoulder wound. The women were followed by police officers. They hardly noticed Bolan.

The Brigaders had figured it right, he thought. They could have walked out, too.

As he walked toward his motorcycle, Bolan activated the Handie-Talkie.

"Mack! Did you—"

"Did I miss everybody? Was anybody hurt?"

"What do you mean, did *you* miss everybody?"

"Explain it later. Is everybody okay?"

"Absolutely. Did you get the launcher?"

"I put a bullet through the aiming system before I walked away from it. They've got a mess to straighten out in Warbury. The rector of the church is dead."

"That's unfortunate. The innocent always suffer. Get back to me as soon as you can."

TIMOTHY FINNERTY stood on a hillside two miles from Salisbury Road, watching through binoculars. He'd seen the missile explode a hundred yards from the road, two hundred yards from the maroon Rolls-Royce. And he'd waited for the second missile.

"Damn!" he grunted to himself as the procession of cars passed along the road out of range.

He swung his binoculars around toward the church. He could see the crowd converging. Something had gone wrong. Finnerty swung his leg over his bicycle and pedaled toward Chippenbridge and a telephone.

"TOO DAMN CLOSE," Townley growled, "but she's at the horse show now. We've got two hours to plan the return trip."

"That could have been their last MILAN launcher, but I doubt it," Bolan said.

"So do I. And still no sign of Finnerty. I want that man!"

Bolan turned to the trestle table. The aerial photograph had been rolled up and put aside and another one lay in its place, marked with the route Townley proposed to use to get the queen safely away from Chippenbridge.

Scanning this route, Bolan's impression was that it was safer than the one they'd used before. This time the motorcade would follow a road marked with numbers but also flagged on the photo with the name Upavon Road. Coming to an intersection, the motorcade would turn south for two miles, then take a road almost parallel to the first and marked Andover Road.

This route avoided all villages. The roads ran through open country where there was nothing but farmsteads to check. It looked easier.

FINNERTY, TOO, HAD a map. Back in the caravan he sat with a highway map unfolded and spread out over his lap. Molly looked over his shoulder.

"I'm going to assume she won't be driven back the way she came," Finnerty said. "That means there are five possibilities—assuming they don't go off to the west somewhere and make a wide circuit. Of those five we can cover three. From this intersection—" he put his finger on the map "—we can move within five minutes to three good firing points. The key is *this* intersection." He touched the map again. "When they pass this point, we'll know which route they've chosen. If the boys move fast enough, they can be in position to get a good shot at any of three roads. We've got a three-in-five chance of getting her this time."

"They'll hunt you down like an animal," Kathryn told her brother. "You'll never know another moment's peace or safety a day in your life."

Finnerty looked up at Molly, then cast a scornful glance toward Kathryn. "Little sister always wanted peace and safety. Her priorities. I gave up peace and safety many years ago. And they *won't* hunt me down. Today will make me the most important Irishman who ever lived. And speaking of peace and safety, I'll dictate the terms on which *they* get peace and safety."

Kathryn lowered her eyes. She stared again at her bruised wrists and ankles, at the handcuffs and leg irons.

HER MAJESTY, FOLLOWED a pace behind by the Duke of Edinburgh, strolled through the grounds of the

Chippenbridge Show. From time to time she paused to speak a word of greeting to someone she recognized—though she had a special talent of making everyone her eyes touched supposed she recognized him. Other people pressed up to the security men, identified themselves and were allowed to approach the queen.

She was gracious to all of them, but what she had come to see was horses. She moved with enthusiasm from one horse to another, pausing to touch their flanks, to speak a word to their owners or handlers, sometimes to ask a question.

She knew a rocket had been fired at her car. She'd seen the violent explosion in the field by the road, had seen enough of it to know what it would have done if it had struck the maroon Rolls-Royce. But in public now she was as calm as if the only incident on the road from London had been a flat tire. No one in the crowd knew what had happened, and to them the queen was her usual charming self. The security men and women who knew about the explosion marveled at her calm.

In Dublin Duncan Rafferty had received the news in his office at the headquarters of the Irish Constabulary. Timothy Finnerty had failed again. Of course, he didn't know enough of the details of Finnerty's plans to know there was another MILAN launcher and a second chance.

He supposed Finnerty was dead, or that Finnerty was a prisoner. And if Finnerty was dead, then probably Molly was a prisoner. And maybe Kathryn

O'Connor had been rescued. Chances were very great that someone was talking. He knew what technique Sir Reginald Townley would use to get a prisoner to talk. The same ones he'd use, had used.

As Rafferty appraised the situation, he had very little time. He jammed a Walther PPK into his soft-sided leather briefcase, tossed some files in on top of it and left the office, leaving no word as to where he could be found that evening.

The critical factor had been that damn American! He, Rafferty, had watched Kathryn O'Connor become enamored of the American to the point she couldn't be trusted to keep a secret from him. Then Harrigan had developed not just admiration for the American, but loyalty to him. Rafferty had arranged the transfer of O'Connor, but she indicated she'd resign from the constabulary rather than be transferred.

Of course, there was another problem with O'Connor. She was Finnerty's half sister and was obsessed with the idea of destroying him. She meant to pursue and harass him until one or the other of them was dead.

Harrigan had never suspected Rafferty. He'd confided in him as a superior officer, which had been lucky for Finnerty. Rafferty had sent the warning to Dr. Kelly to get O'Connor out of his house and out of Dublin if possible before the American arrived with guns. Rafferty had also telephoned O'Neill with the warning that Harrigan had located the house in

Thurles and was coming with a force that included the American.

Rafferty had been forced to kill Harrigan. That is, he'd sent the orders.

It wasn't going to take a smart detective long to figure most of this out. Harrigan would have figured it out if he'd had the information. Rafferty knew he had very little time.

THE VAN PULLING the horse trailer was stopped at the side of Upavon Road, six miles to the east of the command trailer and only half a mile inside the zone of highest security concentration. The horse stamped uneasily on the floor of the trailer, and the three Belfast men played a charade of trying to make a quick repair on the engine of the van.

A motorcycle policeman pulled over ahead of them. He walked back. "Trouble, gentlemen?"

The one called Kevin looked up from the engine and grunted, "The trouble is having two idiots for uncles. I told them this damn carburetor—"

"I can radio for help."

"Thanks," Kevin replied, "but I can fix it. I've done it a dozen times."

The policeman walked around the van and trailer, checking it out thoroughly. He took his time circling the rig, but when he was finished he walked back to his motorcycle and roared off. He radioed a report of the stalled van and trailer to the mobile headquarters.

BOLAN ACCEPTED a roast beef sandwich and a cup of coffee from Townley. The warrior had cruised the roads for an hour, looking for a hiding place the terrorists might use for a MILAN launcher. He'd seen nothing.

What was more, security was even tighter now, if that was possible. The attempt on the queen from the Warbury rectory hadn't increased the number of personnel available to protect her, but it had increased their vigilance.

Helicopters crisscrossed a broad area. Some of them carried television cameras mounted on their underbellies, and screens in the command truck flashed with pictures of the roads and the areas on both sides. Four women stared constantly at the screens.

A tanker truck rolled slowly along the Andover Road. "God knows what's in that," the woman who saw it on her screen muttered. She reached for a microphone and spoke to a patrol car. "Check the tanker on Andover four east of the intersection."

Bolan watched. As the patrol car came up behind the tanker, the tanker accelerated, apparently on a slight downhill grade. Presently it rolled past the intersection of the road connecting to Upavon Road and proceeded west. It was no longer a factor in the queen's security, and the patrol car turned around and came back.

"They got their van and trailer moving, I see," Townley commented.

They had kept an eye on the stalled van and horse trailer ever since the motorcycle officer had radioed in the report on it. Now they could see it moving west on Upavon Road toward Chippenbridge some eight miles away.

"Once he crosses A3086 he won't be a factor," Townley said.

He meant the van and trailer would be off the route the queen would be traveling on her way back to London.

Upavon and Andover were two roads that ran parallel at Chippenbridge, Upavon to the north of the village and just south of the show ground, Andover directly through the village. The two parallel roads were connected by three roads in the security area.

The westernmost of those connections was a village street that extended out to the show ground. Next to the east was a country lane for which no one seemed to have a name. It ran directly north and south, perpendicular to Upavon and Andover. Finally a highway designated A3086 ran diagonally across both Andover and Upavon, connecting them.

East of A3086, Andover began to curve northward. Ten miles beyond A3086 it merged into Upavon Road. Ten miles east of that merge, Upavon merged into the motorway, the direct route to London.

The queen's motorcade would leave the horse show at 4:15. It would proceed east on Upavon Road to the intersection with the unnamed country lane, where it would turn south into that lane. At the intersection of the lane with Andover, the motorcade would turn east on Andover and would follow it until it merged with

Upavon. Then it would follow Upavon Road to the motorway.

This was the route the security chiefs had chosen. It was meant to avoid a couple of possibly dangerous spots on Upavon Road and perhaps to confuse any terrorists who might be lurking about.

Townley was right when he said the van and trailer would be off the queen's route if it passed the intersection of A3086 and continued west on Upavon.

Timothy Finnerty understood that. When he said the Belfast men would station themselves where they wouldn't be more than five minutes from any one of five routes the queen might take, he knew the van and trailer must not continue west on A3086 on Upavon Road.

That was why the van turned south on A3086 and half a mile along the road pulled over and stopped. Kevin got out again and opened the hood.

It was the right place to be. If the motorcade took the most direct route from the show ground to the motorway, it would come along Upavon Road—half a mile away. If it took Andover Road instead, the van could pull the trailer two miles south and be in position to fire on Andover. If the motorcade came out from Chippenbridge on Andover and turned northeast on A3086 . . . well, they wouldn't be that lucky.

Timothy Finnerty stationed himself at the intersection of Upavon and the unnamed country lane. He was running out of men, so Molly was waiting where the lane met Andover Road.

Kathryn lay facedown on a bed in the trailer, tied down with ropes, her hands cuffed behind her back, gagged and blindfolded.

They hadn't risked radio transmissions. Many frequencies would be monitored. Now they would. They had arranged a code.

IT WAS 4:10. Two police cars were stopped fore and aft of the van and horse trailer.

"I tell you I can fix it," Kevin snapped, feigning irritation. "I've fixed it before."

"You're in a special security zone from which we want you moved, sir."

"Well, I want to be moved meself, but I can't push the damn thing, can I now? What's the security zone for?"

"Her Majesty the Queen is leaving the Chippenbridge Show to return to London. She's traveling by car."

"Is she coming along this road?" Kevin asked.

"That I can't tell you," the policeman replied.

"Well, if she's coming on this road, you can hold us at gunpoint till she goes by," Kevin said. "It'd be good to see her, God bless her. And if she's not coming on this road, what harm are we doing?"

The policeman glanced at his superior, who stood nearby listening. The superior laughed. Kevin's logic was irrefutable.

IN THE COMMAND TRUCK Bolan and Townley watched the television screen that covered the exit of the mo-

torcade from the show ground. The exit went
smoothly through a cheering crowd held back by police. They glanced at the screen that showed the van
and trailer. Two cars were with it. It was the only unauthorized vehicle in the security zone, but it was
covered.

FINNERTY WATCHED the motorcade approach. He saw
the maroon Rolls-Royce, and hatred boiled up in him
like acid from his guts. Also fervor. This time it was
going to work. The attempt from the Warbury rectory had been the secondary plan. This was the primary.

The motorcade leading the motorcade turned
south. Finnerty keyed his radio and spoke. "Charley,
Charley."

Molly heard and acknowledged. "Charley, Ro-
ger."

The Belfast men at the van didn't hear the signal,
but they weren't meant to. Knowing the van might be
thoroughly searched, they weren't even carrying a
Handie-Talkie.

Finnerty swung onto his bicycle and pedaled south,
following the motorcade at a respectful distance as it
sped away from him.

"Bobby, Bobby," Molly's voice said over the Handie-Talkie.

Okay. The motorcade had turned east on Andover
Road. Finnerty stopped. He dug into the saddlebags
of his bicycle and pulled out two little radio transmitters. Each was clearly marked with large black letters

on white tape. He dropped one back into the saddle-bags.

They were the transmitters for radio-controlled garage doors, nothing more. Their range was only a hundred yards or so. Only a hundred yards or so—unless your receiver was equipped with a long antenna wire.

He shoved down the big white button on the little transmitter. In a field a mile west of the intersection of A3086 and Upavon Road, a powerful explosion sent a shudder across the land for a mile, and an eruption of earth and rocks shot high into the air.

CONCUSSION ROCKED the command truck. One of the television screens showed horizon and sky as the camera-carrying helicopter was thrown onto its side and the pilot struggled to regain stability. The roar of the explosion followed the concussion.

Miles separated the motorcade from the explosion, but the drivers accelerated. Cars and motorcycles roared onto Upavon Road and sped toward the roiling cloud of smoke and dust thrown up by the blast. The two cars guarding the Belfast men and their van and horse trailer shrieked away on A3086.

"Back to your stations!" Townley yelled into his microphone. "That's a diversion! You're being decoyed!"

KEVIN SLAMMED DOWN the hood of the van and scrambled in to get behind the wheel.

He knew where to go. An explosion on Upavon Road meant the royal party was moving on Andover Road. He himself had taken part in setting the two charges, affixing the detonators and their radio controllers and stretching their antennae across the grass and up into trees. If the explosion had gone off to the south, he would have known the motorcade was coming on Upavon.

Now he had to drive two miles. Two miles, if the Brits didn't figure him out and catch up. Two miles to go, plus getting the horse out of the trailer, tearing up the false floor and getting the launcher out and set up—before the motorcade covered about seven miles.

They'd rehearsed it many times, he and the two men. They could do it. His only horror was that today the damn horse would get stubborn and refuse to back out of the trailer.

"THE HORSE TRAILER'S GONE," said the policewoman watching the television monitor that covered A3086.

The chopper carrying the camera above that road was the one blown over and nearly crashed by the explosion. The pilot had righted the aircraft and gotten back on station, and the policewoman was looking at the picture she was supposed to see for the first time in four or five minutes.

"Chopper Eight, do you have that van and trailer in sight?" Townley transmitted. "Where the hell is he?"

"I don't see him, sir. Where should he be?"

Bolan didn't hear this conversation. He was out the door. "Son of a *bitch!*" he muttered as he swung onto the BMW bike.

He skidded as he turned into A3086, but he didn't lose control and soon he was speeding southwest at seventy miles an hour and accelerating. At that speed he had only two minutes to go before he reached Andover Road.

But he didn't need to reach the road. He spotted the van and trailer.

The horse was out of the trailer and on the road. As well, the van and trailer had been turned around so that the tail end of the trailer faced Andover Road.

He saw the significance of that immediately—the MILAN launcher was inside.

To his right, on Andover, he could see the motorcade approaching. The explosion had panicked the security people, and they were speeding toward London as fast as the motorcade could move.

Hitting his brakes, Bolan skidded the big bike to a stop. If he needed any confirmation about what was in that trailer, he had it at once. A burst of automatic rifle fire chopped the shoulder of the road, kicking up dirt and gravel. Some of the slugs hit his bike and crippled it.

One slug ripped through Bolan's jacket and grazed his left arm above the elbow. He felt the burn, but it didn't slow him down. He threw himself to the ground, rolling into the water of the roadside ditch, and when he stopped, the Desert Eagle filled his right hand.

He couldn't give a second to the man with the AK-47. He leveled the muzzle of the big automatic on the horse trailer and fired two quick shots. The .44 Magnum slugs tore through the flimsy aluminum of the trailer, but what they hit he couldn't know.

Kevin stepped boldly out from behind the van and lowered the muzzle of his AK-47 at the warrior. Bolan let him have one shot, which he couldn't take time to aim with much precision. The huge high-velocity slug gutted the young man, blowing his inside out through a gaping hole in his back.

Bolan took aim on the horse trailer again and fired several more shots through it, placing them so that no one could remain alive in there.

No one did. When he went around to look, he saw that he'd probably gotten the two men with his first rounds and had only chopped up their bodies with his second volley. They were sprawled grotesquely over the floor of the trailer, one of them half hanging out the rear, one half decapitated by a slug that had gone through his neck.

One slug had disabled the MILAN launcher. The control box was blown apart as if a charge had been set in it.

The motorcade screamed past. A chopper landed in the field across the road, and a squad of SAS soldiers jumped out. Police cars screamed up one after another.

However, the work was over.

CHAPTER NINETEEN

But it wasn't over as long as Mack Bolan didn't know what had happened to Kathryn O'Connor; it wasn't over as long as no one had avenged the death of Mike Harrigan; it wasn't over as long as the remnants of the once-arrogant band of fanatic terrorists called the Curran Brigade still believed they had the advantage of possessing a powerful, charismatic leader.

As far as the Executioner was concerned, the work was nowhere near over.

Sir Reginald Townley felt that way, too. The difference was that Bolan could go over to Ireland and do something about it. Townley couldn't, but he could give Bolan access to the best information the Special Branch had.

"He's got nobody left but the hard-core fanatics," the Briton told Bolan, "and very few of them, I'd judge. So where does he go when we've driven him to ground? Back to his origins, I'd guess. Back to Dublin to be swallowed up in the city. To hide. Lick his wounds. Scheme."

"I thought the worst fanatics were in Belfast," Bolan said.

"And about half of them would like to kill Timothy Finnerty. He's a rotten failure, don't forget. How many men have died for him in the past three weeks? Too many. He led them to disaster. They won't forgive him for that."

"Dublin?"·

"If he's got any friends left, that's where they'd be."

"Okay, Dublin."

"I'll get you into the country with your weapons. I want you to memorize a phone number. You can call it if you need help."

TIMOTHY FINNERTY HAD SHAVED off his beard, revealing a puffy face and a weak chin. He sat reading the newspaper.

Kathryn sat in a tub of hot water, trying to soak the aches out of her muscles. Molly had taken off the handcuffs and leg irons at last, though Kathryn knew very well they'd be put on again as soon as she got out of the tub. That was why she wanted to lie here until one of them came in and prodded her out.

Molly was in the kitchen cooking. She had said she was tired of living off garbage. For once, anyway, they would have a decent meal.

They were comfortable. There were only the three of them left, and they were anything but safe, but for the moment they were as nearly comfortable as they had been since they'd left O'Neill's country house.

And why shouldn't they be? This was a comfortable place. It was Kathryn's flat in Dublin.

Odd, she thought. The rent had come due since she'd been gone, but no one had so far objected to their moving in here. Her things were still here, everything in place. The big living-room window had been replaced. Apparently it had been broken. But the flat was still her home, essentially intact.

Finnerty was reading the *Irish Times*—an account of the two attempts to murder the queen.

"An American," he said to Molly, who could hear him through the door between the living room and the kitchen. "'An American security officer, on loan from the government of the United States to the government of the United Kingdom, brought his special antiterrorist expertise to the successful security operation. Although the Special Branch emphasized that the queen's life was never really in danger, it also praised the anonymous American for his courage and resourcefulness.' American! That same damn American *she* brought on us!"

He'd flung out his arm toward the bathroom, so Molly knew who he meant. "She didn't bring the American on us," Molly replied. "We brought him on ourselves. There's an American expression, I think. I don't know how it goes exactly, but something like this. 'If you want to play in the big leagues, expect big-league opposition.'"

"What the hell does that mean? We've been attacked by a murdering mercenary soldier."

"Try letting your brains run your mouth for once, Tim," Molly said in the calm tone she knew infuriated him.

He said nothing more. He rattled the newspaper and went on reading.

Kathryn had heard the conversation. There was justice in the world, after all. Her half brother was a loser. He'd always been a loser. He'd tried to compensate by making himself . . . well, what had he made himself?

"Damn!"

Something else had angered him.

"No wonder I couldn't reach Duncan Rafferty on the telephone. But wouldn't they have had the decency to tell me? Listen to this. Funeral notices, for God's sake! 'Chief Inspector Duncan Rafferty will be buried tomorrow morning after a private service at the Church of the Most Holy Heart of Jesus. The late officer of the constabulary was found dead in his office, the victim of a self-inflicted bullet wound.' And so forth. And so forth."

"One more gone."

"I started with no one, and how did I build a following of men willing to die for me?"

"For the cause," she reminded.

"For *me!*" he yelled. "Because I'm their leader! I built my following and I'll build it up again. There are cycles in the fortunes of man. I'm at a low ebb right now, but I'll rise again!"

"What goes up must come down."

"You bitch . . ." he muttered.

CARRYING THE PASSPORT with the name Tom Grady, Bolan entered Ireland as Finnerty had done—off a fishing boat, walking ashore without passing through any kind of check. Carrying a cheap canvas bag that contained the weapons he most relied on—the Desert Eagle and the Beretta 93-R—he caught a bus for Dublin and arrived there early in the morning.

He checked into a cheap hotel, put on his harness under the ragged jacket of a Dublin workingman, hung his weapons in their leather and left the hotel two hours after dawn.

Half an hour later he walked into the King James Pub—the place where he and Kathryn had taken the Curran Brigade's supply of cocaine, plus their cash, and had burned it in a valise on the sidewalk outside. It was where he had smashed the ribs and dislocated the shoulder of two bonecrushers. The last word spoken to him and Kathryn as they'd left the pub had been that they were a dead man and woman, that the fighters for the freedom of Ireland would never forget them, never forgive them and would have them sooner or later.

Four men were drinking this early in the morning, one at the bar, two together at a table, one at a table alone. He stepped up to the bar. "Lager," he said to the bartender.

The bartender shoved the glass across the bar dully with no sign of recognition.

Bolan took a sip of the barely chilled beer. "Remember me?" he asked.

The bartender shook his head.

Bolan put a .44 Magnum cartridge on the bar. "I was told men would remember me. How about the two bullies? One of them must still be wearing his arm in a sling. Or does Dr. Kelly do miracle work? What about the boys downstairs? Did they enjoy our little bonfire?''

The bartender backed away from the bar. For an instant Bolan wondered if he was going for a weapon. Then he realized the man was just afraid, was retreating.

"Hmm? You do remember, don't you?''

"What do you want?'' the bartender asked hoarsely.

"I want Tim Finnerty.''

The bartender shook his head.

"Don't tell me you don't know who I mean. Finnerty, the guy who runs away every time there's a fight. How many men have died? And how many times has he run? There ought to be a hundred men willing to turn him over.''

The bartender kept shaking his head.

Bolan rolled the cartridge toward him. "Have somebody deliver that to him. Let him know I'm in town. And let him know this time I've got nothing else to do but hunt him down. Tell him he knows how to buy himself a running chance. I'll give him a day's start. He knows how to buy it. If he doesn't buy it . . . no chance.''

WITHIN THE HOUR the cartridge was brought to the flat.

"Tell him there's no deal,'' Finnerty snarled. "Tell him I dare him to come near me.''

The messenger was the bonecrusher whose ribs Bolan had broken on the street not far from the pub. "I'd be careful about that," he grunted. "He's no ordinary guy."

"And what the hell am *I*?" Finnerty screamed at the man. "*Ordinary?* You think so?"

When the man had left, Molly stood with her hands on her hips and glared at him. "What he thinks is that you're drunk before noon, which is what he's going to tell the street."

Kathryn hobbled out of the bedroom. She was wearing her own clothes again—but only a white bra and panties, all that Molly would let her put on before she locked the leg irons and handcuffs on her again.

"You call me a drunk?" Finnerty yelled.

"Why shouldn't she call you that? Or worse?" Kathryn sneered. "Truth will out."

Her half brother slapped her across the cheek.

MACK BOLAN WALKED into the waiting room of Dr. Robert Kelly.

He handed the nurse-receptionist a .44 cartridge and told her to take it back to the doctor immediately. She did, and in a moment the doctor came out.

"My office," he said, nodding toward the room Bolan had seen that early morning when he'd explored all the rooms in the house.

They went in, and the doctor sat down behind his desk.

"I don't know where he is," Dr. Kelly said. "I don't know where *she* is. No matter what you threaten or what you do, I can't tell you where they are because I don't know."

"Frankly, would you tell me if you did?"

The doctor nodded. "At this point, yes. I thought he was a fighter for the freedom of Ireland. Now..." He shrugged. "I've read the newspaper accounts of what he did in England. I've seen the reports on the telly. Yes, I'd tell you where he is."

"Are you afraid of him?" Bolan asked.

The corners of the doctor's mouth turned down. He put his hands together in front of his chin, then he shook his head. "Not anymore."

"Kathryn?"

"I treated her injuries. She was alive the last time I saw them. What he's done to her since, I don't know."

BOLAN RETURNED to his hotel. He needed an hour or so of sleep. When he asked for his key, the desk clerk nodded at a man sitting in the tiny lobby, and the man rose from his chair. "Mr. Grady?"

Bolan nodded. That was the name on his passport.

"I'm Inspector William Hanrahan, Irish Constabulary," the man announced, showing his identification—a laminated card with his picture on it.

The ID was the same kind Kathryn had carried, and it looked genuine to Bolan.

"I'd like to talk with you. Here? In your room? How about a bite to eat?"

"I wouldn't mind a sandwich."

"Yes. An overnight sea voyage, plus a good deal of activity this morning would tend to make a man hungry," Hanrahan said dryly.

Bolan was surprised at how much the man knew.

They stepped out on the street and down the block a few paces to a coffee shop. The inspector ordered coffee and a sugared roll, Bolan a ham and cheese sandwich.

"I was a friend of Mike Harrigan's," the inspector said. "I'm also an admirer of Kathryn O'Connor's. I don't know if you've paid any attention to the news in Dublin. I'd rather doubt it, since I have a very good idea what you've been doing the past few days. Anyway, if you'd been here, reading the newspapers, you'd know that our chief inspector, Duncan Rafferty, committed suicide yesterday. Shot himself with his official weapon. You understand what I'm saying?"

"The bad apple in your barrel."

"We've others, I imagine," Hanrahan went on, "but I suspect Rafferty was the cause of many of our recent troubles."

Bolan nodded, glanced out the window at the street and waited for the inspector to continue.

"You've come to Ireland to kill Timothy Finnerty," Hanrahan said bluntly.

Bolan shrugged.

"I'm an officer of the law. I'm not supposed to let foreign agents enter this country and kill people. But, well, frankly, Mr. Grady, Colonel MacKenzie, or whoever you are, if you should happen to put an end to Timothy Finnerty, I'll pretend I never heard of you."

Their coffee was placed before them. Bolan took a sip.

"In fact," Hanrahan went on, "I'm going to tell you where to find him."

"You know?"

Hanrahan shook his head. "Not really. But I've got a clue. We *do* keep track of things. We don't just let things happen. Did you suppose no one but you was looking for Kathryn O'Connor?"

"Not really."

"Rafferty was interfering, sending the men assigned to her case off on all sorts of wild-goose chases. But I have a bit of information that may be useful. Kathryn has been missing for more than two weeks. Her rent came due Friday. It was paid. With cash mailed in an envelope from a post office here in Dublin."

"They're using her flat?"

"I'd say so. It's possible Finnerty is hiding there now that he's fled England after his spectacular failure. I thought you might want to check it out."

"You want *me* to check it out?"

"If you find him and there's a shoot-out, it's well done," Hanrahan said. "If I apprehend him and arrest him, there'll be screaming from some quarters that the law is harassing a hero."

"He's committed enough crimes to—"

Hanrahan interrupted. "To deserve whatever happens to him."

BOLAN WALKED through the street just as he had done before. He stopped at the telephone booth and pretended to search for a number while looking up at Kathryn's living-room window. It had been repaired since the night he'd thrown Finnerty's bonecrusher through the glass.

He could see no one in the flat, and no one seemed to be standing guard on the street. He could approach from the rear, through the back door he'd used that night, or he could just walk up to the front door and go in.

Bolan crossed the street. A woman was coming down the sidewalk from the other end of the street. She climbed the steps and went into the apartment building. She was a heavy woman in her forties, with sandy-red hair, and she carried a bag of groceries.

Could she possible be Molly Finnerty?

He didn't run, but he walked faster. If she went into apartment 2B, the door would be open for a moment.

TIM HAD SLOSHED down whiskey all morning. Now he was asleep. Or maybe he'd passed out. Anyway, Molly had gone out for groceries. She'd left Tim to guard Kathryn, with a firm warning to him not to go to sleep.

But he'd kept on drinking and he'd gone to sleep. Kathryn had watched him for a while as he snored and sputtered. She'd risked getting up and hobbling to the telephone, but the instrument had been dead when she'd picked it up.

She shuffled into the kitchen, awkward and off balance, jerking against the chain between her ankles. Shortening her steps, she made her way to the kitchen sink and to the drawer to its right.

In there was a little luxury she'd bought herself a year or so ago—a set of Sabatier knives, the full assortment, from short paring knife up through a thick-bladed butcher knife. She pulled the butcher knife from the drawer.

Tim wasn't moving. She jerked her way across the living room toward the couch where he lay. He didn't waken.

Kathryn stood above her half brother, the butcher knife clutched in her manacled hands.

Brother...yes, once he'd been a brother. Tears came to her eyes as she remembered. But a different kind of emotion welled up as she thought of Mike Harrigan. And how many others? Including an elderly rector bludgeoned in his little church. With no thought. No regret.

No. They all died to serve his purposes, to carry out his will. Scores of men who thought they were Irish patriots were Tim's victims as much as the people whose murders he had ordered.

And he said he'd build a following again, do it all over.

Kathryn firmed her determination. She paused one last instant above him, then drove the blade of the butcher knife into his throat.

He coughed out a gurgling cry, and his hands closed around his throat as if he could stop the blood, regain his breath. His eyes focused on her face, fixed in a furious glare of burning hatred. He struggled, trying to get up, to grab at her.

But his blood poured from between the fingers clasped around his throat, and his gasping breath sputtered through the huge wound. He rolled off the couch and onto his hands and knees.

Tim clutched at his chest. At first she didn't understand, then she realized he was trying to pull the pistol inside his jacket.

She struck again, driving the butcher knife into his back. He fell to his belly, and she stabbed him repeatedly.

A piercing scream rent the air. Kathryn looked up and saw Molly standing in the doorway.

Kathryn was on her knees beside Tim, and she knew she had only a moment before the frenzied Molly would pull the pistol from her handbag and fire. She knew Molly would do it, even if by doing so she gave up her only chance of escape and delivered herself to life in prison. It would be pointless to plead with her. Kathryn just knelt, looking at her, and waited.

Molly went for the pistol, her hand digging into her handbag. Suddenly she grunted, her back stiffened and she dropped to her knees and toppled onto her face.

Standing behind Molly, his hand holding the pistol he'd used to knock Molly unconscious, was Mack Bolan.

BOLAN CARRIED Kathryn into the bedroom so that he could take off her chains and she could dress without being seen by the people who crowded into the living room.

Neighbors first, who ran out screaming, then constables. Finally Inspector William Hanrahan, who took charge and brought order out of chaos.

A medical team carried Molly Finnerty down to an ambulance. She'd suffered a concussion, possibly a skull fracture.

Kathryn refused to go to a hospital, so Hanrahan called in a doctor. Except for the bruises and sores on her wrists and ankles, he pronounced her fit.

There were too many questions to be answered, too many things to explain, too many secrets to be kept. Kathryn packed some clothes, and Hanrahan spirited her and Bolan out the back door and into a waiting car. Within minutes they were at Dublin Airport, where they boarded a small jet that carried them to Heathrow.

Sir Reginald Townley met them. He came aboard the little jet and sat down in one of the seats.

"I've got two offers for you," he said. "Hal Brognola suggests some down time, a little R and R. He offers passage to New York on the Concorde, then a few days at a private beachfront estate in the Florida Keys. Her Majesty's government offers a cruise in the Mediterranean aboard a yacht. Both governments would like to offer public honors..."

"Are the offers for the both of us?" Bolan asked.

Townley glanced back and forth between them, an indulgent smile on his face. "Well, Brognola and I *assumed*..."

"It's dangerous to assume." Bolan looked down into the bemused, upturned face of Kathryn O'Connor. "Do you want to go on a vacation with me?" he asked.

Kathryn nodded. With a finger she wiped a small tear from the corner of her eye.